A TIME FOR JUSTICE

Graham Pears (www.gpears.com) joined the police cadets in 1974 and retired as a Chief Superintendent with Northumbria Police in 2007. Whilst in the middle of a busy career he took an arts degree as a diversion from the day-to-day issues of policing, following on with an MA in creative writing. Although he had originally started work on his first degree to give him a break from police work, it seemed natural for him to write about crime. He has now dedicated himself to writing page-turning crime fiction, with a twist of humour. His first crime novel, The Myth of Justice was published in 2009 by Red Squirrel Press (www.redsquirrelpress.com) and was very well received. It introduces Newcastle detective, 'Jet'. A Time for Justice is the second in the Jet series. He is now working on the third.

He was born in Wallsend and has always lived in the North East of England. He currently lives in Stocksfield with his wife June and their many pets.

A TIME FOR JUSTICE

GRAHAM PEARS

CRIME

First published in the UK in 2011 by
Red Squirrel Press
PO Box 219
Morpeth
Northumberland
NE61 9AU
United Kingdom
www.redsquirrelpress.com

Cover design by Andrew Pears

Graham Pears 2011

Printed in the UK by
Martins the Printers
Sea View Works
Spittal
Berwick upon Tweed
TD15 1RS

ISBN: 978-1-906700-39-3

For June, Andrew and Adelle

Journal - Murder One

The second blow killed him. I knew it when I heard the crack and his skull shattered, just like the boiled egg I had for breakfast, but with blood. A lot of blood. The third time I got the hammer stuck in his head, had to give it a real yank to get it out of his brains. He had stopped making any noise by then. Queers are just too keen to turn their backs on you.

It seems easy now I've started it and there's no going back. All systems go. The wind of opportunity blew and it was too good to miss.

By the time you are reading this you will know what I did. But not the whole story. That's why I'm writing this for you. To tell you why I did it. What was it Oscar Wilde said about *De Profundis*? 'I don't defend my conduct. I explain it.' The pleadings of a puff; how apt. I am no poet. My record will be briefer than Wilde's. But by the time you are finished reading this you might see parallels. I am not as forgiving. I am doing this because my life was over before it began. And I do blame. And I know who to blame.

These glorious final acts will be my explanation. The world will not forget me. What better way to be remembered forever than as a mass murderer. I wonder what nickname the press will give me? Let me suggest

'The Avenger'. Nice ring to it. So I write my story in blood. More attention grabbing than ink. You might still be counting the number of victims in my war. A war against perversion? Definitely. Like all wars there may be some casualties you judge innocent. I don't. The way to the truth is drenched with the blood of innocents. And here's me saying I'm no poet. You might judge me harshly, but at least you will now have the chance to judge. Remember that I once was a victim. But now I choose not to be at others' mercy. Now I am in control and I will make a better fist of it.

I still have his prick. Do I have your attention now? It was harder to cut off than you might think. My trophy. A signature. Don't all good murderers need one? There were only two things I took. I needed them for my campaign. I am not a thief, but I do like to make a point. Any case he won't need them now – will he?

Don't feel sorry for him, I have given him fame. Like Polly Nichols, the common prostitute Jack the Ripper plucked from obscurity. Better than spending his life mooching around in the dark looking for more queers. That's no way to live. So he's better off now I've helped him on the way. And he has helped the cause. As soon as the press publish my journal he will become famous, a hero. Until then he will just be another corpse. Let's hope the press do right by him. Maybe he will become somebody after all.

Medical Notes from Bereavement Session Five

Patient still occasionally hears voice of his dead wife.

States he bears no malice towards anyone for her death.

Suicide risk low due to his character and upbringing – programmed to survive.

States he is taking medication when required but not regularly.

Still having problems with sleep.

No risk to others.

To be kept under review. Next session arranged.

Patient now on holiday for a week. Two sessions booked for following week to catch up.

No reason to believe he is not fit for full operational police duties.

Day One – Morning

'Bollocks!'

Jet surveyed the damage to his fence. The wind that had been playing with the branches of the cherry tree last night had not been so whimsical with his front garden fence. The larch lap panels, overcome by nature, now lay on his lawn.

'It certainly got up wild last night.' Jet had not heard anyone approach and looked up to see a face he vaguely recognised from a house further down the street.

'I didn't think it was so bad when I went to bed.' Jet tapped one of the panels with the toe of his shoe; as if it were going to revive.

'Those panels catch the wind; you really need something lets the wind through in an exposed spot like this.'

'It's only been up a couple of years.' Jet kicked the fence again with a hint of malice.

'Looking at them I would think it's probably been a bit longer than that. Time passes so quickly. I've been here close to a year now and they looked fragile when I first saw them.'

'You could be right, my wife Julia used to look after this sort of thing.'

'I was really sorry when I read about what happened

5

to her in the news. It was before I moved here so I didn't know her personally, but I've heard so many good things from other people, she must have been very special.' The weathered faced man's tone had changed to a one Jet had come to recognise over the year since his wife died - sombre.

'She was.'

'Look, when I saw the fence down I thought I'd pop over. I do landscape gardening for a living and as we are almost neighbours I could offer my services at a reasonable rate.'

'How much will it cost?' Jet kicked the recumbent fence once more.

The tanned face of the gardener grinned, 'It's not going to get up you know.'

'More's the pity.' Jet smiled.

'To put the same up again, for you, two hundred and fifty quid. If you want something that's going to stay up longer, it'll be a bit more.'

'Two hundred quid!'

'Two hundred and fifty to put this back up.'

'For a flimsy fence?'

'Yeah, tell you what, for three hundred I'll get rid of this rubbish and put up a really solid five foot fence. That's neighbour's rates.'

Jet looked at the wreckage on his lawn. 'When could you do it?'

'I have a few jobs on this week but I could fit it around those.'

'You're on.' Jet thrust out his hand, 'I'm Frank, people tend to call me Jet.'

'I'm Terry. That's my pickup down the street, outside my house.'

'Surprised we haven't met before.' Jet gave his fence one last kick.

'We're all busy people.'

'Hell, you're right.' Jet looked at his watch, 'Must dash. Work to get to.'

'Don't worry about the fence, I'll sort it.'

Jet dashed up the garden path, pushed at the front door and being reassured it was secure went to his Ford Fiesta and slid into the driver's seat. Jet threw the envelope he had picked up from his doormat onto the passenger seat. Another thing he had become used to was the constant stream of cards. They had been especially abundant over the past few weeks on the first anniversary of Julia's death. He admired the skill of the well-wishers who seemed to be avoiding him and delivered their cards with ninja-type skill. Cards were often waiting for him when he got in, or, as this one, when he got up. But he rarely saw or heard the delivery. He was no slouch himself, but he was never up early enough to catch the ninja-post-people. He was content, it was the thought.

Jet walked up the stairs in the police station. It was still early enough to feel empty. The only person guaranteed to beat him in was Jean the cleaner who was currently using a yellow cloth to wage war against the grime on the brass plate of the swing doors that led to the station corridor.

'Hi Jean. Nice morning.'

'Be better when I get out of here.' Jean kept rubbing the duster with what Jet thought was admirable vigour. 'Got the grandkids to pick up from school this afternoon, first day back after summer holidays. Wish I had teacher's holidays.'

'Me too.'

'Can't be late, don't want one of them paediatrics to get them.'

'Not worth the risk.' Jet had known Jean long enough not to worry about a slip of the tongue. Her mispronunciation was the stuff of legend.

'I'll be at the gates, three clock sharp, come rain, hail or shite.'

'Well it's not raining or hailing at the moment so you should be fine.'

'Aye. They're canny kids.'

Jet pushed the door and disappeared into the darkness of the corridor, then into the CID office.

He flicked the kettle switch causing it to rumble, then sat at his desk and for the first time considered the envelope in his hand. He pawed the white paper, feeling a bulge in the centre. The handwriting seemed scrawled and Jet thought almost childlike. He tore open the top and removed the contents with his fingertips. He was surprised to see a folded plain buff card and when he opened it a watch fell on to his desk. It was a grubby looking silver watch, the broken glass of the timepiece showing the hands stationary at one thirty-five. The black-ink handwriting on the card did not contain the expected message of sympathy but said only 'times up for everybody sometime.'

Mark Groom interrupted Jet's thoughts as he cycloned into the room.

'Did you have a good week's holiday?'

'Yeah, all right.'

'What was Spain like?'

'Hot.'

'You don't look like you've caught the sun.'

'No, I avoided it. Stayed in the shade, sightseeing, that sort of thing. Didn't have to worry about sunburn here, come back to gales. My fence was down this morning and it's going to cost three hundred quid to put it back up.'

'You had an estimate already?'

'An enterprising neighbour with a fencing business turned up.'

'Sounds cheap to me. Any case we need to get our skates on and I don't mean the fish.'

'You know, that wasn't funny first time you said it.'

'Come on. Uniform are at the Gardens, there's a body been found. They want us to have a look down. A lot of blood apparently. Probably someone fell down those stone stairs, but they don't want to touch it in case it's something more sinister.'

'Yes Sarge.' Jet had a hint of sarcasm in his voice for Detective Sergeant Mark Groom who, over the last year, he had come to consider more as a friend than his immediate supervisor. Groom had been in the drug squad until his arrest on suspicion of murder. The trial had collapsed when the real offender emerged and once Groom had been sent back to work he was transferred to the CID at Newcastle. In reality no one knew what else to do with him, but as drug dealers had been involved in the case which led to his charge, it did make sense not to return him to that world. Groom had returned to work with the zest of a man who had stared into the abyss and not enjoyed one second of the view. He was now annoyingly finding joy in his work and all the other things life had to offer. This suited Jet most of the time, who, after the death of his wife, often yearned for some sort of normality, but on occasion the enthusiasm grated. Groom had applied his renewed vigour to his body-building hobby and the baggy clothes he wore could not conceal the solid mass of muscle beneath. Three weeks ago, Jet and Groom had gone to arrest a local burglar at his home and on being told the reason for their visit the suspect had unwisely thrown a punch, which Jet guessed had been aimed at Groom's chin, but had fallen somewhat short into his chest. Jet could see the pain register in the burglar's eye, having seemingly shot up his arm. Groom did not move as Jet turned towards him and said, 'Did that hurt Sarge?' Groom shook his head as the offender amended his strategy from recalcitrance to outright submission. Groom's zeal had even led to Jet studying to take the sergeant's examination and when he was handed the piece of paper that said 'Detective Constable 7390 Francis Whittle: result – pass' Jet nearly passed out himself. His wife had nagged him for years to take the exam but he had resisted. There was irony in the fact that what really drove him now was her memory. There were times when he was trying harder than he ever had done to make her proud of him. There were others when the dark clouds that circled him descended and his thoughts turned black. He was being choked in the space between two worlds. No wonder, Jet often reflected, he was receiving psychological counselling. And, by the way, hating every moment of it. Trying to convince people you were all right was quite a strain, especially when you were not. And Jet knew he was not well. Since Julia's death, he had found it a great strain to keep his emotions locked away inside him, where they belonged. It tormented him. He did not know if it was the depression his doctor had told him was natural and he would get over. He did not really know what depression was or how it was supposed to feel. He knew he felt anger and guilt. Where was the justice? For Julia or him? Sometimes anger and guilt got knotted up in a huge ball of pain in his stomach. It made sleep difficult. He did try to rationalise, to come to terms with the situation and himself, but sometimes no matter how he resisted, it consumed him. Jet did not know if this made him evil. But he did know that sometimes it felt that way.

Jet slid the envelope and its contents from the surface of his desk into the top drawer then followed Groom into the corridor. 'Should I drive?'

Groom smiled, 'No, let's give the Fiesta a rest. I've got the keys to the new CID car, just delivered last week.'

The new Ford Focus had a little more legroom for Groom's large frame. It took ten minutes for Groom to drive and then by Jet's standards, to carelessly park the car at their destination.

The Gardens is a small park in Newcastle's city centre. A wide steep bank of paths and shrubs. Too precipitous to be overcome by the commercial buildings that surrounded it. Its splendid intention, to provide an area of recreation, had succumbed to a different kind of rendezvous, other than friendly picnics or chats between friends and colleagues. The labyrinth of paths, which spread like cracks in a windscreen, had a reputation for prostitution and other indecent acts which took place in many of the Gardens' dead ends. Such was the reputation of the place that it was avoided by most people, even through the relative safety of daylight.

Jet and Groom looked down to the scrum of uniforms which were located near one of the path's cul-de-sacs. It was fifty metres down the steep incline and another twenty metres to the left of the main stone stairway which ran down the length of the Gardens. Jet followed Groom down the steps. A piece of string was tied from a shrub across the footpath to a metal fence, obstructing the way to where the activity was. A uniformed officer approached as Groom pulled at the string. 'Is this supposed to be a cordon?'

'It was all we could find.'

The officer's lack of embarrassment clearly irked Groom. 'Is there a body in there?'

'Yes.'

'And you haven't cordoned off the stairs that run down the whole place,' Groom sounded angry, 'but you have used a bit of string to stop people getting into that small enclosed space?'

'Yes.'

'And that makes sense to you?'

'It's all we could find.'

Groom looked at Jet and pulled the string again. 'Well it does look like a fine piece of string. Is it force issue?'

'No, we found it in the hedge.'

'Is your sergeant here?'

'No he's tied up at the nick with prisoners.'

Groom moved to where the other officers stood chatting to each other. The body of a man was lying a little further down the bank from the huddle. Groom pointed to one of the officers, 'You go to the top of the stairs and stop people from coming into the Gardens.' He pointed again, 'You do the same at the bottom.' The officers seemed to be taken by surprise, 'Well, chop chop!'

The two randomly selected officers suddenly kicked into action, leaving three others looking startled.

'Who was here first?'

'Me, it's my beat.' Jet recognised Steve Manson who had worked in the city for a couple of years.

'Right then, you stay here and you two - one of you go to the top, the other to the bottom and talk to anyone you can find. See if there is anyone who was about here or knows something, or might have seen anything that might help. Get loads of names and addresses. Got it?'

'Yes, Sarge.' They both shot off to their allocated missions.

'Now....' Groom searched for a name.

'Steve.'

'Now Steve, what we got?'

'Anonymous person reported a body lying about an hour ago. He's cold and stiff so been here a while. Face

14

down, trousers around ankles.'

Groom looked down at the figure. The back of the head was crushed and bent out of shape. The bare backside faced up. Prominent and waxen.

'The way these shrubs are, it could have lain here unseen for a while.' Groom looked at the main stair and realised the person who spotted the body must have moved off the main thoroughfare.

'Looks like a couple of puffs have fallen out to me.' There was no emotion in Manson's voice.

'That's quite a conclusion to jump to Steve.' Jet made his first contribution to the conversation.

'This place is over-run with puffs at night doing all sorts of unnatural things to each other. It's one of their meeting places. And they're always falling out. I'm always chasing perverts who have been fighting each other from here.'

'He could have just fallen and hit his head on this steep bank. It might have been an accident.'

'Might have been, but if it is, he accidentally cut his dick off as well.'

'You turned the body over?'

'When I first came - to see if he was dead or not.'

Groom rolled his eyes at Jet, then turned his attention back to Manson. 'Will you man the string Steve,' Groom curled his lip. 'And make sure nobody gets anywhere near the body from now on? Me and Jet better go and call the cavalry.' Groom nodded to Jet and they both walked away.

As they walked back to the car Groom spoke. 'This is going to be fun. The scene's been trampled all over. Better get the Detective Inspector down here – let's hope he doesn't have a stroke or we could have two bodies to look after.'

Jet was struggling to keep up with Groom's long strides back up the steep bank. Groom stopped to allow him to catch up and turned to look back down to the scene. 'Do you know that cop?'

Jet was slow and short of breath. 'Not very well. He's worked on this beat for a long time.'

'Seems quite a character.'

'Not big on sympathy.'

'Let's not make him the family liaison officer then.' Groom was not smiling. 'His prints and DNA must be all over the scene.'

'Suppose.'

'I thought everyone was trained to be politically correct these days?'

'You can lead a horse to water.'

'Yes, Jet, I was thinking that.'

Both men stared as Jet caught his breath. Groom looked at his unfit colleague. 'Didn't you tell me you have an appointment at headquarters today?'

'Yeah, but I can put it off.'

'No need for that, we're going to be here for hours yet.' Groom wore the grin of someone who knew the sound of a man searching for an alibi. 'You go to your appointment. I'm sure we'll still be here when you get back.'

'Thanks Sarge.'

'No problem Jet.' Groom's weak grin metamorphosed to broad smile. 'Do you want to ring Ormond and give him the news? Don't think there's much doubt that we have a murder, do you?'

'No. Ormond's going to do his nut.'

'I bet you a quid he says we'd have been better off if the Chuckle Brothers were protecting the murder scene.'

'He always says that.'

'He's very astute.'

Bereavement Session Six

Jane Metcalf's affair with the Chief Constable was a poorly kept secret. It was not absolutely certain whether her paramour's position had been used to her advantage, but it was clear, so far, it had done her no harm. Her position as the force's senior psychologist had the potential to lead her into conflict with peers within the organisation, but others avoided risk of disagreement, lest their lack of diplomacy led to pillow talk and them being metaphorically shot at dawn. Such was the Chief Constable's self belief that it was rumoured he often wrestled with the morality of the shootings of those who displeased him, becoming somewhat more real than metaphorical. James Stavers was the Chief Constable and had an iron grip of the force, and even if some doubted whether this grip always extended to reality, it was abundantly clear he was not a man to be trifled with. To most people's surprise, the position of senior psychologist had recently been created after a force inspection of the department. Surprise was replaced with suspicion when Jane triumphed at interview for the post over her four other psychologist colleagues. Two of whom, at least on paper, seemed to be better qualified for the job. She now had a better title and enjoyed an increment in her pay but was not sure what else the promotion brought, other than another monthly force management conference to go to.

Jane was sufficiently trained in the workings of the mind to know why her imminent fortieth birthday was significant, but disappointed her skills did not extend to avoiding the accompanying feelings of panic. She stood in front of the full length mirror on the inside of her office door and reviewed the result of her careful grooming. Turning sideways she brushed her stomach which looked pleasingly flat and wondered how long she could maintain the regime of abstinence and exercise it required. Since her divorce she had lost several pounds and although there were times when the attention this attracted made her feel powerful and alive, she wondered how long it would be before the forces of nature tipped the balance in favour of the chocolate and white wine she adored in front of the television.

The knock on the other side of her door did nothing to ruffle Jane's tranquil façade and pulling the handle she activated her professional smile. The swift and personal response led to Jet wearing more a look of startle than cordiality.

'Frank. How nice to see you. Come in.'

Jet obeyed. In their previous sessions he had never disclosed he much preferred Jet to Frank and guessed she would not know of his widely used epithet. After all, she worked at headquarters - Fantasy Island, as it was un-affectionately referred to by all in operational posts –

those in the real world! How could she know? He doubted she even knew the man who invented the Jet engine was also called Frank Whittle.

'Let's sit down.' There was no need for Jane to indicate to the low chairs that surrounded the coffee table. They both sat in the same thick-cushioned chairs of previous visits, leaving two other fake-leather seats empty. As he lowered himself on the chair Jet wondered whether anything was being made of his tendency towards routine. But as Jane did not alter her choice of chair either guessed he was the one over-analysing. Jet could still not make up his mind whether Jane realised he was playing the game, coming along to these bereavement sessions because it was a lot easier than resistance, and professionally the wisest thing to do. There had been times during the sessions when he had forgotten about the game. When Jane had asked about his wife's death, it had been easy to talk about her and he did feel better after he had spoken of Julia. Her death had left a huge hole and he knew he was never going to be able to fill it. Sometimes talking about her was too easy and he slipped into it. But he knew he could not be totally forthright with his force appointed counsellor. She had stressed the confidentiality bond that existed between them, but Jet knew there were no secrets - there never are. So he tried to say the things required and at the end of his sessions leave her with the impression he had been through a tragic experience but was now well on the road to recovery. She could write that in her notes and then people would leave him alone. There had been mention at the very beginning that he would have to attend at least ten sessions and then the situation would be reviewed. Jet had set himself the objective of satisfying Jane that ten was enough. He found it ironic that sessions designed to help him were more a hurdle to be crossed, but needs must.

'So how was your holiday?' Jane settled down in her chair as she spoke.

'Fine.'

'Where did you get to again?'

'Spain.'

'Very nice. What did you get up to?'

'Not a great deal. Hired a car and toured the countryside. It was very nice.'

'That's really good. I imagine it has done you the power of good.'

'I don't know. Hope so.' Jet knew the holiday had made a big difference to him. For better or worse, he did not really know. He certainly wasn't going to disclose this to Jane Metcalf.

'First holiday since your wife passed away?'

'Since she was murdered. Yes.'

'Had you been to Spain before?'

'No. We did have a week in Ibiza a few years back but

it's the first time I've been to mainland Spain.'

'So what made you choose there?'

'As good as anywhere I suppose. Found it on the internet, self catering, very quiet.'

'Sounds nice.' Jane crossed her legs and tucked her skirt between her leg and the chair, using this motion to change the subject. 'How are you sleeping now?'

'Better.'

'Nightmares?'

'Less frequent.'

'When was the last time one woke you up?'

'Not since I went on holiday.'

'You haven't dreamt about the man who killed your wife since then?'

'Ray Harris. No. Not since my holiday. Let's hope he's gone from my dreams now.'

'That's good.' Jane renewed her clip-on smile. 'Any plans to see the lady you were going to the cinema with when I last saw you?'

Jet wished he had not mentioned Trish at a previous appointment. It had seemed like a good idea at the time. Evidence of him making emotional progress. But he had continually felt lost for words and their night out had ended in less than promising circumstances. Him sitting in the Fiesta declining her invitation for late night coffee, citing early morning work starts, but both knowing Julia was still there, stopping him. It had always been so natural to be with Julia, effortless. Trish had smiled so warmly at Jet as she kissed his cheek and thanked him for a nice evening. She had suggested dinner sometime soon but Jet did not know whether the vagueness of detail meant Trish had drawn herself to the conclusion that they were wasting each other's time.

'No we've no plans to see each other.'

'I'm sorry to hear that.'

'Think it's just too soon.'

'That's all perfectly understandable. You mentioned to me hearing your wife's voice, last time we spoke.'

Christ, Jet thought, he really had let his guard down at the last visit. 'I think it is just the shock of everything. I heard her voice for a lot of years, it's going to take a lot of time to get used to her not being here.'

'It's very natural you know.'

'That's reassuring.'

'We all move at our own pace.'

'Well I've never been known for my speed.'

'There is no guilt attached to any of the past you know?'

'I know.' If Jet knew one thing, it was this was not true. Guilt was all around. He felt guilt that he was still breathing and his beloved Julia, wife of eighteen years, was not. Guilt that he had not been able to protect her, after all it was his main job. Guilt was abundant. Sometimes he even thought it was the only thing keeping him going.

'Your holiday has obviously done you the power of good. How do you feel being back at work?'

'Good. It's busy. Looks like there's a murder in this morning, so that should keep us all entertained for a while.'

'Sounds grisly.'

'Life in the real world is grisly.'

'That's interesting. Don't you think I live in the real world?'

Jet wondered whether the words 'Freudian slip' had crossed Jane's mind as well. 'No. I didn't mean anything, I just meant being a detective, sometimes it can show you a side of human nature that can be disturbing.'

'I'm sure it must.' Jane's smile broadened and Jet wondered if it was as false as he found the meeting's sentiment. 'Well it sounds like you are busy; perhaps we could carry on our discussion about the real world at our next session?'

'Sounds good to me.'

'You know everything we talk about is in strict confidence.'

'I appreciate that.'

'Well we have another four sessions booked. Maybe if there was anything in particular you wanted to talk about we could discuss it at length next time.'

'Sure.'

'Give it some thought. I'm here just to help you.'

'Thanks.'

Jet stood up and walked out of the office. Jane smiled as he closed the door behind him. She realised the session had not been one of her best. He seemed unwilling to talk. She consoled herself this also was natural and it was usually best not to force the issue. There was always next time.

She picked up her pen and in the file she opened in front of her she made her notes.

Medical notes from bereavement session six.
Responding well to counselling.
Had a holiday which seems to have helped his mood.
Feelings of guilt are subsiding.
Currently fit for full operational duties.

She signed the paper and returned to her desk and picked up the next file in her tray. She sighed as she read the front of it to herself. 'Ralph Wilson - another skiving bastard.'

She picked up the phone on her desk and rang the extension to the reception desk. 'Yes, it's Jane. Is Ralph Wilson there? Good, send him up.'

Jane went back to the mirror on the back of her door and reviewed the damage caused by the previous bereavement session. She stroked the front of her skirt, smoothing out the creases and heard a gentle tap. She pulled at the handle.

'Ralph, how nice to see you.' She beamed. 'Come in.'

Day One - Afternoon

By the time Jet got back to the Gardens the scene had been transformed. Blue and white tape zigzagged across the entrance of the Gardens as well as across the road, even preventing cars from passing. Uniformed officers were spread out to reinforce the cordons and Jet could not get his car close to where Groom had abandoned the Focus on their first visit. Jet found a space behind a string of police cars in Forth Street. He left the Fiesta and walked towards the Gardens.

After negotiating several lengths of tape Jet got to the top of the Gardens in time to see the huge figure of Groom emerge.

'I see someone replaced the string with cordon tape.' There was no hint of a smile on Jet's face.

'Ormond came down and did his nut. Let's hope they run out of tape before they cordon off the Central Station.'

'Are forensics down there now?'

'Aye. There's a team doing a fingertip search of the whole area as well. We're still missing a penis. Bloody strange one this Jet.'

'If you say so Sarge.'

'I do. And you owe me a quid as well.'

'Therapy and robbed of a pound. Must be my lucky

day.'

'How did it go?'

'All right. I'm fully fit for operational duties.'

'That's just as well cos I think we're going to be busy.'

'What's to do now?'

'There was a name and address on the body. We need to go and check it out. I gave the CID car away so we'll have to use the Fiesta.'

'Far to go?'

'No, the Old Engineering Works near Stowell Street.'

Like a lot of buildings from Newcastle's industrial past, the Old Engineering Works had kept its dark red brickwork shell, but little else. Its conversion into apartments had been hailed as dramatic transmutation by architects, imaginative regeneration by the council and bloody expensive by everyone else.

Jet and Groom stared at the large mahogany door and all of the intercom buttons that ran down its side. After a minute of no response from apartment 7b, Groom started to push the buttons either side of it and after a few seconds got a squealed hello from 7c.

'Hello, I'm from the police. I'm trying to find Derek Thompson from 7b. Do you know where we might be able to find him?'

'I haven't seen Derek for a few days.' The remote voice

squealed through the metal speaker and Jet thought sounded cartoon like.

'Listen we're a bit concerned about him, could we come up and talk to you?'

A buzzer unlocked the door and they climbed a few short flights of stairs that took them to 7c. Jet and Groom produced identification cards to the dark-haired woman who opened the door.

She looked from Jet to Groom and slowly raised her eyes, scanning Mark's thick chest. She looked directly into Groom's ocean-blue eyes and smiled. 'Come in.'

The spotless cream walls and wooden floor of the hall led to an equally immaculate living room. Jet and Groom accepted the invitation to sit and lowered themselves onto a cream leather sofa. Jet rubbed his hand on the arm of the sofa, subconsciously reassuring himself this was not the feebly deceptive false leather look of psychotherapist's offices, but the genuine thing.

'We're sorry to disturb you....' Groom smiled

'Sarah,' she continued to look directly at Groom's face. 'Sarah Baxter.'

'Sarah,' Jet thought Groom was simpering as he spoke. 'Do you know Derek very well?'

'I wouldn't say very well. We both moved in at the same time and agreed to help each other out as much as we could, to be good neighbours. These places can be so impersonal. We take in parcels and the like for each other.

He seems a really nice man.'

'Does anyone else live next door?'

'No, just Derek. Look I don't mean to pry but can you tell me what this is about? He's not in any trouble is he?'

'We don't really know Sarah. The truth is a body of a man was found overnight and he had Derek's name and address on him.'

'Good God. You don't think?'

'Look, we're sorry to land this on you. All we have is this name and address and we really don't have anything else.'

'That's all right; it's not your fault.'

'Can you tell us what you know about Derek?'

'He's lived here about two years, single. I think he keeps in touch with his mother. She lives in Bath I think.'

'Do you know who he works for?'

'He's a regional manager for one of those national sports store companies.'

'I don't suppose you have a photograph?'

'Sorry.' Sarah gave a faint shake of her head as she spoke and then after a slight pause burst into speech. 'But I do have his key. I think under the circumstances....'

Groom and Jet followed as Sarah opened the front door of 7b and with a few taps on a console disabled the alarm.

They went into the living room which was as bright and fresh as its neighbouring apartment. Jet picked up a photograph of a man in his thirties with an older woman. 'This Derek?'

'Yes and I think that's his mother. Is it him? The body you found?'

'It's impossible to say at the moment. We'll need to make more enquiries.'

'Of course.'

Groom flicked through an address book which lay next to the telephone. All of the entries were made in neat blue-ink handwriting. 'We'll borrow this as well for a while.' He smiled at Sarah, who looked uncomfortable. 'I'm sorry to frighten you Sarah. We really don't know anything at the moment. Who knows, he might come bursting through the front door at any moment. Let's hope it's just some bizarre coincidence.' Something inside Jet made him seriously doubt Groom's words, but he guessed the reassurance was due more to the fact he did not like to see distress on the attractive face.

'Do you know if he had a girlfriend or someone he might be with?' Jet was keen to make progress.

Sarah looked at Groom. 'I don't think he was the type to have a girlfriend. You know.' Sarah raised her eyebrows as she stared at Mark.

'Look Sarah, are you going to be OK?' Jet thought Groom was fawning again.

'I'll be fine.'

'We're done here for the moment.' Groom gave

another sympathetic smile and they followed Sarah back to the door of her apartment.

Groom spoke to her at her door. 'As soon as I know anything I'll let you know.' He handed her a card, 'My mobile number's on there, if there is anything I can do, just give me a call. Can I take your number?'

Groom scribbled the dictated number on the back of another card and put it in the inside pocket of his suit jacket.

'Thanks for all your help. Try not to worry. I'll be in touch.'

Jet and Groom were soon out of the building and in the fresh air.

Groom smiled at Jet. 'I think she likes the strong sensitive type.'

'Yeah, you were well in there, until you said her neighbour was dead.'

'That did kind of stifle things.'

'Never mind. Plenty of time for more visits on compassionate grounds.'

'Exactly my thoughts Jet.' Groom tapped his pocket where the card with her number was.

Whilst he was tapping his phone chirped in his pocket and after a few seconds fumbling he had it to his ear.

'Groom.'

'Mark, DI Ormond. Any Joy?'

'We have a photo and some addresses. We'll be able to

identify him soon if he is Thompson.'

'Good, listen, we have some local press gathering here so I have sent them to the conference room at the station for an impromptu press conference.'

'Yeah.'

'I can't make it, so can you give them a brief statement. Tell them we don't know anything yet and when we do we'll hold a proper press brief. Tell them it's early days, etcetera etcetera. Just get them off my back, I'm sick of them down here and if we don't do something they'll just start making things up and panicking people for no good reason.'

'I'll head on down there now.' Groom put the phone back in his pocket.

'Ormond?' Jet enquired.

'Yes, he's dodging the press again. Sent them up to the conference room for us to speak to.'

'What we going to tell them?'

'Early days, etcetera etcetera.'

'Etcetera etcetera?'

'Etcetera etcetera.'

'That'll make a good headline.'

'Let's hope they agree.'

It took ten minutes' walk to get from the plush apartments at the Old Engineering Works to the square concrete building that is Newcastle Police Station. Every time Jet saw the drab grey building he thought it gave pebble-dashing a bad name.

On Ormond's instructions everyone claiming to be from the press had been ushered into the conference room of the police station. The conference room was a long oblong shape with walnut panelling. It seemed odd to Jet the only room in the police station infrequently used had been selected for the most expensive décor. When he sat at his own desk and looked at the grubby magnolia paint flaking off the wall he wondered whether he was supposed to feel undervalued. If that were the intention it often worked a treat.

A table and two chairs had been left empty at the head of the conference room and as Groom and Jet entered they could see all of the gathered representatives had taken positions to face it. There was no doubt where the hot seat was and Jet thought he could see alarm on Groom's face when he realised he could not avoid it.

Groom sat down in one of the seats and looked behind him to see Jet had decided to remain standing at the door. Jet forced a grin on his face when Groom caught his eye.

'Ladies and Gentlemen. I just have a few words to say, if I could have your attention.' Groom tried his best to smile and ignore the fact he had suddenly become aware of his heart thumping in his chest like an old diesel engine. Among the facing throng he saw a television camera pointing at him and heard the heavy pounding in his ribcage getting louder. 'Early this morning we received the report of a body of a man having been found in the Gardens area. Enquiries are continuing into this and as yet no further details are known.'

'Officer, can we have your name?' The voice came from a reporter sitting at the front of the room, notebook and pen in hand.

Groom winced at such a simple oversight. 'Sorry, I am Detective Sergeant Mark Groom.' Groom felt his face turning beetroot as he spat out his reply.

'There are reports that the body has been mutilated, to what extent has this occurred?' The same reporter spoke as he was still scribbling on his notepad.

'It's too early to say at the moment.'

'Too early to say Sergeant? Haven't you had a chance to look yet?'

A loud burst of laughter shot around the room.

'I'm sure you will appreciate the scene of such a serious crime needs careful examination and it would not be wise to jump to early conclusions.' Jet could tell Groom was using his best speaking voice.

'All we want to know is what you've found. It's not really an early conclusion is it Sergeant? Has he been mutilated?'

'The victim has been seriously assaulted....'

'We guessed that, him being dead and all.' The same

reporter interrupted and seemed to be enjoying taunting Groom. 'Early reports to us suggest he has had his penis cut off. Is that true?'

'It is a very early stage of the investigation.'

'Surely you know if his penis is missing or not?'

'The scene is being carefully examined and the body will be examined by a pathologist.'

'You don't need a doctor to tell you where to look to see if he has a penis or not, do you Sergeant?' Clearly this reporter could smell the blood of an unprepared officer and was determined to take advantage. It would be something to talk about with his colleagues in the bar later on. Jet could see the shade of Groom's face growing deeper.

'Look, all I can say is we're conducting enquiries at the moment and we would appreciate your patience. As soon as we are in a position to provide you with further details....'

'Further details, come on Sergeant, you haven't given us any details. What harm can it do to tell us what you know so far?'

Groom was beginning to wonder why he had found himself in this position and wasn't sure himself why he was not telling them anything. All he knew was Ormond had said tell them nothing. It had seemed a simple instruction when delivered to him. Had he prescience of this meeting he would have sought more clarification or better still formulated a good reason for some other poor sod to be here in his stead. Bloody Ormond, he was like Teflon, got stuck with nothing.

'I am sorry gentlemen but I cannot add any more detail at this early stage.' Groom was feeling very warm now and could feel sweat rolling down his back.

'Perhaps I could add a comment Sergeant.' The room hushed and for the first time Groom noticed the white collar of a religious figure. 'I am father Patrick O'Brian of St Stephen's Catholic Church here in Newcastle City Centre. Whilst our prayers must go out for the soul of any of God's creatures who has been the subject of such an horrific incident, it does need to be said, that we have all been aware of the unholy activities that have gone on around this parish, for too long now. It is against God's teachings and wishes and perhaps this is an opportunity for us all to reflect on our own behaviour. Perhaps it is now time for us all to go back to the house of God and heed His teachings. For too long now we as a community have gone against His teachings and ignored the abhorrent actions that occur on the very streets where our children play.'

Jet could see Groom shrinking and realised this press briefing was turning into a nightmare. The members of the press scribbled furiously on their pads and with every scratch of their pens Groom could feel another arrow in his heart.

'Father O'Brian.' It was the troublesome reporter who stirred. 'Are you saying that this murder might be a good thing?'

'I say no such thing. I simply say that when we allow evil to spread amongst us then evil will begat evil. Perhaps now is a moment when we could stamp out this evil and if good could come out of this atrocious act then perhaps that is the will of God. Now is the time for us all to return to the path of the glorious Lord God.'

Jet walked over to Groom and whispered into his ear. 'I think they have their story now, why don't you pretend I am saying something important to you and make an excuse to wind this up?' Jet returned to the door.

'Thank you gentlemen, I am afraid I must go now, there is a lot to do. As I said there will be a full press conference held as soon as we are in a position to release more details.'

Groom stood up and left the pack gathering up their notepads in readiness to leave. Some gathered around the Priest who seemed quite willing to give further private interviews.

Outside the conference room Groom and Jet strode quickly down the corridor.

'Bloody Ormond. He should have been here. God knows what they'll print tomorrow.'

'God might be in it.'

'What the hell is that Priest doing in here?'

'It's not your fault.' Jet was trying to be as positive as circumstances allowed.

'I'll get the blame.'

'Let's just get out of here.' Jet smiled at Groom. 'They're going to report a story about a murder, how can anyone blame you for anything?' As Jet spoke he was doubting his own words again. He was right to.

Day One – Evening

'Did you see the six o'clock news?' The Chief Constable wasn't really interested in the answer Superintendent York was going to give.

'No I haven't had a chance to see the television.'

'Never seen such a shambles. What sort of operation you running?'

'We've set up the incident room and DI Ormond is organising everything, a DCI from the homicide unit is on hand to advise and oversee.'

'Your man told the press he didn't know yet whether the body had been mutilated. Came across a right idiot. Now we have a Priest saying we're all suffering the wrath of God.'

'I think we just got caught on the hop.'

'Who sent a DS to do a press conference?'

'I think Ormond was tied up at the scene and Mark Groom volunteered to jump in and try to save the day.'

'Save the day? Save the bloody day? Heaven preserve us. Has Groom been on the media training course?'

'I don't know.'

'Don't know! You don't know whether your staff have had the appropriate training before you send them into battle?'

'I think the press conference was called to try and

make things better at the scene. It seems to have backfired.'

'It backfired all right. Listen York, get a grip. You sort the press out and if things don't get better it's not the wrath of God you'll have to worry about. You understand?'

York didn't really understand. 'Yes Sir.'

'And if Groom is going to a promotion board at any time, he better know I won't forget this fiasco. Tell him he's not inspector material. Mark his card.'

'Yes Sir.' York did not add that Groom had recently been interviewed by the Chief following success at the inspector's examination and had passed with flying colours.

'Sort it out York.'

York held the phone to his ear for a few seconds before he realised the absence of the Chief Constable shouting meant the conversation was over and he had hung up. The Chief Constable was famous for his tantrums. When something was not going to his liking he found someone to threaten. There was no reasonableness test, it just happened. If York had been in the mood to apply his usual balanced opinion he would have no doubt appreciated that no matter how random and unfair this approach was, it often got the desired result. But York was not currently in this impartial frame of mind. He felt aggrieved all his previous good deeds accounted for nothing and a press conference he knew nothing of had tarnished his reputation. Superintendent York had been the divisional commander at Newcastle long enough to have enjoyed several such verbal assaults and although he wasn't sure how he was responsible for what the press reported, he knew for certain if it portrayed the police in a bad light he was going to be blamed. He looked at his watch and saw it was nearly seven. He decided to go to the briefing room where he knew all the staff currently working on today's incident were going to meet in a few minutes.

Jet was sitting next to Groom in the briefing room.

'I'll bet Spain seems a long time ago?' Groom was feeling less tense than he had an hour ago at the end of his press conference.

Jet smiled. He knew where he would rather be. It wasn't Spain.

DI Ormond burst into the briefing room and without looking at any of the assembled throng took position at the lectern at the front. He was carrying a green file and opened it, rustling some handwritten notes.

'Right let's have some quiet.' Ormond had a talent for getting to the point. This no frills approach was popular with some. Jet thought a lack of self confidence lay behind Ormond's manner at large gatherings. Which was why he studiously avoided other tasks, like talking to the press. 'We've made a lot of headway since this morning and need to review where we are and make more progress.' Jet noticed York slipping into the room, remaining on his feet, just inside the door. Ormond did not appear to see York and continued his growling. 'Right, let's have a report from the scene manager. Paul, that's you.'

'The two main areas of damage to the body are serious head injuries and the penis has been removed.' Paul Stimpson had been the Sergeant at the Scenes of Crime Department for as long as anyone could remember. 'It's gone to the mortuary now for full post mortem. There was considerable blood around which suggests the murder took place where the body was found. There was no sign in the immediate vicinity of the missing body part. The pathologist did an initial exam at the scene and thinks the cause of death was blow to the head with a blunt heavy instrument. The blood patterns suggest the penis was removed after death. We'll know more after the PM.'

'Thanks Paul.' Ormond seemed more interested in the papers in front of him as he spoke to Stimpson. He rustled the contents of the file for a second then shouted again. 'Roger.' He looked up at the Sergeant in uniform.' You co-ordinated the search of the area. What did you find?'

'Very little. We did a fingertip search and other than hundreds of empty cans and bottles and plenty used condoms, nothing.'

'Dave, how about enquiries in the area?' Ormond looked up at the uniformed Inspector who had his own file in front of him.

'We searched the area; knocked on every door and spoke to everyone we could so far. Nothing of note. Apparently it's the kind of area that has a lot of people going backwards and forwards all times of the day and night. Nobody seems to take notice of anybody else. Those who would speak to us said they saw nothing out of the ordinary.'

Ormond went back to his notes. 'Right. We have an identification – Mark can you tell us about that?'

'We think he's Derek Thompson.' Groom did not need notes to refer to as he spoke. 'Thirty-four years old. A sportswear company regional manager. Lives at the other end of town, on his own, in a nice apartment. No previous convictions recorded. His mother is travelling up from Bath and should be here in a few hours for formal identification.'

'OK, so we have the location and the victim, what about the offender, what do we know about him, her or them?'

There was silence. Ormond rustled his papers about a little more. 'What about motive?'

Jet broke the silence. 'The area's known as a gay meeting place. In view of the injuries, it does seem to be reasonable there was a sexual motive. The mutilation was very personal; might be worth looking at previous partners.'

'Thanks Jet. I agree. Mark, I want you and Jet to find out everything there is to know about the victim. Meet the mother when she arrives and sort out formal ID. Partners, lovers, girlfriends, boyfriends, work colleagues, friends, whatever there is, find out. We know most people are murdered by people they know.' Ormond added to his scribbled notes as he spoke and then after a second's pause barked again at the gathering. 'Anything else?'

'What about the gay community? There might be people who know what happened – aggressive partners, that sort of thing?' As Groom spoke, Detective Sergeant Ian Davison lowered his head. He was the only other DS on duty from Newcastle and had been seconded to this murder enquiry with his usual investigative partner DC Stuart Townsend. Groom had been given the job of victim family liaison and Davison knew who was going to get the job of speaking to the gay community. He summoned all of the positive energy his diversity training had equipped him with and 'bollocks' was the only thought that crossed his mind.

'Ian,' Ormond said raising his eyes from the paper to

Davison. As he did Davison found another word inside his head, 'shit.'

'Yes Sir.'

'You and Stuart set up liaison with the gay community. Start with the bars, get in there tonight and talk to anyone you can. Headquarters have a community relations department, they must have contacts. See what you can rustle up.'

'Whilst Ian is trying to rustle something up the gay community,' Groom kept his face straight but snorts of laughter could be heard throughout the rest of the room. 'Should we think about keeping a watch on the area tonight in case the murderer comes back to the scene?'

'Good thinking Mark.' Any schoolboy innuendo had flown past Ormond. 'We are going to have a support team of officers down there from ten tonight until it gets light. We will speak to anyone who's there; if nothing else we might find some witnesses.'

'Anything else?' Silence followed Ormond's words. 'Right then. Go and get your jobs done and we'll meet here for a last briefing at eleven. We'll include supervision from the team on nightshift in the Gardens so we all know what's going on.'

Ormond lifted his file and as the noise of everyone leaving was starting to take off York raised his voice. 'One second please.' The silence quickly returned. 'There has already been a lot of press interest in this incident. From now on any comments to the press are to be run past me first. I will arrange for a press conference tomorrow afternoon and we'll co-ordinate things from there. It will give us a chance to appeal for witnesses. Given the sensitive nature of this enquiry, please be careful. You will have seen there is a Priest who is already stirring things up a bit. The last thing we need are more problems. Any questions?' Silence reigned. 'Thanks.'

There was a burst of activity as people left for their assigned tasks. York remained at the door. Groom made his way for the door and as he passed York spoke to him. 'Mark, can you and Whittle stay for a second? We need to have a quick chat.'

Groom turned and quickly eyed Jet. 'Of course Sir.'

They followed York to where Ormond was adding to his scribbled notes. He seemed completely consumed by the task and Jet thought he looked startled when York spoke to him.

'Nigel, can we have a word?' Ormond put his pen down and York waited until the last stragglers left the room. York directed his words to Ormond, 'Nigel, what do we know about this Priest?'

'Not a great deal.'

'He was quick to highjack the press, don't you think?'

'He wasn't slow off the mark.'

'Perhaps a little too quick?' York raised his eyebrows.

'Maybe.'

'Wouldn't hurt just to talk to him and see where he was last night. Perhaps at the same time just ask him to keep his comments to himself for the moment. Point out it's not helpful at the current time.'

'Are you talking about putting the frighteners on him?'

'Not the frighteners Nigel. Mark and Frank have a bit of a wait for the victim's mother to come, perhaps they could have a diplomatic word with him now? Before things get any further out of hand.'

Ormond looked at Groom and Jet. 'Can't do any harm to go and speak to the Priest now can it?' Ormond paused to think rather than wait for an answer to his question. 'Groom, can you and Jet go and speak to him. As Mr York says, just ask him what his intentions are and ask for his co-operation.'

'Suggest that we don't need to distract the press from finding the killer, it would be a shame if a murderer was getting away whilst the press printed stories of conflicts between the church and the gay community. Tell him we wouldn't like him to feel threatened, but if he said things that could be construed as anti-gay, he might become a suspect. He might want to think of the field day the press would have with that, if he was arrested?' York was expressionless.

Jet looked on and for the first time in a long while his thoughts were completely away from domestic considerations and dedicated to his professional investigation. He could not recall having been tasked by a superintendent to warn off a priest before.

'I think we're clear on what to do – aren't we Groom?' York looked at Mark as he spoke.

Groom appeared startled. 'Yes, we'll go and see him now.'

'Good, let me know how you get on. The Chief Constable has a personal interest in this as well, so I'll let him know how you get on. When you get back come and see me.'

'Will do, Sir.' Groom spoke and then watched York turn and leave the briefing room.

Jet stood with Ormond and Groom as they watched the door close behind York. Once it was closed Ormond looked at Groom. 'Well you heard the Superintendent. Go and tell the Priest to shut the fuck up.'

St Stephen's Church was in the heart of the city centre and one of many places of sanctuary in Newcastle not used by people in need of it. Open, and lit sufficiently by the highly positioned electric lights, it was a cold building, even on this late summer's day. Groom and Jet walked down the centre aisle, past all of the empty wooden pews.

'These places always make me feel uncomfortable.' Jet

was looking at the pictures of the Stations of the Cross on the wall. 'A lot of torture going on.' They had reached the one where Jesus was being taken from the cross. 'I was reading about those pictures a while ago.'

'You need to get out more.'

'I was looking around a church when I was in Spain.'

'Couldn't you find a bar?'

'On the front of the church there was a huge statue of Jesus on the cross, there were more inside and then these pictures all around the walls.'

'Suppose it would be odd if the priest just had a picture of their lass up.'

Jet smiled. 'Pope might frown upon the priest having a wife, never mind her photo on the wall.'

'Valid point.'

'It seems to me it's all just about death.'

'It is a bit depressing Jet, I'll give you that.'

'If the promise is an afterlife shouldn't there be more focus on resurrection?'

'You mean rather than torture and murder?'

'A constant reminder of the evil of mankind.'

'This lot are not the forgive and forget type.' Groom had not seen Father O'Brian approaching the altar from an anteroom nor appreciated the excellent acoustics of the church.

'On the contrary. God sacrificed his only son to save mankind. Forgiveness is very much a part of our faith.'

Jet thought the Priest looked in his forties. He was wearing a long black robe which contrasted with his ruddy complexion. It looked to Jet like the Priest attempted to force a smile but it would not form on his face and quickly it got lost.

'You're the officer from the press conference?'

'Yes.' Groom really did not want to be reminded of the conference but at least managed a faint smile of his own. 'Mark Groom, this is Frank Whittle.'

'How can I help?'

'We just wanted a word about the incident we're investigating.'

'Well if I can help in any way.'

'Did you know the deceased?'

'I don't know who the deceased was.'

'Does the name Derek Thompson mean anything to you?'

The Priest stood still and silent for a second as if digesting the information and then shook his head slowly at first and then more quickly. 'I don't think so, should it?'

'We think that's the name of the victim.'

'The thing that springs to mind is – what a strange question to ask.'

'You seemed to be very quick to attend the press conference and make comments.'

'As priest here I know only too well the sins that are

committed. Our streets are full of people who have turned their backs on the teachings of God. It is my job to point this out. I work in the service of God.'

'If you didn't know the details of what happened how could you make a statement like that so early?'

'I speak to many people and everyone was aware of what happened. That's why your press conference was such a failure, because you were treating people as if they were stupid, and trying to conceal the truth. I don't conceal the truth. I glory in it, and the teachings of God.'

'You were very quick to condemn.'

'I preach the word of God.'

'There is a victim here, with a family, perhaps we should think about their feelings.'

'You insult me to suggest what I said was insensitive. I only repeat the word of God, that we should all live a chaste life and sexual congress is acceptable only within the bounds of marriage. The word of God is not insensitive. It is the same as you saying we cannot mention the word murder, in case it offends.'

'What makes you think there was sexual congress?' The Priest turned to face Jet as he joined the conversation for the first time.

'Are you saying there was not?'

Jet was feeling frustrated at the Priest's tendency to answer questions with another question. 'We're still making enquiries and it's a little too early to judge.'

'There is only one important judge and it is never too early to spread His word.'

'Where were you last night?' Jet could sense Groom's frustration in his voice.

'I was here until after the late service. I had a few meetings with parishioners and then went home.'

'Where is home?'

'The church owns a house around the corner, which is my home.'

'Does anyone else live there, who could verify where you were?'

'No, I was on my own. You're treating me as a suspect?'

'As we said it is a very early stage of our enquiry, we are trying to establish what happened and appreciate your co-operation.'

'You can be assured I will always co-operate where I can, but it will always be my duty to spread the word of God.'

'It's our duty to catch murderers.'

'Rest assured I will do nothing to interfere with your duty. I trust you will not do anything to interfere with mine?'

Whatever they had hoped to achieve during this meeting Jet sensed they had failed.

Groom smiled at the Priest and Jet thought he had reached the same conclusion. 'Thanks, no doubt we'll be seeing you soon.'

Jet followed as Groom turned and walked up the aisle and out into the street.

'Well that went well.' Groom did not smile.

'I don't think anything's going to shake him from his cause.'

'I have the feeling we've not heard the last of the Priest.'

Mrs Greta Thompson looked pale and shell-shocked as she entered the police station. The police woman who had met her from the train took her to the peace of an interview room and went to make her the cup of tea she felt obliged to accept when offered.

With all the democracy that exists between a sergeant and constable it had been decided it would be better if Jet dealt with this sensitive issue on his own. There was something about Groom's muscle-bound frame that seemed to put him at a disadvantage in these tender moments. He never said that and nor did Jet. Jet was content it was a discussion they never needed to have.

Jet immediately felt sympathy for the mother of the victim of this hideous offence. A plump woman in her sixties, dressed in her Sunday best, she looked every bit the experienced mother in gravy adverts of days gone by. She should have been smiling, wearing an apron, catering for her loving family, not sitting in a police station dealing with the consequences of violent death.

Jet smiled as he sat on the chair next to her. 'I'm Frank Whittle, I'm really sorry for your loss.'

Greta smiled and rubbed the damp looking handkerchief she had in her hand on her nose. 'There's no doubt it's Derek?'

'No. We will need a formal identification but we have a photograph and with the identification on him, I don't think there's any doubt.'

Greta winced.

'Look, I can't even imagine how hard this is for you and we don't need to do anything you don't want to.'

Greta shook her head slowly.

'All the formalities we can leave for the time being.' Jet's voice was low. 'But there are some things you could tell us that would help us to try and find out who did this to Derek.'

The door opened and the police woman held out a cup in front of her.

'There you are Greta.' Police Constable Alice Burn had a lot of experience dealing with grieving relatives and had often told Jet that she had never enjoyed a moment of it. She placed the cup in front of Greta and sat down on the other side of her.

'What can I tell you?' Greta was trying to rally herself.

'What do you know about Derek's friends here?'

'Nothing really. He occasionally went out with people he knew at work but he was a quiet lad, kept himself to himself. His job brought him here but I don't think he intended to stay.'

'Did he have a partner that you knew of?'

'No, he was a quiet boy. I don't think he had a girlfriend here.'

'Did he have a girlfriend in Bath?'

'No. He was always very shy. He went out with a few girls over the years but nothing special. His father always used to say he was a mummy's boy.' Greta attempted a laugh but it would not come. 'His father died ten years ago.'

'What did he do in his spare time, hobbies that sort of thing?'

'He loved his computer, a keen photographer and he read a lot. He used to enjoy cooking.'

'Did he do anything where he might have met other people, clubs, night classes, anything like that?'

'No.'

'He had a wallet with thirty pounds and two credit cards, was that usual for him to carry – I mean did he usually carry more money? I'm just wondering if anything was stolen.'

'He just carried what he needed.'

'What about jewellery?'

'He always wore the watch his dad gave him. He

usually had a gold ring on, and of course his crucifix.'

'Crucifix?'

'Yes, gold, on a gold chain, it was his confirmation present.'

'Confirmation?'

'Yes.'

'Was he a practising catholic?'

'Yes. Never missed church.'

'Did he go to church here in Newcastle?'

'Yes, every Sunday. He would never miss.'

'Do you know which church?'

'St Stephen's.'

'Did he tell you anything about the church, if he'd met anyone there, anything like that?'

'No, he was just going to the service on Sundays as far as I know.'

'Thanks Mrs Thompson. I think that's all for tonight. I understand your daughter is coming to meet you?'

'Yes, Alice here has booked us into a hotel for tonight. I imagine there'll be a lot to sort out tomorrow.'

'There's no rush for anything. The important thing is you look after yourself. Perhaps Derek's sister could help us with the formal identification tomorrow?'

Greta nodded and gave a little sob into her handkerchief. Jet rose.

'I'll see you tomorrow after you've had some rest and your daughter is here. Please try to rest and take care of yourself.' Greta's head was bowed as she blew into her handkerchief. Jet smiled at Alice Burn as he quietly left the room.

Jet walked into the briefing room just before 11.00pm and scanned the tired faces until he saw Groom and sat next to him. Ormond burst in, still carrying his green file. The fatigue felt by the staff in the room meant Ormond did not have to compete hard for their immediate attention.

'It's been a long day, so let's keep this brief.' Ormond opened his file. 'DS Davison, what have you got for us?'

'Not a lot. The bars and clubs are quiet. Not many people talking. Certainly no suspects being put up. Headquarters have come up with a volunteer as a liaison, Jake Swinton, he works for a local organisation which promotes gay issues; he's coming tomorrow to help us.'

'Ian,' Groom piped up. 'Are you going to wait until Jake comes for you tomorrow?' There were snorts of laughter and Ormond looked confused. 'I mean, is he going to come just for you?' Groom's smile was not returned by Davison.

Jet thought Ormond had not noticed Groom's emphasis on the word 'come' and clearly could not see any purpose in this line of enquiry as he pressed on. 'DS Davison will act as liaison with the gay community throughout this enquiry. Ian, find out how this man Swinton can help us.'

The sniggers had subsided as Ormond returned to his notes. 'Groom, what have you got?'

'Priest says he didn't know Derek Thompson but his mother reckons he was a regular churchgoer there. Jet spoke to the mother and checked with the mortuary. He still had a gold crucifix on him and a gold ring. We can't be certain but it may be the only thing missing from the victim was his watch.'

'You found his cock then?' Davison's retort did not enjoy the accompaniment of laughter from elsewhere in the room.

'Groom, check his apartment and see what we can do about the watch. If it's missing we need to circulate it. It could be a good lead. If it was the motive for the crime we need to know. Let's hope the killer's still got it and will try to sell it. Let's talk about the Priest after the briefing.' Ormond shuffled his papers again. 'Anything else of note?' There was silence. 'OK, you have your jobs for tomorrow morning. We'll work from the incident room and the next briefing will be here at noon.'

Groom and Jet stayed where they were as everyone else but Ormond quickly left.

'What do we know about the Priest?' Ormond had his file tucked under his arm.

'Very little.'

'Is he going to shut up?'

Groom twisted his face. 'We've done everything we can. I don't think there is much more we can say to him unless we start treating him as a serious suspect.'

'Seems an unlikely one to me, but you and Jet take a good look at him tomorrow. If there is anything to know about him, I want it.'

'Sure. What about Mr York?'

'What?'

'He asked for a briefing about the Priest.'

'I'm going to see him now. There're a few things we need to sort out. The budget being the main one. I'll tell him you're on to the Priest, just keep me informed. Go home and get some rest. I'll see you tomorrow.'

Jet and Groom rose then walked out of the room. They headed down the corridor towards the exit.

In the quiet of the corridor Jet spoke. 'Why do you keep winding Davison up with all those schoolboy jokes?'

'Schoolboy Jet? I thought they were quite sophisticated.'

'Just because Ormond doesn't get them, doesn't mean they're sophisticated.'

'Don't worry about it Jet. Just having a bit of fun.'

It was almost midnight when Jet parked the Fiesta on his drive. He had forgotten about the fence and surveyed the two new posts that had been put in his front garden. A length of string pulled tight traversed them, marking the line of the new fence. Jet spoke sotto voce as he eyed the perfectly straight line. 'Well, at least someone's made some progress today.' He thought Julia would have been pleased with this gardening improvement.

Jet was tired. He set his alarm for seven, then emptied his pockets onto the chest of drawers in his bedroom. He pulled out the packet of paracetamol tablets bought today at the chemist he passed on his way back from headquarters. He opened the top drawer and counted the other slim packets of the tablets he had collected. He had six. So he now had ninety-six pills. He remembered the days you could go to the chemist and buy a bottle with a hundred and no-one blinked an eye. He had seen people take more and survive. He would have to remember to buy something to stop him from vomiting. He had seen too many attempts fail when pills were returned from the stomach by a person's natural defence mechanism. He could not bear the thought of waking up in a hospital ward. That would be the worst of all worlds.

Journal - Murder Two

There was poetry in this one's death. He gurgled as he fell to his knees. The first swipe of the hammer took him down. A queer hanging around the public toilet like a refugee. He saw me pretending to take a piss and he knew what I was after. Or at least he thought he knew. It took just minutes and he had his trousers around his ankles. He got much more than he thought. He was well past caring when I cut off his prick. Another trophy for my collection. It will grow, my collection that is, not his prick. His prick will never grow again. It was his undoing if you think about it.

I don't know what his name was, I did not ask him and I did not introduce myself. That is how queers live you know, anonymously. They shag strangers in the shadows of public places because they are embarrassed at what they do. Ashamed of their affliction. Quite right most would say. Better they are hidden away out of the sight of good solid upstanding people. They have no right to be seen in public doing normal things with normal people. They deserve to be kept in the dark and never spoken about.

I have made another hero. If this one had a secret then the world will find out about it. But he has given his life for the cause. The fight against perversion. He might not be as well remembered in years to come as last night's hero. But still his death will mean more than his life ever did.

It is strange writing this now because you will know that he is not going to be the last. But think about this, I have not yet selected tomorrow's hero and yet you know who he is. I wonder if you know the names of all of the heroes I have created. I think I will call them the pervert martyrs. Does that have a nice ring to it for your front page headlines?

Day Two – Morning

'There's another body.'

'What?' Jet was barely conscious. The bedside phone had woken him and automatically he'd picked it up.

'There's another body been found. They just rang me. You need to wake up Jet and meet me at the station.' Groom sounded far more alert.

'I'll get straight down there.'

Jet pulled himself from bed and went to the bathroom. He sat on his toilet and at the same time ran his electric razor across his face. Multitasking. A shower, clean shirt and yesterday's suit took a matter of minutes. Soon Jet was opening the door of the Fiesta. He slumped into the seat and closed the door, then noticed through the windscreen an envelope tucked under the wiper-blade. He strained to reach out of the door window to grab the envelope. The handwriting was the same as the mysterious delivery he found on his mat yesterday and he felt stupid that events had made him forget about it. Now he had another. It felt bulky. He leaned over the empty front passenger seat and tore open the top of the envelope, using his fingertips to pull out a buff coloured card. As he tilted the envelope to remove the card a silver coloured watch fell out onto the empty seat. The face was cracked and the dials had stopped at twenty minutes past

67

two. He opened up the card and inside the black-ink handwriting said 'time's up for someone else.' Jet felt a shiver run up his spine.

The Fiesta took an extra rumble before bursting into action, as if it too did not appreciate unexpected early starts. During the twenty minute drive to the station Jet was conscious of the sound of the watch sliding on the passenger seat with the motion of the car as he negotiated the still sleepy streets.

Groom was sitting in the incident room when Jet walked in and jumped to his feet. 'Come on, we need to get down to the toilets in the Bigg Market.'

'Something odd's happened, Mark.'

Jet had a plaintive look and Groom stopped in his tracks. 'Yeah?'

'This was on my car this morning.' Jet handed Groom the envelope. 'A similar one came yesterday. I didn't have time to think much more about it.'

Groom opened up the envelope and gently examined the contents. 'What did you do with yesterday's?'

'It's in my desk.'

'Let's go to your desk then.'

The incident room was on the same floor as the CID office and within seconds Jet was opening his desk drawer and pulling out yesterday's envelope. They placed both envelopes on opposite ends of the desk surface, with the notes and watches adjacent.

'It could be nothing.' Jet said hopefully.

'It's fucking strange Jet.'

'With all that happened yesterday I forgot all about it and when I opened this morning's I thought of the watch missing from Thompson's body.'

'And they were on your car?'

'That one was pushed through my door.'

'Lock them in your drawer, we better get to this morning's body. Ormond's going down to the scene as well, we can speak to him there.'

The public toilets in the Bigg Market are circular. They are sunken into the ground and the round frosted glass roof sits only feet above road level. The glass in the roof carry the stains of urban pollution and it is hard to determine whether it is the design or the dirt which prevents the light from piercing the old structure. Whichever, the building is an unwelcoming one. Blue and white police tape had been wrapped around the wrought iron railings which circle the toilets. The tape crossed the open gateway that led to the stone steps which sank down to the toilet entrance. Jet lifted it up as he and Groom walked down the stairs. The tall Victorian urinals ran in a semicircle against the wall and on the opposite wall was a row of toilet cubicles. A uniformed officer stood at the cubicle door furthest from the entrance.

Jet recognised the figure guarding the toilet door. 'Hello Steve, we'll have to stop meeting like this.'

Steve Manson remained straight-faced. 'I can think of better things to do.'

'I see you've used the tape this morning. It's good to see the scene properly cordoned off.' Jet knew Groom was trying to deliver a compliment but Manson did not seem to appreciate it. No doubt there were plenty of fleas in ears after Ormond had seen the second-hand string used yesterday.

'What we got?'

'Same as yesterday.'

The circular line of the wall made the row of cubicles oddly shaped and each more spacious than usual. The vandal resistant stainless steel toilet pans were a cold and hostile modern addition to the Victorian facility. Jet stretched past Manson and looked into the cubicle he was guarding. The twisted body lay on the floor beside the toilet, the torso had come to rest chest to the floor but the head was turned and looking up from the rear wall, as if it were trying to gaze out of the door. The body was clothed but the trousers were pulled down below the knees. Jet could see blood around the groin and there was a pool of it on the floor under where the head had come to rest.

'Looks like his penis has been removed.' Jet's

comment was meant for Groom, but Manson added. 'Yeah, he really did get his end away.' His mischievous smile was not shared.

'You think this is sexually motivated?'

'No doubt. This place is notorious. They even cut holes in the cubicle walls where they put their knobs through. The council are often here patching up the holes. They've even tried to stop them by putting stainless steel partitions in but the puffs still get down here. Gets so decent people can't use the place. Maybe this'll quieten the place down a bit as far as the puffs go.' Manson was still smiling.

'So you see a positive side to this?'

'Every cloud and all of that.'

'Have you touched the body?' Groom looked directly at Manson.

'Just enough to confirm he was beyond mouth to mouth.' Manson's smile now had a touch of venom.

'Two bodies in two days, and your DNA on both of them. People will start to talk.' Jet was not certain how light-heartedly Groom meant his comment.

Jet knew he should not touch the body but could not resist pulling gently at both sleeves. 'He's not wearing a watch.'

'Not everybody does. Let's not panic.' Jet thought Groom's mind was spinning as much as his.

'I don't think he'll be needing a watch. Do you?'

Manson was still grinning. 'I think his time's up.'

'You're cheery for someone who's been on duty all night and left guarding a public shithouse.' Even Groom's sense of humour could not stretch as far as Manson's.

'Take pride in my work.'

'When was the body found?'

'Cleaner found it at six this morning. She's gone home for a lie down, lives not far away.'

Groom turned his back on Manson and tugged Jet's arm. 'Come on, we need a chat.'

Groom sucked a deep breath of air as they emerged from the underground toilet. He turned to face Jet as they stood in the cobbled street. The Bigg Market was deserted. The pubs and takeaways that surrounded them were locked up and it would be a good while before their neon lights burst into life again. 'I'd better wait here for Ormond. It's going to take most of the morning to get the body and the scene sorted out. Can you see the Priest and then Thompson's mother and I'll see you at the briefing at twelve? I'll tell Ormond about the watches and we'll speak later.'

Jet was turning to walk away when a thought crossed Groom's mind. 'Jet?'

'Yeah.'

'How well do you know that idiot Manson?'

'Not well, he's been on that uniform shift for a few

years. Why do you ask?'

'Nothing. Just getting frustrated, I suppose. He's been at both scenes and he's getting on my wick.'

'Yeah, Manson will do that.' Jet smiled, then turned and walked away.

As Jet left the scene he found his mind a fog of watches, priests, grieving relatives and missing penises. Once he had decided on an order to approach his current tasks, his mind, as usual, returned to Julia. The image of his dead wife, smiling, and he felt a smile grow on his face too, the one that when he was on his own, was often followed by tears. He could never forget her, never wanted to, but also he could not stop the feeling of a red-hot sword being plunged into his chest every time he did recall. These emotions were tearing him up inside, killing him, he knew it. He could not stop it. He told everyone the pain was easing - isn't time the great healer? – counsellors, Julia's sister, Julia's mother, Groom; he lied to them all. During their life together Julia had become his reason for living. After her murder he knew there were things he needed to do. His sense of justice had made him hold on to see things finished. Justice for Julia. Soon all would be complete. He was getting close to being able to implement his final exit plan – he didn't tell anyone about that.

Jet did not know what time catholic priests started work but guessed it might be early. On his way to the church he called into the police station and walked into the room he knew was the control room for the CCTV cameras that monitored the city.

He always felt dazzled by the urgent images thrown out by the bank of twenty screens that lined the wall. It reminded him of the migraine attacks he sometimes suffered; fragments and colours jumping uncontrollably. He felt his stomach turn a little in sympathy at the thought. He moved his eyes from the screens to the operator and did not recognise the slight figure in the fabric-covered swivel chair. Waves of auburn hair swayed freely as the head turned looking at the screens and, as delicious as it was, looked incongruous with the white uniform shirt.

'Excuse me,' Jet thought the operator surprised as she turned her head away from the screen. She smiled. Jet felt the warmth. 'I'm Jet, from CID; I'm working on yesterday's murder. I was wondering if you could show me where the camera in the Bigg Market was pointing through the early hours of this morning.'

'Of course. I'll check the hard drive.'

'That sounds complicated.'

'Not really, all the images captured by the cameras are stored on a hard drive for a week, then backed up on disc after that.' She was tapping away at a keyboard in front of her and then the main monitor in front of her changed view and showed 'Bigg Market Cam 12' at the bottom of the screen. 'This is midnight.'

The view from the camera high upon a building on the corner of the Bigg market covered the wide cobbled road. It showed the car parking spaces in the middle of the street which ran to the edge of the toilet, but the toilet building itself was too far away down the gentle sweep of the road to be seen by the camera's chosen position. The street was busy with people and vehicles running up and down.

'Could you fast forward it?'

'Sure.'

At the press of a button the screen became a comical scene of people speeding up and down the cobbled street, with the odd glare from a headlight thrown in.

A thought shot into Jet's mind. 'Did you know Benny Hill's still popular in America?'

'I didn't.'

'I read it somewhere; I think the Americans have just caught up with his sense of humour.'

'Really?'

'Yeah.'

'Who's Benny Hill?'

Jet sighed. 'Probably a bit before your time.' Jet was close to her seat now and caught a subtle whiff of scent. Arousing. 'Could you spin this forward to twenty past two?'

The screen sped up further and Jet watched time

75

hurry through. When a car headlight hit the camera full on, it flashed violently and for a split-second looked as if the screen burst into flames. Another childhood television reminiscence, Bonanza, jumped into his brain. He decided not to share this with the auburn-haired beauty. It got to 02:14. 'Slow it down there please.'

Jet and the operator watched. The street was transformed from streams of lifeblood customers of pubs and takeaways, to the barrenness of a place no longer awake. The camera still watched over the cobbles and Jet could make out the edge of the public toilets on the left hand side of the screen. Activity was now restricted to the occasional car, Jet guessed probably taxis passing through the street. Then a car slowed down and stopped in a parking bay near the toilet. A figure got out of the car and walked away.

'What make of car is that?' Jet was squinting.

'Ford Mondeo.' She said without hesitation.

'You know your cars.'

'Get an eye for them doing this job.'

'Don't suppose you can make out the registration number?'

'No. It will have to go to headquarters to be enhanced if you want any more detail.'

The car remained in position for nearly ten minutes, then the figure returned, got back into the driver's seat and drove away.

'Has that anything to do with the body found down there this morning?'

'I just had a feeling about something and wanted to check.' Jet didn't want to start explaining about broken watches. 'What's that?' Jet saw another figure coming from the direction of the toilets, crossing the road.

'Dunno.'

Both sets of eyes stared at the screen as the figure made its way to the other side of the street. As it passed under a street light it became a little clearer.

'It's all right; it's just the beat bobby.' Jet thought her voice like velvet.

He too could now see the outline of a police cap. The figure was strolling in the silence of the Bigg Market towards the cathedral that proudly stood at the bottom of the Bigg Market, out of sight of the camera.

'I wonder which officer that was.'

'Tell you in a jiff.' She thumbed her way through the duty sheet which lay on the desk at her side.

'That's very efficient.'

'We need a copy here, so we know who to call if we see anything happening. Need to know who's on duty and closest. PC 6904 was on that beat last night, that's Steve Manson.'

'Thanks, you've been a big help.' Jet smiled.

'Pleased to help. My name's Claire by the way.' She thrust out her right arm and Jet accepted the warm soft hand. As he did he noticed her shirt tighten over the curve of her breast as he reluctantly let her hand go.

'Thanks Claire, I owe you.' Jet smiled and felt rooted to the spot.

Claire returned the smile. 'My relief always meet up at the club after late shift, you should join us next time. You can pay me back by buying me a drink and telling me more about Benny Hill.'

'That sounds good.' Something in Jet's brain reminded him he needed to get moving, so with a smile he turned and walked out of the CCTV room.

He felt a slight tingle and grinned to himself as he walked out of the station. He knew that was the best offer he'd had in months. He also knew he wouldn't have the courage to do anything about it. What would Julia have said?

When Jet looked up at St Stephen's Church he wondered how much Father O'Brian would give to have the same amount of visitors as the pubs in the Bigg Market. He walked through the huge doors and down the aisle and made a mental note to get a telephone number from the Priest for future visits, rather than relying on him being in the church. He was just about to give up and walk out when he saw the familiar figure of the Priest walk across the altar. Father O'Brian nodded his head but did not smile when he caught his eye and Jet thought he detected the signs of an inward sigh.

'Officer, I would have thought you'd be busy at the scene of today's crime?' The Priest walked through the low gate of the altar and stood opposite Jet near the front pew.

'You're well informed.'

'I do keep my ear to the ground. The press have also been on to me for a comment.'

'Have you made one?'

'I've decided to call a little press conference later this morning so I can answer any queries they might have in one go.'

'Do you think that's wise?'

'The wisdom of the word of God is beyond question.'

'We don't even know what's happened yet.'

'Details of current events don't concern me. I know you find it hard to believe but I'm just trying to make things better.'

Jet didn't believe. The thought of making hay whilst the sun shined crossed his mind. 'Even so, the wrong comment might be insensitive to someone's feelings. A relative or friend of a deceased perhaps?'

'There is much wrong in this community and we all have a responsibility to make things better. God sacrificed his only son, you could say that was insensitive to His feelings but it was for the salvation of mankind.'

Jet realised he was kicking water uphill. 'You told me yesterday you didn't know Derek Thompson.'

'That's true.'

'Can you have a look at this photograph and tell me if you recognise it?'

Jet produced one of the many copies they'd made of the photograph taken from Thompson's apartment. The Priest took a cursory glance at the picture and started shaking his head.

'No I can't say that rings a bell.'

'Strange that, because his mother says he was a regular Sunday attender.'

'Really.' The Priest did not change his expression and quickly scanned the photograph again. 'I suppose he might have been in the church at some time. I have quite a large and varied congregation. Perhaps it's just a poor likeness.'

'He's been a staunch catholic all his life. He's been living in Newcastle for the past two years and been coming to your service all that time.'

'That's not so surprising is it?'

'No. But I am a little surprised you didn't see him.'

'A lot of people come to the services; I don't get to chat to them all individually. It's possible I have met him but just don't recall.'

'Might it cause you some embarrassment?'

'What are you talking about?'

'Well you are being vocal about people's life choices and the victim is a practising catholic.'

'Are you suggesting I should not do my duty as parish priest?'

'No, I just wonder if a little sensitivity at this time might be wise for everyone. Things might be said people will regret.'

'You accuse me of being insensitive? How crass. All that is necessary for evil to triumph is for good men to do nothing, I do believe it was an Irishman who coined the phrase, it's as true today.' Jet was as interested in the sayings of 18th Century Irish politicians as the Priest was in modern-day political correctness. 'And what you call life choices, I call a sin against God.'

'Times change.'

'The word of God has not changed. We should heed it.'

'Where were you last night?' Jet changed the subject.

'I was here and at home. Does that matter to you?'

'Routine enquiries into a serious incident. I'm sure you understand.'

'I understand all right. I also understand my duties to my church and my God.'

Jet did not know why he was surprised the Priest had a mobile telephone but still he was. He took the number and left the church, no further forward than when he'd arrived.

Jet thought there was nothing discovered from the Priest that required special attention and as he had a little time to spare he pointed the Fiesta toward home. Outside of his house he was pleased to see a pickup and Terry beavering away with a fence post on his garden.

'Looks good.' Terry had not seen Jet approach and looked startled.

'Yeah, it's going all right. I want to get all the posts up and then I'll be able to get the rails and boards up when I get them. That all right?'

'Fine by me, I'm grateful you could get it done so quickly.'

'Not such a big job, it's just fitting it around others.'

'I'll need to get the cash for you, any idea when it'll be done?'

'Depends on getting the materials and other jobs, a few days I would have thought, I'll let you know when I'm going to put the final boards up, if that's okay?'

'Fine by me.' Jet paused a second. 'Listen, I was just wondering if you saw anyone put an envelope through my letter box yesterday morning, when you saw my fence down?'

'Been getting hate mail?'

'No. Just got an odd delivery yesterday morning and was wondering who had left it.'

'Don't remember seeing anything.'

'Anyone on the path, or maybe a vehicle?'

'The street's pretty quiet, I don't remember anything.'

'Thanks, if anything does come to mind would you let me know?' Jet produced a card with his mobile telephone number.

'No problem, I'll give it some thought.'

Jet admired the line of the fence again and then made a check of his front door and was relieved to find out there had been no further mysterious deliveries. He made his way back to the Fiesta. Julia had often wondered why Jet had been content as a detective constable and he had always defended himself because he'd enjoyed the work. But watching Terry constructing the new fence Jet felt envious. Perhaps had he gone into a similar line of business for himself he would be leading a more contented life. With Julia alive, perhaps using her talents to keep his business accounts in order. She could easily have done it. He looked at the pickup laden with fencing rails and bags of fertiliser, and then at his Fiesta. The Fiesta that Julia always hated. The things that could have been.

He did not want to be late for his next appointment with Mrs Thompson which was due in thirty minutes so he slid into the Fiesta and headed back to the police station. Back to reality.

At St Stephen's Church a large crowd of reporters gathered at 10am. Some with early afternoon deadlines were keen to make progress; others stood in the sun outside the church and relaxed in its pleasant rays. Three sets of TV cameras followed their reporters, awaiting the arrival of the Priest. All sensed a unique angle to a familiar story. People killed other people every day of the week. Crusades by priests on the back of them, that was different. No matter his motive, this is what the viewing public wanted. Some would hail him a hero, telling the world how it is. Some would think him a relic who had no right to preach to them. Consensus among the reporters was it did not matter if he was eloquent or made a real fool of himself. Either way would make a good story.

The Priest appeared on the broad steps outside the church.

'I would just like to say a few words.' He had a piece of paper in his hands, which was folded in front of him, but he did not raise it to read. There was a sudden burst of noise as cameras whirred and photographers seized their opportunity. The television cameras focused upon him as he stood on the edge of the shadow being cast by the tall stone building of the church. 'There have been some tragic events in this city over the past two days, and first I would like to extend my deepest sympathies to the victims and their families. I do not wish to add to the grief of anyone during a difficult time.' The Priest turned his head as he spoke, gazing at those gathered who hung on his every word. Most of the audience did not return the look, but scribbled on the notepads they held out in front of them. 'That said, it is known by all who live in this city, and I have no doubt Newcastle is no different from any other, that a large part of our community have turned their back on God. Dramatic events, such as those we are witnessing now, are a time when we can, and should, examine our behaviour, and I call for everyone to do this and to come back to the path of the Lord. God sacrificed his only son to save mankind and lead us into the light. We risk feeling His wrath if we do not amend our ways and live by His teachings and His will. So I call to all our community to examine our souls and to come back to the house of God.'

'Father O'Brian.' The reporter was Groom's tormentor from the last press conference. 'Are you saying we should come back to the church or something of biblical proportions is going to happen to us?'

'I am saying we should remember the lessons God has taught us and remember His will is we live by His word.'

As the Priest spoke a headline was forming in the reporter's mind along the lines of 'Priest warns of Sodom and Gomorrah vengeance on Newcastle if we don't mend our ways!' This crazy Priest was making things interesting!

'The police have been reluctant to provide any information but the indications are these incidents involve members of the gay community. What is your message to them?' The reporter had now moved in his mind to 'Priest speaks out against homosexuals.'

'This church is open to everyone; we must all heed God's word. The act of homosexuality is intrinsically disordered.'

'Are you saying that all gays are disordered?' The reporter could smell a good story.

The Priest looked irked by the interruption. 'It is not those who have homosexual desires that are evil, but it is acting upon the desire that is wrong.'

'So gay people shouldn't have sex?'

'Sexual intercourse is only acceptable within the bounds of marriage, only then does the act fully symbolise the creator's dual design, of an act of covenant love with the potential of creating new life. Outside of that solemn bond it is wrong.'

'Father O'Brian.' The reporter was beginning to sense other opportunities. 'You mentioned the risk of us feeling the wrath of God if we did not mend our ways and using these events as a lesson to us all, is that right?'

'Yes.'

'Forgive my ignorance but in the Old Testament aren't there examples of God himself exacting revenge on the world to teach mankind lessons? Noah's Ark comes to mind.'

'Yes.'

'So you could say, in the same way, these murders are a good thing, as they point out lessons. Do you think good can come from these murders?'

'I am saying we need to get ourselves back onto the path of the Lord. Now is the time for change.'

'So are you saying these murders are a good thing?'

'I am saying that from any evil act, we must learn and mend our ways. We must now come back to the path of God.' The Priest's stolid expression showed no sign of change. 'Now is the time for us to change our ways.' The reporters scribbled on their pads. 'Thank you for coming this morning.' The Priest turned to go back into the church but was prevented by individual requests for comment and interview; each member of the press being interested in reporting their own particular slant on things. The Priest obliged and it took him another fifteen minutes before he could resume his normal church duties.

Day Two – Afternoon

'Come on, we've got a lot to get through.' Ormond was trying to interrupt the garrulousness of pre-briefing gatherings without immediate success.

Jet looked around the room and could see the staff numbers were growing. He pointed this out to Groom who was sitting next to him.

'Yeah, serial murders do seem to attract a lot of attention.'

Silence spread and Ormond shuffled his notes around. 'We have another victim and the MO is the same as yesterday. So we have a serial killer. Paul can you tell us all about today's scene?'

DS Paul Stimpson did not refer to any notes. 'SOCO are finishing off at the scene and the body has gone to the mortuary. Cause of death looks to have been a number of blows to the back of the head. The skull is caved in. The penis has been removed and is missing. It's a public toilet so there's fingerprints and DNA galore. The post mortem of the first victim was done this morning and it confirms the cause of death was brain damage and the penis was cut off after death. The second one looks the same.'

'Thanks Paul, what do we know about the victim?' Ormond looked up and scanned the room. His eyes settled on one of the recent additions to the enquiry.

Ormond addressed the crowd. 'DS John Jardine and his colleague DC Colin Needham have been seconded to us this morning from Gateshead; they're taking on liaison with the second victim's family. John, what can you tell us?'

'Precious little, if I know Jardine.' Groom was whispering into Jet's ear.

'Another friend?'

Groom winked but did not reply to Jet's under-the-breath enquiry.

'Oh yes,' Jardine was fumbling with a folded piece of paper. 'Justin Gallagher, thirty-two years old. Estate Agent, lives with his partner Peter Russell in an apartment on the Quayside, 35 Sailors Wharf.'

'Do we know if anything was taken from the body?' Ormond stared at Jardine as he read from his paper.

'Oh yes, we've spoken to his partner and the only thing confirmed missing is his watch.'

Jet's heart sank.

'Do we know if he had any connections with the first deceased, Derek Thompson?' Jet thought Ormond's public interrogation of Jardine was like pulling teeth.

'Oh yes; no.'

'Can we pursue that and make absolutely sure. If there is a connection we need to know.'

'Oh yes.'

Groom again spoke to Jet in a hushed tone. 'If you're

wondering if he's always like that, the answer's, oh yes.'

Jet tried to keep a straight face.

'There was a vehicle caught on the CCTV camera.' Ormond's voice boomed to the assembly. 'It's a white Ford Mondeo reg number NH57 EGA. That number refers to a Renault so it looks like it had false plates. It was caught on the CCTV camera parked next to the toilets. We have uniform out looking for it. We'll put it out to the press and see what comes back.'

'Smart bit of detective work.' Groom whispered to Jet. Jet allowed himself a smile as Ormond continued.

'DS Ian Davison has been responsible for liaison with the gay community and we now have a representative who is going to advise. Ian, can you explain?'

Davison looked no more comfortable than previous briefings. He stood up and turned his back on Ormond to face the rest of the gathering. 'This is Jake Swinton. He works for an organisation here in Newcastle called NEGRA which is North East Gay Rights Association. They have a lot of links in the community which I am sure will be of use to us. Justin, can I ask you to explain your role?'

'Jake. I think Justin is the other gay, the one who's dead.'

Davison winced as Jake Swinton spoke while he got to his feet. Swinton looked more comfortable than Davison in front of the assembly. Davison attempted a smile by way of reconciliation but it got lost in the embarrassment of such a public error.

'What a tit.' Groom was whispering to Jet again.

Jet decided on reticence in this public gathering.

Jake broadly smiled. 'I'm the only full-time employee of the organisation which has been in existence for twenty years here in Newcastle. Our aim is to work to try and overcome prejudice and promote the rights of the gay community. We are not perverts or a threat to anyone; we are just part of the community who wish to coexist in harmony. We have a communication and support network and will be pleased to help in any way we can. As you can imagine, there are a lot of worried people out there at the moment.' Jake looked around the room as he spoke. 'It is actually a very busy time for us here in Newcastle as we are hosting our first national conference, it starts the day after tomorrow, a lot of high profile people are attending to address the conference. There's a function arranged tomorrow night to welcome everyone attending. So we're going to be very busy, but I assure you we will do our best to be of whatever help we can to assist you to solve these crimes.'

'Thanks Jake. Does anyone have any questions for Jake?'

As usual Jet's mind had raced ahead. 'You mentioned a national conference. What does that entail?'

'We're trying to raise the profile of the gay community

in Newcastle, to dispel the seedy myths. We want to be seen as an asset to the community not the reverse. The national conference is designed to bring a lot of people together from different places to learn about what goes on elsewhere, look at good practice, that sort of thing. The goal is to produce a plan of action that we can take forward.'

'Has there been any resistance to it? I mean, has anyone objected?'

'Not really. There doesn't seem to be any reason why anyone should. It's just a two day conference.'

Jet nodded, 'Thanks.'

'Any more questions?' Ormond raised his voice at the same time as he lifted his head up from his notes.

There seemed to be a mass shake of heads and a smiling Jake Swinton sat down.

'Right, we're all up to date, get on with your jobs and we'll meet here at six tonight.' There was a loud collective rumble as chairs moved and people made for the door. 'Mark, Jet, can you wait?' They remained seated after Ormond's instruction.

'OK.' The room was now absent of staff and noise as Ormond spoke as he walked towards Jet and Groom. He turned a chair around to sit and face them. 'Where are we with these watches?'

Jet felt uncomfortable as he spoke. 'Mrs Thompson has identified the first one I received; it was a present to her son from her late husband. Apparently it is quite an expensive make, her son always wore it.'

'The second one?'

'Don't know yet. The relatives are coming in later. I've bagged it. I guess as you've asked DS Jardine to be family liaison for the second victim you'll want me to pass it to him?'

'Yes, brief him will you? He's seeing them this afternoon. We'll find out if it belongs to the victim then.'

'Jardine, boss; what happened there?' Groom looked earnestly at Ormond.

'You know what happens when we ask for staff from other divisions, they always send the dummies.'

'You know he's known as Thrombo by the staff at Gateshead?'

'Thrombo?' Ormond's eyes narrowed.

'Aye, as in thrombosis - a slow moving clot.'

'Look there's nothing we can do. Let's just get on the best we can, and Mark,' Ormond's tone markedly changed to stern as he spoke and looked directly into Groom's eye, 'it doesn't help if you're going to take the piss out of him all the time as well, so leave him alone, will you?'

'Model of diplomacy me boss, as long as you know the calibre of the staff you're working with.'

Ormond's eyes shifted from Groom. 'Jet, have SOCO seen the watches yet?'

'Yeah. I don't think they found anything of use to us.'

'I understand there were notes?'

Jet took a notepad from his inside pocket and flicked it open. 'First one said, "time's up for everybody sometime". The second one said, "time's up for someone else".'

'Does that mean anything to you?' Ormond looked puzzled as he spoke to Jet.

'Nothing, other than it refers to the victims.'

'I think we need to put some observations on Jet's house.' Groom looked directly at Ormond as he spoke.

'I agree. Jet, any idea why this is being targeted at you?'

Jet was slow to respond. 'I've been racking my brain. All I can think of is when my wife was murdered, it got a lot of press coverage and with the funeral and such, I suppose a lot of people would know where I live. I guess it would be easier for the murderer to deliver things directly to me rather than the police station. If he's smart I think that'll stop now.'

'I'll arrange for your house to be watched.' Ormond scribbled a note on one of the many pieces of paper in his file. Jet was alarmed at the disarray of Ormond's system but said nothing.

'On the CCTV Jet found, there was a cop. Have you had time to think about it?'

'What are you getting at Mark?' Ormond raised his

head.

'It's just Manson has been first at both scenes and should we say, his comments have been less than sympathetic. I wonder if there's something we need to have a think about?'

'He was on patrol, it was his beat. Before we start to make giant leaps and point the finger at our own we should have some evidence.'

'I wasn't pointing the finger at him; I was just wondering whether we should take some precautionary measures.'

'Get to your point Mark.'

'I was wondering whether we should transfer him to another station for a while or maybe another beat?'

'Can you imagine what the Federation would say about that? We don't suspect him of anything but we want to move him just in case. Might as well just cut my own bollocks off and post them to York now.'

'He was at both scenes and on the CCTV.'

'Mark, he was supposed to be, he's the beat copper. Come on man. We both know the person who's doing this is some demented cracker out there. Not one of us. Let's stick to the facts. Focus on our lines of enquiry and we'll catch him. Right?'

'Just thought it needed to be raised.' Groom shrugged his huge shoulders.

'Do me a favour Mark. Don't mention this to anyone

else. I don't want any disharmony among the staff, and whilst you're on, don't take the piss out of any of your colleagues on the enquiry. Please.'

'If you say so.' Groom's subdued expression was interrupted by the swift opening of the door. Supt York swept in. He had in his hand a newspaper.

'I thought you might like to see the early edition.' York held out the front page so all could see the headline 'Time for us to repent.' York's stern expression needed no interpretation, he read from the paper. 'Local Priest Father Patrick O'Brian has issued a warning that we could all suffer the wrath of God unless we mend our evil ways. He said events around the suspicious deaths currently being investigated have highlighted how we have shifted away from the teachings of God and if we do not return things will get worse. Now is the time for change, the Priest said at a press conference he held this morning. Father O'Brian's response to these tragedies is in direct contrast to that of the Newcastle Police, who have been conspicuously tight-lipped and seemingly clueless.' York's anger was now bubbling very close to the surface. 'I thought you were going to do something about this Priest?'

'We went to see him but he wasn't in the mood to co-operate.' Groom spoke and Jet thought was oblivious to the fact Ormond appeared in the early stages of mouthing something of a more thoughtful response, which was now extinguished by Groom's words.

York turned to face Groom directly. 'I've had the Chief Constable on the phone and I can tell you he's not in the mood to co-operate either and let me tell you the difference.' Jet thought he already knew the difference, but he also knew it was his place to keep quiet as York was getting into full flow. 'The Chief Constable will have the four of us directing traffic in Berwick by the end of the week unless we start doing the things that generate positive publicity.'

'In fairness....' Ormond was red-faced.

'Fairness has nothing to do with it.' York interrupted; he had clearly filled his daily quota of listening with the Chief Constable and was now in the mood to talk. 'Let's start seeing some progress and do something to shut this Priest up.'

'Well we're pursuing lines of....' Ormond could not finish.

'Arrange a press conference here at five o'clock. I'll head it up. See if you can get some of the victims' relatives to make a plea for assistance. We'll also make an appeal for anyone who knows where the car with the false plates is. Let's start feeding the press what we want. Groom, you make the arrangements and Whittle, you go and see that Priest and tell him he better shut the fuck up. Mr Ormond here will accompany me at the press conference in case there are any specific questions to answer.' York scanned the three faces around him. 'Everyone clear?'

Three nods. York threw the paper onto one of the empty chairs and made his way as swiftly out of the briefing room as he had entered.

The door clicked shut before Groom spoke. 'Mr York really doesn't want to do traffic duty at Berwick.'

'For fuck's sake Mark.' Ormond's outburst clearly indicated he thought Groom's levity mistimed. 'Let's make sure we get everything right for the press briefing. You'd better prepare a statement for the Superintendent as well. Not like we don't have enough to do.'

Jet eyed the paper which lay on the chair. 'The Priest thinks time's up as well.'

'What?' Ormond seemed preoccupied. Jet thought him having a public role at a press conference was going to trouble him for a while.

'The notes I got said time's up and so did the Priest.' Jet added.

Ormond looked plaintive and seemed to groan before he spoke. 'Don't you start as well. Mark suspects a police officer and you suspect a priest. Let's get back on track here.'

'What do you want me to say to the Priest?' Jet looked directly at a wilting Ormond.

'Tell him he's not helping and point out the fine line that exists between free speech and obstructing a police enquiry.'

Jet and Groom rose leaving a lamenting Ormond making more entries on his disorganised lists.

As they were walking down the corridor Jet straightened his jacket and spoke to Groom. 'The Detective Inspector is asking a lot if he expects you not to take the piss out of people for the whole enquiry.'

'Aye, I can't see that lasting, especially with Thrombo about and that's before I ask Davison if he wants a badge made up with his new title of gay liaison officer.'

'Do you really want to be on traffic duty at Berwick?'

'This job's done worse to both of us.' Groom smiled but Jet could see there was a hint of pain in his face.

'Fair point.' Jet had a trace of a smile as well and then changed the subject. 'Listen, as my immediate supervisor, do you think you could ring the force counsellor and tell her we're too busy for me to go to my appointment tomorrow morning?'

'As your supervisor and your friend I will ring them up and ask her to make it an early appointment. But you're not missing it Jet. You bottle things up and this might do you some good. And more importantly it's free, so go.'

Jet was forming a counter-argument in his head when his mobile phone rang. He plucked it from his pocket and heard the voice of Terry Luton.

'Hi Terry, what can I do for you?'

'It's probably nothing but I was thinking about what you asked me this morning and I remembered when I first saw your fence down, early morning, a car was near your house. I didn't think anything of it at the time, it just drove off as I was walking up the street.'

'Did you get the make?'

'I think it was a Ford Mondeo, a light coloured one.'

'Did you see who was inside it?'

'No, sorry, I didn't get very close. It seemed to be parked near yours and all I saw was it drive off when I got close.'

'Did you see the registration number?'

'I tend to notice if things are local and I think it did have a Newcastle plate, started with NH I think, but other than that I don't really know. As I said, it was probably nothing but I thought I would let you know in any case. Sorry to bother you.'

'No bother at all, it's a big help. I'm grateful, thanks Terry.'

Jet placed the phone back in his pocket and Groom spoke. 'Anything interesting?'

'A neighbour of mine said he saw a light-coloured Mondeo near my house, about the time the first watch was delivered. It could be the car from the CCTV.'

'What kind of car does Manson drive?'

'Don't know. You're not getting a bit paranoid about him are you?'

'Don't you start.'

'What do you think I should say to this Priest?'

'You could ask him if he has a Ford Mondeo hidden somewhere.'

'Right thanks I'll do that. Good luck with the press conference.'

Jet decided not to ring the Priest to make arrangements, as he wanted to avoid the inevitable question about the purpose of the meeting so close to their last encounter. He lost his train of thought as he walked into the church which was now empty and silent. As he looked around it occurred to him that the last church service he had been to was Julia's funeral. The tall building was cool and Jet thought it had a strange atmosphere of calm about it. He walked down the centre aisle and his eye was drawn to the altar. The huge gold candlesticks shimmered in the dim light and Jet stared at the ornate fabric which surrounded the tabernacle. The thick cloth covering the altar was spotless but awkwardly folded over the harsh angles. He stood still and his mind drifted, as it usually did, to Julia. How he wished he could believe she was in heaven waiting for him to join her. What would he not give to see her face again? Radiant smile, perfect teeth, round cheeks, he knew he would give everything he owned just to kiss her lips once more. But he also knew she was dead and he would never see her again. Memories, photographs and guilt were all that remained. He had even stopped hearing her voice. He had been convinced she spoke to him and pulled him through the depths of his depression. Even this part of her had left. Now he was alone. Dying inside.

'To what do I owe this pleasure officer?' Jet had not noticed the Priest approach from the rear of the church.

Startled, Jet turned around and smiled. 'I didn't hear you. I was just admiring your church, it's a beautiful building.'

'It's the house of God, it should be.'

'Must be a nightmare to maintain?'

'It keeps me busy. Where's your church?'

Jet was caught off-guard by the question. 'I'm not really a churchgoer, weddings and funerals that's all.'

'We all need something to believe in, the house of God welcomes all.'

'Judging by the headlines in this afternoon's paper it doesn't welcome everyone. Not much of a welcome if you're gay.'

'You misinterpret. All are welcome. But we should follow the will of God.'

'I don't understand the logic. You believe God is the creator of all things. So he creates gay people, but he condemns them as well?'

'He only condemns sin. We must resist temptation. A man being attracted to another man is not a sin against God but acting on temptation is. I am sure you are familiar with the fate of Adam and Eve who gave into temptation in the Garden of Eden.'

'I confess I struggle to understand the lack of compassion. There are people who simply want to go about their own business, not hurting anyone. They're probably not even aware of the many rules you follow.'

'A policeman complaining about following rules?'

'The laws of the land seem different.'

'The laws of God were here first and like your laws ignorance is not a defence. It is my role to deliver the word of God and that is what you take offence at? Surely you can see why I have no choice.'

'I think my boss is concerned because it might have the effect of causing alarm in the gay community and it might also cause people who are anti-gay to start persecuting them more.'

'The consequences of not following God's law are severe. Sometimes in this life but always when we face him on our judgement day. There is time for us all to repent and he will forgive. What you are doing is making excuses for those who choose to ignore the word of God and that could never be acceptable.'

'Are you going to hold any more press conferences in the future?'

'There is nothing planned but I will not remain silent if that is what you're asking.'

'If your comments stir up trouble and make things worse, it might be considered as obstructing the police in their duty.'

'I think I have made the position clear. My God will be my judge.'

Jet realised there was no compromise and thought of York's instruction to tell the Priest 'to shut the fuck up'. Jet decided it was a message York was going to have to deliver personally. There was something inside Jet that admired the Priest's conviction. He had a belief and nothing was going to sway him from it. Jet imagined it was the sort of certitude that in the past could get you burned at the stake or likewise make you believe you were righteous enough to burn someone else at the stake.

'If these murders are by someone who is targeting men because they are gay, could that be justified?'

'The sanctity of life is beyond question. God gives life and only He can take it.'

'So someone doing such an act, even if they thought they were doing it to promote Gods word, could not be forgiven?'

'No one is beyond redemption. But if you are asking if the person who is committing these acts is doing so on behalf of the church, then the notion is preposterous and offensive.'

Jet could see he had reached a boundary and decided not to push at it any more. He smiled at the Priest. 'Thanks for your time.'

The church felt distinctly colder as Jet walked out and made his way back to the station. He called into the chemists on the way.

Jet walked into the Briefing room and saw Groom lifting a table to place it at the front of the room in preparation of the press conference. Jet knew the table was a lot heavier than it looked but in Groom's powerful arms it could have been made of paper.

'Multitasking?'

Groom had not heard Jet enter the room and turned when he heard his voice. 'There's supposed to be someone from the press office coming to help but no sign yet.' Groom put the table into place and then looked up. 'This had better go well, I have a feeling we're all on thin ice.'

'As long as we're all on it together.' Jet picked up a chair to place it behind the table Groom was arranging.

'The rule of thumb tends to be, the lower the rank you hold, the further out on the ice you are.'

'That's comforting.'

'How did you get on with the Priest?'

'Pissing in the wind.'

'Good. It will stand you in good stead for where we're going now.'

'Where's that?'

Groom picked his jacket up from where it lay on a windowsill and pushed his arms roughly through the sleeves. 'York arranged for a crime profiler, he's talking to Ormond now and we have to join them.'

As they walked towards Ormond's office, Groom straightened his jacket. 'I got a call from Sarah Baxter asking if there's anything she can do.'

'I know what you'll have in mind.'

'Now now Jet. She's the neighbour of a murder victim, I need to be professional.' Groom brushed his jacket sleeve with his hand. 'At least until we have cracked this case.'

'Well at least you're motivated to see it resolved.'

'Does the Priest have a Ford Mondeo?'

'I didn't ask him, but I think it might be worth checking.'

'What'd he say?'

'That it was wrong to kill people but it might not be so bad if you repent afterwards.'

'You think he just hates puffs?'

'No, worse than that. I think he's spent his life telling people they're not doing the right things and he's sick of saying it. I think he might be using the rules to justify taking matters into his own hands.'

Groom nodded. 'Let's get the incident room staff to run a check on his background. See if there's anything of interest.'

Ormond's office door was closed and Groom's knock was met with Ormond's customary growl.

As Groom yanked at the door, Jet thought it quite miraculous that he did not damage more door handles than the few he had already witnessed.

Ormond sat at his desk and opposite was the slight figure of a woman in her mid-thirties. She got up to face Jet and Groom. She thrust her right hand out to greet them as Ormond spoke.

'This is Miss Shepherd, she works at the University.'

'Rosie, I teach criminology and specialise in criminal psychology.' She added as she shook hands with Groom and then Jet.

'I'm Mark Groom and this is Frank Whittle.'

Ormond had five hard chairs scattered around his office for visitors. Groom and Jet selected one each and all four sat.

'I've explained to Miss Shepherd what has happened so far.'

Rosie looked at Jet. 'It must feel strange to be receiving messages direct from someone thought to be the murderer? Quite unnerving I would imagine.'

'It does feel odd.' Jet felt uncomfortable. Empathy was a double-edged sword, his counselling had taught him that.

'We were just discussing the relevance of the messages you received and the penis being removed from the victims.' Ormond did not look comfortable and Jet thought he would rather be scowling at someone or making more notes.

'The removal of the penis seems a clear message. It could well be a souvenir. It does seem to be an object of great hatred.'

'Hatred?' Ormond sounded bemused.

'Yes. It could be that the murderer is repulsed by the penis and this is an act of outrage and revenge.'

'A gay person who doesn't like gays?' Ormond seemed more mystified.

'Possibly. Or why would it have to be a gay person at all?'

'Someone who just doesn't like gays?' Jet had always thought this was the most obvious conclusion.

'Yes, and making the point.'

'What sort of person would be sending me messages about the murders and why the watches?'

'The watches are more significant than the penises. More alarming.'

'Why?'

'It is a taunt. They're not going to stop.'

'Why a watch?'

'There might be no underlying reason other than the

clear reference that time is up. But the penis being taken as well would suggest there is a deeper meaning.'

'Why?'

'Well, the penis is a symbol of masculinity. It is hardly going to be any use when the victim is dead but it has still been cut off, it's significant to the murderer. So if that is why he or she is doing it, then it is fair to assume the watch also holds some symbolic significance and that is more difficult to assess.'

'Why do you say they're not going to stop?' Jet asked.

'Most murders are crimes of passion. People in a rage killing someone they love or hate, but usually someone they know. This is more than a heat of the moment crime of passion. For whatever reason your killer has thought all of this through. Probably planned this for weeks, maybe months, even years. Now they've passed the point of no return so they will go on. If this is being done because of hatred of homosexuals, then why stop at two? No, this person is going to go on and on, until you catch him or her, or they implement some other end to the game.'

'Other end to the game?' Jet wrinkled his forehead.

'Yes. Suicide is a common one; wreak revenge on those you harbour ill feeling towards before you kill yourself.'

'Common?' Jet felt a shiver through his spine.

'Yes, perhaps a familiar example is American kids going on the rampage in school with a gun before turning it on themselves. It can be a more elaborate form of suicide.'

'Seems far-fetched to think a person would go to all of this trouble if the plan is to commit suicide.'

'I agree, this is a well planned suicide, if that is the plan. But it is fair to assume this is a truly disturbed individual you have here.'

'What sort of person do you think fits the profile?' Ormond wanted to get to the point.

'Very difficult to say, it would be pure guesswork at this stage.'

'Is it likely this person would have come to our attention before? Started with assault and built his way up to murder?'

'You keep saying he. I'm not even sure you can rule out a female offender.' Jet could see Ormond was fidgeting in his chair as Rosie spoke. 'It is possible the offender has a violent past, but not certain.'

'So we are looking for a man or woman who may or may not have convictions. That narrows it.' Groom seemed to be enjoying himself.

'It is worth checking your records for offenders and victims of violent offences.'

'Victims?' It was Jet's turn to sound surprised.

'Yes, how about a male or female victim of rape? If an individual can't get over the trauma of an attack they might want to satisfy themselves by taking revenge.'

'We do have people in the incident room doing a lot

of background work already. Victim of male rape sounds plausible. Is there anything else they could look at?' Ormond was still shifting in his seat and Jet thought he was growing even more uncomfortable.

'If you let me meet with the people you have working on it, I will happily look at what they are doing and advise. Mr York did suggest I could stay with the team and help.'

Ormond smiled through clenched teeth as he turned to Groom. 'Mark, do you think you could take Miss Shepherd to the incident room and find her a desk to work from?'

'No problem.' Groom stood up, his huge frame towered over the diminutive criminologist as they walked out of Ormond's office. Jet followed and as he did Ormond shouted. 'Mark when you're done I'll see you and Frank at the press conference.'

It took only a few minutes to settle Rosie Shepherd into a vacant desk and she quickly became engrossed in conversation with the two criminal intelligence officers already designated to do research work. They clearly appreciated someone taking an interest in what they were beavering away at. 'Birds of a feather' Jet thought as he and Groom left them bent over a computer screen.

Groom kept his voice low as he and Jet walked away. 'I can't see how any of that helped.'

'Early days yet.' Jet was trying to be optimistic.

'I can't see a woman having anything to do with this, can you?'

'It is difficult to imagine, but I guess it is best not to rule things out at the moment.'

'Is it comfortable sitting on the fence Jet?'

'It doesn't do to jump to conclusions.'

'My money's on that Mondeo, it's the only thing we've got to go on.'

'Let's just hope putting it out to the press works for us, not against.'

'You worried about traffic duty at Berwick Jet?'

'If I were using a car and I heard it was wanted in a murder enquiry and I was a suspect, I would put it in the river or burn it. I wouldn't keep using it, would you?'

'Yeah, I would have kept the car details under my hat for a while as well but I think York wanted to get it out so it looked like we were making progress.'

The briefing room now bustled with activity and cameras seemed abundant as reporters readied themselves.

Groom and Jet took a position at the back of the briefing room where they could watch the proceedings with as much anonymity as possible. The familiar face of the reporter who had given Groom so much trouble appeared. He was characteristically the last to arrive on the stroke of five o'clock. His rounded stomach protruded his open sports jacket and he pulled the ring-bound notebook which had been jutting out of his side jacket pocket. He casually looked around the room to scan all present and after a few familiar greetings his eyes rested on Groom and he smiled.

'Are you not doing this today?'

'No, just watching.' Groom tried to summon a smile but it transformed itself during construction into a grimace.

The reporter sat down.

Ormond and York appeared with someone Jet did not recognise, he guessed it was the press officer from HQ. Ormond was still carrying his ever-growing file of papers. York had a neat leather document holder which he opened in front of him as he sat at the centre of the table which faced the press. The press officer left the room and then returned with a figure Jet recognised as Mrs Thompson, her daughter had her arm across her shoulder and they sat down next to York. Soon the figure of Peter Russell appeared. He was neatly dressed and held a grim expression.

York introduced the first victim's mother and the second victim's partner and both read a short prepared statement. As they spoke everyone concentrated on their words which were only interrupted by the regular whirrs of cameras as photographers got their exclusive shots. It was standard stuff, beautiful people taken by an evil act, the vile actions of a person who must be stopped. Appeal for witnesses and vital public support. York appealed for anyone who had information about who was using the Mondeo to call the police. Jet often wondered whether these gatherings were worth the effort. They seemed more like the done thing. Distressed relatives made good press photography but he could not remember the last time anyone actually rang up as a result with anything of use to the enquiry. He had never heard of a murderer ringing up to say they had watched the television and did not realise the relatives of the victim would be so upset and now wanted to give themselves up. Witnesses were the same; if someone had seen something then they wanted to talk to you or they didn't. They had their own motives and these were not changed by adding further anxiety to distressed loved ones.

When the assembled throng was asked if they had any questions Groom was disappointed there was only one, a query about a possible motive. York dealt with it quickly, saying it was too early for elaboration and he had been made aware of the comments of others that he thought were less than helpful as the full facts were not yet known. The cruel taunting Groom had been subject to was missing. Jet thought the press had probably had their fill of that and would now run with the relative's perspective and the concomitant sympathetic approach. They had what they wanted, for the moment.

As York and victims' relatives got to their feet the

members of the press scribbled.

'Two-faced bastards.' Groom spoke in hushed tone. Jet had to agree.

Day Two – Evening

The briefing room had recovered from the press conference and at six o'clock a growing crowd sat awaiting Ormond and his further instructions. Jet thought Ormond was looking dog-eared as he burst through the room and took up his familiar position with his bulging file.

'We have a few new faces. Rosie Shepherd is working with our analysts in the incident room. Rosie is a criminal psychologist and will be helping us on the intelligence side of things and trying to formulate a profile of our offender.' Ormond looked up and watched as Rosie raised her head and circled the room saying hello with her eyes, but remained silent. 'We also have Deborah McQueen joining us. She is going to take on the role of administrator and budget manager. Deborah is there anything you want to say at this stage?'

Before this moment Jet had only known Deborah McQueen as the civilian finance officer for the division. He had seen her occasionally disappearing upstairs to her office next to the superintendent's but that was the extent of the interaction. She stood up and uncomfortably shuffled from side to side as she began to speak. 'Hi everyone.' She smiled warmly and also circled her head around the room to indicate her welcome was for everybody. Inclusive, Jet thought, new management techniques in unfamiliar territory. 'I have overall responsibility for the finance of the division and have been asked to oversee the finance for this enquiry. We've been allocated an adequate budget but it will be easy to quickly spend it, if we're not careful. So I will monitor things and report to Mr York on progress, so we can manage the event. In the past things have tended to get out of hand on these major enquiries and we have been left with a huge bill. We want to try and manage this better in future.'

'She's going to go down a bomb.' Groom was whispering into Jet's ear again.

Jet remained silent.

'Is there anything in particular you would like us to do Deborah?' Jet thought Ormond was trying his best to conceal his anxiety at the addition of something else to worry about. No doubt he remembered the days when murder enquiries were a free-for-all and detectives made hay while the sun shined and no one questioned the cost. These days maybe traffic duty in Berwick would not be so bad after all.

'Overtime is the main issue at the moment; we need to make sure any additional hours worked are necessary and authorised by a manager. Also subsistence, we need to make sure, where possible, no additional costs are incurred, so people should come back here to take their meals in the normal way to avoid unnecessary claims.'

'Thanks, Deborah.' Ormond then addressed the throng. 'Deborah will have a desk in the incident room as well; make sure we all do our best to help her with the difficult role she has to perform.'

'He's shagging that you know.' Groom was whispering again.

'What?' Jet gave Groom a surprised glance as he replied under his breath.

'I'm telling you.'

'Ormond?'

'Aye, it'll be scribbled on one of his notes in that file.'

'I don't believe it.'

'My information is always spot on.'

Jet watched Deborah McQueen in a new light as she shuffled on high heels back to her seat. The previously anonymous woman suddenly became more human. She looked in her late thirties and was always dressed as if she was a wedding guest, perhaps a distant relative of the bride. Jet knew she had worked as a manager within private industry until a year ago when she was appointed to the financial manager's role at Newcastle Police Station. A transition to test the patience of Mother Teresa herself, given the number of junior members of police staff willing the failure of anyone directly appointed from outside the organisation to be their senior. It seemed to Jet that the permanent smile worn on her attractive face was held together with make-up as a defence mechanism. An impenetrable mask. Her quest for the look of respectability and an air of authority made her look uncomfortable and somewhat out of place. He had noticed her walking up the stairs recently in cords and a brown leather jacket and even this casual attire had a formality about it. The belt of the jacket hung untied but its leather shined pristinely and like the corduroy trousers, brand new, like one of the rich kids he remembered from school, going to the Christmas school disco after much preparation, achieving a look of awkwardness rather than the desired 'cool'.

'She has two rare breeds of cat, Ormond went to admire them and he's been stroking her pussies ever since.'

'I didn't think Ormond liked cats?'

'Didn't think he liked women.'

'Or people in general.' Jet looked shocked.

'Can we have an update on the first victim?' Ormond looked up and his eyes found Groom. 'Mark?'

'His watch has been identified by his mother, so we can assume the murderer is responsible for sending us a note and the broken watch. SOCO say the watch is clean, no marks or fingerprints. Mrs Thompson appeared at the press conference and made an appeal for public help. Thompson was a regional manager for a national chain of sports shops, a director from the firm is going to meet us at his office tonight with Thompson's secretary. We know he kept himself to himself at his home, we'll find out if anyone he worked with could be of any help.'

'Thanks, Mark, we'll come back to the watch in a moment. John, any update on the second victim?'

Jardine looked startled as Ormond's eye homed in on him. 'Oh yes.' He reached into his pocket and produced a folded piece of paper. He read from it. 'The identification has been done by his partner, so that's been confirmed.'

'Confirmed it's him or he's dead?' Groom was whispering again to Jet who remained straight-faced.

Jardine turned his piece of paper over again. 'His partner has identified the watch we received with the note. It's definitely his.'

Jardine went silent and for a few seconds Ormond stared at his blank expression, then he spoke. 'You were going to find out if there was any connection with Thompson?'

'Oh yes.' Jardine looked at his bit of paper. 'We have interviewed Peter Russell and he does not know Thompson and he doesn't think Justin did, but he can't say for sure.'

'It's important John. Do you have a list of his friends and associates?'

'Oh yes.'

'Can you start going through them please; we need to

know if there is a link between the two victims.'

'Oh yes.' Jardine scribbled something on his piece of paper.

'Do you know what he does with that paper?' Groom was whispering again.

Jet shook his head.

'He fills the paper with writing, then puts it in the bin and starts again on another one.' Jet did not know whether to believe the report Groom delivered quietly to his ear.

'Ian, what do we have from our liaison with the gay community?'

'We're using the NEGRA links to try and reassure the community that we are doing what we can and they are providing a service to receive and collate information. If an informant wants to, they can leave anonymous information. There's been a few snippets so far which is being fed into the intelligence system in the incident room.'

'Thanks Ian.' Ormond's eyes returned to his notes. 'Will you keep the feelers out and make sure we act on any good intelligence immediately?'

'Boss.' Groom shouted for Ormond's attention but waited only until he had lifted his head. 'Whilst Ian is feeling up the gay community, do you think he could keep us informed about the conference they have coming up, just in case there is anything of relevance?'

'Good point,' Ormond said, oblivious to the muffled snorts around the room. 'Ian is there anything on the conference?'

Davison tried to ignore the snorting. 'There's nothing further on the conference, as Jake said last time, there's no reason to think there will be any problem with it.'

Groom had fixed his eyes on Davison and had an impish smile on his face as he spoke.

'Right,' Ormond was changing subject as he went through his scribbled agenda. 'Intelligence updates. So far we have been inputting all the data. I have set the first priority for the intelligence team and that's to produce a likely list of suspects. Violent offenders and some victims, so far six names have emerged and I will allocate them for further enquiries. So look forward to getting your fair share of people to check on. I want to know where each one of them was when the murders happened and I want alibis checked. If you have any further suspicions or uneasiness about anyone you see, let me know.' Ormond shuffled his notes again. 'We have uniform teams out doing patrols around the toilet area tonight as well as the Gardens.'

Ormond looked up at the faces and closed his file. 'The incident room co-ordinator will have jobs for each of you so make a start. If you have suspects to look at, remember one of them is a murderer so be thorough. Unless there are any questions get cracking. Mark, John,

Ian and Frank, stay here.'

There was an explosion of activity.

As staff hurried themselves to their jobs Jet turned to Groom. 'You didn't really want to know about the conference did you?'

Groom shrugged. 'I do have an enquiring mind.'

'What have you got against Davison?'

It looked to Jet as if Groom was considering his response when Ormond interrupted. 'Right lads, time for us to do a bit of real police work.' Ormond had everyone's undivided attention. 'The only concrete thing we have is after each murder there's been a delivery to Jet's house. While we have everyone else tied up in the city where the murders happen, we're going to keep surveillance on Jet's house and with luck, catch this bastard.'

Groom smiled at the thought of a bit of action and excitement. It was clear from Jardine's expression he was in deep thought. 'Oh yes. Will that be an early start then Inspector?'

'Of course, to be on the safe side we'll be in position by 4 a.m. This is a murderer we're waiting for. I trust there's no problem?'

'Oh yes. No - I'll have to ring the wife.'

After Ormond's instruction to be alert and ready to go at

Jet's house by four o'clock the following morning Jet and Groom were keen to get to their appointment with Thompson's work colleagues as swiftly as possible. Jet thought he could feel the gears of the Fiesta developing an unusual shudder as he moved through them whilst driving to the meeting.

Jet pulled the handbrake of the Fiesta on and he and Groom got out of the car and walked across the empty car park of the Newcastle Riverside Business Park. The orange brick buildings were new and black metal bars ran across each window in circular decorative patterns. Jet thought the bars' elaborate design could almost make you believe they were there to add aesthetic value, rather than protect from the marauders he knew would come, if the bars were not solid, when night swallowed the daylight.

Jet pushed the door of office suite 12b. The rented accommodation for the Newcastle regional manager consisted of two offices, his secretary sat in the first space they entered and another door led to Thompson's office. The walls were cream, clean and devoid of any decoration which Jet thought made it feel sterile. A fubsy middle-aged woman sat behind the secretary's desk and a tall thin man stood beside her. He was dressed in a light-grey suit that looked perfectly tailored. He smiled and walked towards Jet and Groom.

'You must be the police officers.' He thrust a hand out which Jet accepted.

'Yes, I'm DC Whittle and this is DS Groom.'

'Mark Donaldson and this is Violet Bridges, Derek's secretary.'

Violet did her best to smile through her discomfort. Jet guessed being on her own with one of the directors of the company was probably a rare experience and on top of the loss of Derek Thompson she must have known many better days. Violet appeared to Jet to be the mothering sort and from the little he already knew about Derek thought he'd probably been a good candidate for it.

Donaldson shepherded them all to a small conference table in the regional manager's office where there was a tray with four cups and a plate of expensive biscuits. Violet quickly pulled a glass jug of fresh coffee from its holder and all four settled into chairs around the table. Violet poured coffee into each cup.

'Everyone in the company is in total shock at what's happened. Derek was so well thought of. If there is anything we can do, then we'll be happy to help.' Groom added milk to his coffee as Donaldson spoke and managed to dribble milk from the spout so it ran on to the tray. Jet looked as Groom examined the jug in an apparent attempt to illustrate the spillage was due to poor design of the jug rather than him being ham-fisted. Jet thought it was probably fifty-fifty.

'What was Mr Thompson's role in the company?' Jet

pulled out his notebook as he spoke and got his pen ready.

'He oversaw the running of the north east stores. Stocks, trends, staff and management issues. He had a great deal of responsibility and was very good at his job.'

'Presumably he travelled a lot to the stores?' As he spoke Jet noticed Donaldson had lifted his cup towards him, placing it closer but did not drink. At the same time Groom placed a biscuit in his mouth, snapping it in half between his teeth, keeping the remains in his broad fingers and oblivious to the crumbs escaping down his shirt.

'Did he have any close friends in the company, people he would go out with and maybe confide in?'

'Not that I knew of, Violet here might know more?'

'I don't think he really had time to make many friends, he'd been here two years and visited the stores regularly but he just stayed long enough to do what he needed to. I don't suppose it's easy making friends like that.'

As Violet spoke Groom took a gulp of coffee and Jet watched two drops of milk from the bottom of the cup fall to join the crumbs on his shirt.

'Do you know if he ever socialised with anyone from work, Christmas parties anything like that?' Jet enquired.

'No, he never went to any of them. He was a nice quiet young man, kept himself to himself. He talked about his mum in Bath, he used to go home a lot and the only friend he talked about recently was someone he met at his church.'

'Church?'

'Yes, he was quite a religious man. He never thrust it upon you but when I used to ask him what he did over the weekend he always said he'd been to church.'

'Do you know which church?' Jet asked, suspecting he already knew the answer.

'The catholic one near his house, I'm not sure what it's called. But I know he was a strict catholic. He was such a nice young man. Really lovely, I don't know why anyone would want to hurt him.' Jet thought Violet's eyes were going to well but she managed to restrain herself. At the same time Jet noticed Groom had picked up his second biscuit.

'Do you know who he'd met at the church?'

'All I remember him saying was he was going to meet his friend Paddy, I think he'd met him there and they'd been socialising for a few months.'

'Any idea where they'd been socialising?'

'They were both keen photographers and I think they went out various places taking photos together. Derek showed me a camera he'd bought himself a while ago, it was one of those huge things with all sorts of lenses and dials and things.'

'Was Mr Thompson his normal self when you saw

him on that last afternoon?'

'Yes, he seemed fine, I think he had been a bit lonely in the north east and found it difficult to make friends, so he was happy he was finally getting out and about.'

'What other hobbies did he have?'

'He was mad on computers as well, always talking of downloading his pictures onto his computer, he enjoyed his music and I know he read quite a lot because we used to lend each other books.'

'What do you know about his friend Paddy?'

'Nothing much, just he had met him at the church. I think he was going to see him the last night he left here.'

'Why do you say that?'

'We were just chatting as I was leaving and he said he was going out that night for a drink with Paddy. I think they'd fallen out over something the night before.'

'What makes you say that?'

'He looked a little out of sorts and when I asked him he just said they'd had an argument.'

'Over what, do you know?'

'No. I don't think it could have been much because he was still going to see him that night.'

'No idea what it might have been about?'

'No. He looked tired and he just said he hadn't slept much because of an argument with Paddy. But he didn't go into the detail. None of my business. Derek was a lovely man.' Jet thought Violet close to tears again, she paused for a second, inhaling while recovering her brave face then continued. 'He said they'd been at the George and Dragon. They always met there.'

'Did you ever meet Paddy?'

'No, he never came here.'

'What about lady-friends? Do you know if Mr Thompson was seeing anyone over the time you knew him?'

Violet seemed to squirm a little in her seat and the slight shake of her head was subconscious. 'No, I don't think Derek ever had a girlfriend. Not that I knew of.'

Jet looked at Violet and decided not to pursue the point further. 'Is there anything else you can think of that might help me?'

Violet hesitated then spoke. 'I don't know if it's anything but a few weeks ago Derek came in with a black eye and his hand all bandaged up. He said he'd fallen down, but now I think about it....'

'You think someone attacked him?'

'I don't know. Probably nothing.'

'Do you think Paddy might have hurt him if they'd fallen out?'

'I don't know about that. I just thought after this happened. Well, you know, I should mention it.'

Jet smiled. 'I understand and am very grateful. Don't worry. I think that'll do for the moment. Is there anything else you can think of Sergeant?' Jet looked at

Groom who looked a little startled.

'No, that's fine thanks.' Groom brushed the crumbs from his shirt as he spoke.

'If there is anything else you think might help us, please ring me on this number.' Jet placed his card on the table. 'We'll arrange for full statements to be taken soon, so we'll be in touch.'

As they left the table three of the cups still had black coffee close to the brim, the brown stagnant fluid now uninviting. The fourth cup was empty with traces of coffee dribbles running haphazardly down the empty vessel. As Jet looked at the crumbs on the table scattered around the stained milk jug and cup, he remembered the last time he had been at an Indian restaurant with Groom and thought the regional manager's office had gotten off lightly.

As they walked across the car park Jet spoke. 'Low on carbs?'

'Low on everything. These enquiries knock me out of my routine, do you know I haven't been to the gym in two days? If I'm not careful things'll begin to sag and I'll start looking like you.'

As they reached the Fiesta Groom's mobile phone rang. After a yes and a brief period of listening he said OK and put the phone back into his pocket.

'Back to the station I'm afraid.' Groom was not amused.

'I thought we were getting some rest before our early start.'

'The Chief Constable is paying a surprise visit to the incident room and we need to be there to look pleasantly surprised when he does.'

'Bollocks.'

'My thought exactly.'

York straightened his uniform hat in the mirror and then made his way from his office to the back door of the police station where the Chief Constable was to arrive. The Chief's staff officer had rung when he had left headquarters. The Chief demanded to be met by the superintendent of every police station wherever he went and duly saluted as befitted his status. General opinion was the Chief was 'not too tightly wrapped' and the longer he was Chief the looser the wrapping had become. York thought as everyone pandered to the Chief's whims he had now firmly come to believe he was a superior being. The Chief had two basic strategies. He threatened those very close with often unrealistic demands and if they dared to fail he exploded. York had witnessed these explosions and knew they were to be avoided if at all possible. When he had first arrived as Chief Constable his explosions had actually been quite popular as they happened at headquarters and an early one had led to people in the training department being transferred to operational duties within the blinking of an eye. Skivers getting their comeuppance was the general opinion throughout the workforce. Encouraged by the feedback the Chief just kept on exploding and now it was usually for no good reason. But no one was ever brave enough to point this out to him. An act of occupational suicide no one was prepared to commit. The second was the antithesis of the first strategy, where he would make outrageous promises to people, usually constables, and leave others to deliver. This was a stroke of genius because it made him very popular with the rank and file. York had suffered personal financial loss during a recent visit to an officer who had been assaulted on duty and the Chief had told him the force would pay for him and his family to take a foreign holiday. 'Enjoy two weeks recovering with your family soaking up the sun, it's the least you deserve.' York remembered the smiling Chief's words. The officer had been excited to the same measure York was depressed when he discovered there was no budgetary provision for such trips. The finance department just laughed at him and told him to take it up with the Chief. Advice they were clearly used to giving and well aware was never taken. So once he had exhausted all possible funds on which he could legitimately draw money for such a trip, he had still come up short and so had taken the cash from his own pocket. Rather this than try to explain to the

Chief he had failed in the simple task of securing a promised holiday.

A red Jaguar pulled up with the Chief sitting in the back. The Chief's staff officer had travelled ahead to meet the Chief's car as it arrived. The role of staff officer required silence as well as deference and as it was usually reserved for those destined for greater things, Chief Inspector Henry Hardwick was content with it. Hardwick opened the rear door of the Jaguar and the long legs of the Chief Constable appeared. He put his hat on as he straightened up. York threw his right hand swiftly up in a salute and was always relieved when this was achieved without sending his own hat flying from his head. The Chief's return of salute was far more relaxed and then followed by a handshake.

'Good to see you Sir.' York lied, then added to his false statement. 'I'm sure the troops in the incident room will appreciate your visit.'

'Just want to make sure all is going well and show my support. Important for morale you know.'

York wondered whether the Chief had been truly listening when the subject of morale was covered on his senior command course, at Bramshill National Police Training College. Maybe he had been off colour and having become confused, left thinking it was his morale that needed to be lifted, as undoubtedly these royal visits did. Self importance oozed infinitely.

Tradition dictated they went to York's office first so the Chief could impart his pearls of wisdom and the visit could begin from there. The Chief made his way straight to the coffee cups which had been put out in preparation and told York to close the door so they would not be disturbed. A shiver ran down York's back as he indicated to Hardwick where he could go for coffee and he shut the door so he was now the exclusive entertainment of the Chief. York did not really know why the Chief did not like him; he just knew it as a fact. He had reflected on it in less stressful moments and knew that the Chief came from a well-to-do background. He was a keen yachtsman and had his own craft, followed rugby and enjoyed all of the formal engagements that came with his position. Much different to York's working class northern roots. The gulf between them was never going to be traversed even if the Chief had harboured the desire.

The Chief sat down and took a sip of his coffee, twisted his face slightly in apparent disgust, then replaced the cup on the table as he spoke. 'Remember Ray Harris, who we took into the witness protection programme?'

'Don't think I'll ever forget him. A bent cop whose evidence brought down two of the main criminal families in the north.'

'He was resettled a few months ago after he was released early from prison.'

'Very nice. Less than a year for all those serious

offences he committed.'

'The witness protection people told me last week they've lost contact with him.'

'What does that mean exactly Sir?'

'A handler from the team makes contact every week, just to make sure all is well and he hasn't been able to get a hold of him. He's just disappeared off the face of the earth.'

'I don't suppose that's so unusual in these cases. We always thought he had a fortune stashed away from his drug money. He could be anywhere.'

'If he has done a runner he's left his wife and son at the place we set up for him.'

'Do you think Waters or Patterson have found him?'

'I know they were big criminal names in the north but the system is very tight. If they'd have done something to him it might be more obvious. I think we would have heard from their solicitor about a formal appeal. They wouldn't hang around. They'd know if we couldn't produce the main witness they may get off. Why rot in prison? But there's been nothing so far. Not a thing.' The Chief seemed to be contemplating his coffee cup again as he paused for a second but decided not to re-engage with it and then continued. 'There was someone else who harboured a grudge against Harris, wasn't there?'

'Are you talking about DC Whittle?'

'Yes, that's him.'

'How would he know where he was?'

'I don't know. I've got people looking at any possible breaches of security.'

'Whittle's not the sort. He blames Harris for the death of his wife but he's not the violent or vengeful type.'

'How's Whittle doing now?'

'He seems to be fine. He's getting regular counselling from the force's senior psychologist, we've kept a good eye on him.'

'Oh, is Jane seeing him, that's good. He is being well looked after then.'

'Yes Sir. Whittle is actually very heavily involved in this case at the moment. He's the one that's been getting the messages and the watches from the murderer at his home. He's been kept very busy.'

'I see.'

'If Harris has been found I would have thought it most likely that Waters and Patterson have got to him. If they have....' York shrugged.

'No, it doesn't look good.'

'What will happen to his wife and son?'

'The team will keep looking for a while and see what they can find out. If he doesn't turn up we'll probably just bring them back to their home here. No point keeping them out there.'

'Out there?'

'Yes.' The Chief was playing his cards close to his

chest. 'They're out of the country.'

'Very nice.'

'Any case, keep this under your hat, as it was your case I just wanted you to know he was gone. If anything occurs to you that might be of use, let me know.' The Chief suddenly got to his feet. 'Right. Show me around this incident room then.'

Groom and Jet had just got back to the incident room and were following Ormond's instruction to look natural and busy for the Chief's imminent arrival.

'I wonder how long this is going to take?' Groom was hungry.

'No idea.'

'We need to be at your place for four o'clock in the morning.'

'If you like you can use my spare room tonight, after all, you and I are supposed to remain inside the house.'

'Good man Jet. I'll pop home and pick some things up after we're finished here.'

Ian Davison came thundering through the door. He looked at one of the computer analysts who was tapping at a keyboard. 'Has the Chief been yet?'

'No we're still waiting to be surprised.'

'Good. Thought I'd missed it.'

Groom smiled at Davison, 'Ian, shouldn't you still be

out feeling up the gay community?'

Davison rolled his eyes.

York came through the door first and the Chief followed closely behind. Following the Chief was Henry Hardwick, who clutched a clipboard and pen.

'Stand up.' York shouted, indicating the reverence required for the visit. All obeyed and eyes turned towards the Chief.

The Chief smiled and basked in the attention. He waved his right hand and Jet was not sure if it was some sort of instruction for people to relax and take their seats, if they had one, or a royal wave to his subjects. After a few seconds of people looking around, those who could sit down did.

'I just wanted to pop in and tell everyone what an excellent job they are doing. This is a very important enquiry and the reputation of the force is at stake here. So, good luck, I know you'll not let us down.' The Chief paused for a second and his face changed from broad smile to look of considerate concern, the transition looked slow and deliberate, like a traffic light changing from green to amber. Once fully set on amber he continued, 'I know some of you have been working very hard and I appreciate this, which is why I have told Superintendent York everyone is to have two days off so you can be fully rested, I don't want anyone suffering from fatigue. Your welfare is my main priority.' Jet looked at York and thought he could detect his eyes widening as he heard the Chief's promise. The Chief's face was still on amber as he continued. 'I have also told Superintendent York resources cannot be a problem and whatever you need to use or spend then we will find it.' Jet thought he saw York's eyes twitching this time, but decided this could not be a shock to him as common sense would dictate it be fully discussed before such a public announcement. Jet thought the Chief must have provided York with a surprise bottomless pit of money, which the Chief no doubt had access to. The Chief again paused as his expression changed to one of a sterner outlook, amber to red, and he asked. 'Does anyone have any questions or points they want to raise with me?'

All in the room had heard enough stories to know not to speak. After a few seconds of silence the Chief bade farewell and disappeared, with York and his staff officer following in his slipstream.

Jardine, who had been hovering at the rear of the incident room was the first to break the silence. 'Oh yes, two days off, that's good.'

'That doesn't apply to us, we've got Jet's house to look after soon.' Ormond looked the most tired of any of the group, but fatigue had clearly been overtaken by frustration at the thought of staff abandoning the incident at this critical time.

'Oh yes, but the Chief said we were to take two days

off.' Jardine persisted.

'He didn't say when though. We can't just drop everything.' Ormond raised his head and then his voice. 'Can I have everyone's attention please?' The growing chattering died. 'I know the Chief has just made a promise of days off but I just want to clarify the situation. You know we're at a critical stage and I'm afraid we cannot let anyone go at the moment. We will look at giving people time off when we can, but we'll need to stagger it. So let's stick to the plan for now and I will speak to Superintendent York and we will do what we can to make sure everyone gets what they need.'

'Boss?' It was Groom.

'Yes?' Ormond didn't sound in the mood for questions.

'Can I stop looking surprised now the visit's over?'

Ormond's face creased and although he laughed Jet thought he was close to tears. 'Thanks Mark. Yes.'

'Good. Surprised isn't a look I'm good with.'

Jet had made a detour on the way to his home but was still there well before Groom.

Jet admired the straight rails of the fence and noticed there was now a huge pile of fencing boards lying on his garden. He had forgotten all about Terry's promise to have the job finished soon and resolved himself not to forget to call and get the cash. He smiled to himself as he again reflected how Julia would have been pleased with the new fence. He knew, had she been home, he would have been treated to an excited update on the day's progress. Details of all the activity which had led to the fence's current state. More bitter than sweet the thought stung and his smile evaporated.

Once indoors, Jet placed the videotape he had acquired on the way home on his coffee table and then went upstairs. He walked into his bedroom, the room he had shared with Julia, some might say he still did, and he replaced his suit with jeans and a checked shirt. He opened the top drawer of the chest and added today's strip of pills with the rest he had collected.

As he walked down the stairs he heard a knock and opened it to find Groom wrestling with a holdall, a suit on a hanger and a huge pizza box.

'I didn't know they made them that big?'

'Yeah, I hope you're as hungry as me. You got any beer?'

They settled in the front room and Groom got his eye on the videotape that rested on the coffee table. 'I hope that's not the Sound Of Music.'

Jet picked up the tape and inserted it into the recorder and pressed play. 'You might change your mind when you see it.' The screen flashed. 'It's the entrance to the George and Dragon; remember Violet Bridges said Thompson was going there the night before he died.'

The colours of the images were vivid and Jet thought it looked unnatural but nevertheless it was a clear view of people coming in and out. There was a large foyer and it was easy to identify the regulars as they came straight in, the strangers tended to dawdle, peering in the choice of doors they had, of bar, lounge, stairs and private flat.

'How do you know about the tape?'

'I went to a burglary of the owner's flat. They had this installed later. The system's getting on a bit now but it's still OK.'

Groom and Jet sat back as they watched the real-time comings and goings of the foyer of the George and Dragon pub.

Groom took a sip of his beer. 'I wonder if Jardine got permission from his wife to come to work early tomorrow.'

'It did seem an odd thing to say. Even if I did have to get permission from the wife, I think I would have kept that bit of information to myself.'

'Me too.' Groom's voice was obscured by the munching of pizza, then he licked a finger. 'Mind you, when he was a PC he couldn't go to public order training because his mother said it wasn't safe. So his wife has just taken over where she left off.'

'Get away?'

'I'm telling you. There was a bus to take them away

for a three day course and he didn't turn up. It left without him and two hours later he turned up to see his inspector and told him his mam said he couldn't go. He'd gone home and told her he couldn't wear nylon socks because they were going to throw petrol bombs at him and that was it, she wouldn't let him go.'

'Didn't he get into bother?'

'No, they just accepted it. I don't think they thought there was a risk of it becoming a trend and in any case the training isn't compulsory.'

'They never told me that when I had to go.'

'No, me neither, and I wore nylon socks.'

'Trust you not to heed the warning.'

'They were right an' all. Nylon isn't good with flames. Burned every hair on my leg.'

Jet chuckled and then decided to change the subject. 'What's the story with Ormond and the finance woman?'

'Did you know Ormond's wife's an alcoholic?'

'Everyone does.'

'She's been in hospital a few times for treatment but nothing seems to work.'

'I heard she was found unconscious at the bus station.'

'They hushed a lot of it up for Ormond's sake.'

'It's hard keeping things like that secret.'

'You're right. She's the only one who thinks people don't know.'

'Can't be easy for Ormond I suppose.'

'Don't suppose him working every hour God sends has helped.'

'Probably happier at work.'

'With her drinking problem and the hours Ormond puts in, I think it's many years since they've had a normal life. So Deborah McQueen came along and showed him a friendly face and a bit of compassion.'

'Not a match made in heaven then?'

'Who knows?'

'Does his wife know?'

'If she does she doesn't care.'

'Really.'

'She's usually too drunk to know what's going on.'

'Ormond must have his time in now.'

'He can retire any time he wants, but I don't think it's his style. What would Ormond do without work?'

'What's that?' Jet pointed at the television screen. 'Isn't that our man?'

The figure of Derek Thompson stood in the foyer near the main entrance door, occasionally looking out.

'Looks like he's waiting for someone.' Groom moved towards the screen.

A second person came into the foyer and spoke to Thompson. The two appeared to exchange a few words and then, as if they had jointly made the decision to go into the lounge they moved away together. For a split-second they got close to the camera and Jet rewound the

145

tape until he had the image frozen on the screen. It flickered in front of them.

'Is that who I think it is?' Jet strained his eyes at the wavering image on the screen.

'Who do you think it is?'

'Last time we spoke to him wasn't he wearing a dog collar?'

'Bloody hell, I think you're right.'

'I'm away at headquarters tomorrow, I'll call into the technical unit and see if they can get it enhanced and we'll get a few stills.'

'I think I'd better ring Ormond. It is going to be worth someone watching his place tonight to see if he comes out to play.'

'Ask them to check if he has a white Mondeo lying about as well.'

Day Three - Morning (4am)

'I just spoke to Ormond. They're in position. So we just wait in the comfort of your house and hope our man turns up.' Groom spoke as he walked towards Jet who was looking out of the window of his front room. The small gap in the curtain was not conspicuous from outside and masked further by the net curtain which hung close to the window pane. From the darkness of the room he had a clear view of the drive, garden and the path leading to the front door.

'What about the Priest, have they seen him?' Jet was sitting on one of his dining room chairs which he had strategically placed to sit in comfort as he secretly watched his own garden.

'No, they don't think he's at the address he gave us.'

'Strange.'

'Strange all right. My money says we should just find and arrest him.'

'For what?'

'He's told us lies for a start about the first victim. He's hiding something. Religious fanatics. He could be befriending them and then punishing them on behalf of God. You heard what he said.'

Jet frowned, 'I'm not sure if religious fanatic applies to a catholic priest.'

'I knew when I saw him at that press conference he was trouble.'

'Bit obvious though.'

'He's murdering homosexuals. He doesn't want it kept a secret.'

'Why would he make himself a suspect though?'

'It's a war as far as he's concerned. It's not that long ago since the Pope sent the Spanish navy across to try and invade, they're a violent bunch you know.'

'The Spanish Armada?'

'Aye, that's the one.'

Jet smiled, Groom had a habit of crossing the border of serious debate to comically bizarre without warning. It had taken Jet some time to become tuned to it and since then had witnessed others' failure to understand his humour to lead them to believe Groom was quite strange. Jet formed the opinion that Groom did not always mean what he said, but his frequent impish moods meant he enjoyed the confusion he caused. A few months ago Jet was dealing with a case of alleged damage caused to a butcher's shop by local animal liberation activists. As part of his enquiries Jet had gone to speak to representatives of a local animal liberation group at a community centre and took Groom for support. When he saw the large number of their group he had been pleased he had. He discovered their internal politics did not allow them to elect a leader to speak for the group. The meeting was intense and the discussion had somehow turned to the issue of the reason why the group were active. To prove how committed they were to the welfare of animals one young dreadlocked woman looked at Groom and angrily informed him they were all vegans. Groom replied by telling the group that any friend of Doctor Spock was indeed a friend of his. It had not gone down well. There were times when Jet thought Groom could not take anything seriously and made no attempt to. Groom seemed to Jet an odd combination. His huge mass of muscle often at odds with his flippancy. But Jet knew Groom had a keen insight always worth listening to. If Groom thought the Priest was worth looking at, Jet wouldn't bet against it.

'So did Jardine get permission to be out this early in the morning?'

'Oh yes.'

Both men smiled. Groom's imitation of Jardine sounded more like a cartoon character Jet had seen on the television. A bulldog advertising car insurance.

A gentle rattling noise from outside made both men concentrate. Then Jet saw a milk float go past, its load jingling an appropriate aubade.

'I thought those were a thing of the past.' Groom pulled back from the gap in the curtain after the few seconds of excitement.

The silence returned to the street and Jet looked at

Groom. 'You never told me what's with you and Davison.'

'Do you remember a little incident last year which led to me being kept in custody awaiting trial?'

'I'm not going to forget it.'

'Well I found out that whilst I was inside he visited Shirley.'

'And?'

'And he went there twice to see if there was anything he could do for her.'

'I see.'

'Yeah, he obviously had even less idea than I did that she already had a lover.'

'He might have just been trying to be helpful?'

'Provide a shoulder to cry on? I bet that's not all he had in mind. Treacherous bastard.'

'How did you find out?'

'Shirley told me.'

'You see each other much these days?'

'I go to see Dianne, take her out most weeks.'

'How did she take the divorce?'

'She's a strong girl that one. We probably see each other more since Shirley divorced me. She starts her GCSE course at the high school this term.'

'They grow up fast.'

'Yeah. She's coming to stay with me this weekend. Shirley and what's-his-face are going away for the weekend.'

'We better catch this murderer then.'

'Come hell or high water.'

'You know Davison might have been genuine.'

'He didn't come to visit me in prison to see if I needed anything.'

'You're obviously not his type.'

'Exactly.'

'There's movement from the north side.' The radio Groom had in his hand burst into action. It was Davison who was at the top of the street with Townsend. Jardine and Needham were at the bottom of the street. Ormond was in a vehicle on his own ready to go wherever he was needed. 'Male on his own walking towards the target.' Davison's voice was close to a whisper but still clear in the silence of the early morning.

Jet strained his eyes through the net curtain and saw a dark figure in the street light walk down the opposite side of the street. It walked straight past.

'Male has kept on going past target.' Groom also spoke gently into his radio. 'Jardine, are you receiving?'

'Oh yes, loud and clear.'

'There's a man coming your way, once he's out of the street can you stop and have a word with him and get his details, find out what he's doing, just in case.'

'Oh yes, will do.'

Jet smiled at Groom as he heard Jardine speak. 'Do

151

you think he knows he says "oh yes" all the time?'

'He's done it as long as I've known him. Guess it's automatic; nerves or something.'

'Did you ever come across - "oh yes aye yes"?'

'No.'

'He was an old cop who used to work over at Newburn. He always said "oh yes aye yes" to everything. He often used to just burst out with it for no reason. Strange old guy. I was a probationer on his shift when I first started. One night I was called to a disturbance on the main street and when I got there it was him singing an old sailing song about dipping bread in his gravy.'

Groom laughed, 'He was on duty?'

'Yes, in full uniform. When I asked him why he was on my beat he said he liked to be near the street lights. He didn't feel safe on his own in the dark.'

Groom's radio crackled again. 'Oh yes, did you say there was someone coming our way?'

'A male was walking down the street towards you.'

'Nothing here as yet.'

'That's odd.' Jet angled his head so he could see as far down the street as possible but the figure was gone.

'Don't worry, we'll see him if he comes back.'

Jet kept peering down the street but there was no sign of life. After a few minutes of silence Groom spoke. 'All right if I make some coffee?'

'Sure, make me one as well. I think it's going to be a

challenge to stay awake here.'

Jet thought that Groom was making a lot of rattling noises to merit only two cups of coffee.

'Did you know there's a pair of glasses in your kitchen drawer Jet?' Groom raised his voice from the kitchen.

'Oh, aye, is that where they are. They're a pair of safety glasses.'

'Safety glasses, I didn't know you were into DIY.'

'Had them for years.'

'They look like the glasses Bilko used to wear.'

'They're just plain glass, been kicking around for years.'

Groom came out of the kitchen with two cups. 'There you go Jet, let's see if this will keep us awake.'

After an hour of silence the street began to slowly rouse and by seven o'clock there was a lot of movement that now did not warrant radio conversation.

Jet yawned, 'I'll need to get going soon, my session with the psychologist is at eight.' Groom was now perched on the chair in front of the window, they had rotated the job as the morning wore on.

'I don't think you'll miss much here. If our man was going to make a move I think he would have done it by now, don't you? Why don't you make yourself some coffee and then clear off?'

'Good idea. He must have been here earlier than this the past two days.'

'I think we'll be hanging around just in case for a while. I promise I'll not nick the family silver.'

Jet smiled then went into the kitchen to open a drawer and he removed a key on a key ring. He returned to hand it to Groom. 'You can borrow this, will you lock up when you leave?'

Groom looked at the key ring which had the name Julia on the leather fob.

Jet watched Groom examine it. 'It was Julia's key so don't lose it.'

'Are you sure?'

'It's the only spare I've got.'

'I'll be careful.' Groom pushed the key in his trouser pocket. I don't think we'll be much longer. Looks to me like the deliveries to your house have stopped. I suppose after two he'd see it as an unnecessary risk. After all he is a murderer.'

'Suppose so, but why is he making contact like this anyway?'

'We'll find out at some stage I'm sure. Must be a reason.'

Jet returned to the kitchen and flicked the switch of the kettle.

'Have visual on someone who has stopped at garden gate.' Davison spoke. 'He's looking around.' The voice came through the police radio which was on the windowsill.

Groom picked up the radio and cautiously looked out of the window. He spoke carefully into the radio. 'Have visual. He's on the garden path now.' Groom kept an eye out of the window. 'He's coming up the path.'

The letter box rattled as an envelope fell onto the mat.

'Delivery made.' Groom's voice was raised. 'In pursuit.'

Groom shot up from his chair and made to the front door. Jet came through from the kitchen and followed him into the garden. Jet could hear the screech of tyres from a car further up the street. Groom hurtled out of the door as the man started to run. He tore down the path and ran down the street.

'Pursuing male, heading south. Jardine towards you.'

'Oh yes.' Jardine's tone had not changed.

By the time Jet had got to his garden gate Groom was yards ahead striding down the street. He heard Jardine's car come to a halt as Groom ran towards him. Jardine and Needham got out of their car and Jet saw Jardine crouch down as the figure ran towards him. The figure tried to swerve but Jardine lunged in a tackle that would not have been out of place at Twickenham. Both men landed in a crumpled heap on the ground. Groom's sprinting came to a stop and he placed a hand on the figure that was now underneath Jardine. 'We've got him.' Groom shouted down the radio. More screeching of tyres was audible as two more vehicles came from the north end of the street. Davison and Townsend appeared within seconds.

'Get off me!' The figure sounded distressed as the weight of Jardine and the iron arm of Groom kept him in position.

Jet had caught up and decided not to get involved in the melee. He looked on as the figures eventually stopped wrestling. Groom's vice-like grip kept a hold of the stranger as Jardine, then their captive, stood up.

Jet recognised the face as he rose under Groom's supervision.

'Terry, what are you doing?' Jet was looking at the red-faced gardener.

'Running away from him.' Terry looked at Groom.

'Mark,' Jet looked at Groom. 'This is the man who's doing my fence.'

Groom looked at Terry. 'So what did you put through the letter box?'

'A note to say I was going to try and finish it today.' Terry looked at Jet. 'I was wondering whether I might be able to pop around after it was done to pick the cash up.'

Jet smiled. 'I'm sorry Terry, I've had some strange deliveries recently and we thought you were the person responsible.'

'We don't know that he's not yet.' Groom snarled and did not release his grip of Terry's arm. 'Why did you run?'

'You came storming out of the house. I don't know

who you are. I thought you were some madman.'

'What have you got on you?' Groom was unrelenting.

'Wallet, keys that's it.'

Groom looked at Jet. 'You go and see what was put through the letter box and I'll check he's got nothing else on him.'

Jardine had brushed himself off and was now watchfully content that Groom was in control. Jet felt embarrassed but could see that Groom was in no mood for concessions.

'Just be patient for a few minutes Terry, we need to be thorough, we're dealing with a serious case.' As Jet spoke Groom's eyes widened at his apparent displeasure at Jet's attempt to console.

'Let's have a look in your pockets then Terry.' Groom had started patting his jacket as he spoke. Terry reached into his trouser pockets and produced a crumpled wallet, keys and a small amount of change.

Groom handed them to Jardine, 'Check those.' Whilst Jardine performed his close examination of the articles Groom returned to his methodical inspection of Terry's clothing.

The search of Terry's person was coming to an end when Jet returned with an envelope in his hand. 'It's just as he said.'

'Yeah nothing on him either.' Groom sounded disappointed.

Terry still looked shocked and Jet thought wounded by his experience.

'I'm sorry Terry, I hope you understand.'

Terry looked at Groom. 'Can I go now?'

Groom's eyes burned into Terry's face. 'Before you do, how about knocking a bit off the price of that fence?'

Jet put his hand out and touched Terry's shoulder. 'Of course you can go Terry, don't worry.'

Jardine handed the wallet, coins and keys back to the visibly shaken gardener, who then walked towards his house.

Ormond had arrived in the middle of the excitement and watched. As Terry got out of earshot he spoke. 'That's a pity; I thought we had a breakthrough there.'

'I hope he still finishes my fence.'

Terry had now disappeared into his house.

'I'm sure I could have got you some discount there, if you hadn't interrupted.' Groom looked serious.

'I think making him shit himself is probably enough for one day.'

'It looks like we're going to draw a blank here, let's wrap it up and get back to the nick.' Ormond looked pale and fatigued but Jet knew there would be no suggestion of slowing down for a long time yet.

'Boss, do we know if there have been any incidents reported overnight?'

'No, nothing, certainly no bodies found, so that's

something.' Ormond started to make his way back to his car, as he did he shouted. 'Don't forget there's a briefing at noon.'

Groom and Jet left the others to make their way back to their respective vehicles whilst they headed back towards Jet's house.

'Was PC Manson on duty last night?' Jet thought Groom probably already knew the answer to the question he asked.

'No. He'll be on his days off now.'

'No Manson and no dead bodies. I wonder if that's a coincidence.'

'I thought you were interested in the Priest?'

'I have a feeling we will be seeing them both again soon.'

'I think the Priest has some difficult questions to answer.'

'Did you see that rugby tackle of Jardine's?' Groom sounded impressed.

'Yeah, it was certainly full-blooded.'

'Yes, brilliant.' Groom was thoughtful. 'Wasted on your gardener mind.'

The daylight had brought a sky that looked like tarnished silver and the promise of a lack-lustre day ahead.

'Jet, if you want to grab your coat I'll lock your house up and you can get to your appointment.'

'Do you want a lift to your car?'

'No. it's just around the corner. You get to headquarters. I'll see you back at the nick when you're done.'

Bereavement Session Seven

Jane Metcalf sat at her desk tapping the file cover which had 'Francis Earnest Whittle' written on the front. She had come in uncharacteristically early to read the contents of the file. She had written most of it. But as her day consisted mainly of speaking to strangers and then writing brief notes, she found that fine details disappeared and with lack of distinction the days became a synthesis. A mass of fake smiles and ins and outs. But now this one had become something more. She had not broken her own code of ethics. For what it was worth. Not yet. She had not disclosed confidential information to anyone. But she had been told things. Big things. Things she wished she had not been told. Bloody things.

Jane walked to the mirror on the back of her door and considered the reflection. She had not slept much last night. There had been a leaving function and a carefully planned drink with her lover at a nearby pub. Then back to her place. It had been after two by the time the Jaguar had pulled off her driveway.

The early start meant there was no receptionist and she was startled to hear a knock at her door. She pulled the handle and Jet's smiling face peered from the shadow of the corridor.

'Frank, how nice to see you. Come in.'

'Thanks for seeing me so early.'

'No problem. I understand how it is in the real world you know.'

Jet winced. His slip at the last session really had touched a nerve. He felt guilty. That's all he needed from these sessions, more guilt.

He smiled, uncertain of what else to say and anxious not to make things worse.

They sat down in their usual seats. Jane had a clipboard on her knee and Jet could see some scribbled notes he could not make out.

'I was reading in the press about the murders you're dealing with. It sounds horrific?'

'Yes. It is very unpleasant.'

'I understand you've been receiving messages at home from the killer.'

Jet was taken aback. 'Your information is good.'

'I know you think us all out of touch here but it is police headquarters.' Jane smiled. 'How does that make you feel?' She paused then burst in to clarify. 'You know, being targeted by the murderer.'

'It's strange. But I'm not too worried about it. I don't think my address is a big secret. Especially after Julia's death; with the funeral and that. I suppose everyone in the north east knows where I live.'

'I was thinking more about the emotional impact it might have. After all your wife was murdered not long ago and now another murderer is targeting you.'

'I don't suppose I linked the two things together.'

'Really?' Jane scribbled something on her clipboard as they spoke. Jet had not noticed her making notes at previous meetings. 'You said the last time we spoke that you had not thought about the man who murdered your wife for some time?'

'I hadn't dreamt about him. I had been having dreams but they do seem to have stopped now.'

'You must have felt a real sense of injustice when he got away so lightly?'

'Yes. But I understood.'

'Understood?'

'Yes. The person who was paid to kill her is dead now but the man who arranged it, Ray Harris, he managed to make a deal. It was felt there wasn't enough evidence to convict him of the murder, but in return for not pursuing that charge he pleaded guilty to something minor and he gave evidence which brought down some big names in the criminal underworld. Lots of people thought it was a good result.'

'But not you?'

'Not me. But I understood how others might see it was a good result.'

'I understand how you must feel though.'

'There is nothing I can do. He's out of prison now, with a new identity. He's gone and I just have to move on.'

'That is a very healthy way to look at it.'

'It could drive you mad if you let it.'

'Have you ever thought about revenge?'

Jet hoped that the extent to which this question shook him did not show on his face. It took him a second to consider his response. 'I would be lying if I told you I hadn't. Who wouldn't? But what would I do? He's gone now. He's lost his job and his life.'

'It's good to hear it. Not everyone would be able to deal with that sort of trauma in such a balanced way.'

'Apart from anything else; Julia would never have forgiven me for trying to find revenge.'

'Do you still hear her voice?'

'Not now. I think I'm adjusted to the fact she's gone.'

'But you still wouldn't think of revenge because she wouldn't have allowed it?'

'She was a sweet human being. She had powers I could only hope to have. I try to follow her example. She would know the only thing I could now do is to get on with my life.'

'It sounds like you have dealt with this in the best way.'

'What do you mean?'

'Some would find it difficult to be so understanding.'

'I don't think I've understood, I've accepted. There is nothing I can do.'

'Have you found things getting easier as time passes?'

'Yes. There's no doubt. I think I'm making progress now. At first I was bottling things up.'

'Did the medication help at all?'

'A doctor prescribed things, which I took when I needed, truth is I like to avoid it when I can. I was never one for pills. I've seen enough to think that drugs cause more harm than good.'

'Talking about things will help. I hope these sessions will.'

'I'm sure they do help.'

The nib of Jane's pen moved again.

'Things like your holiday will help as well. Part of moving on.'

'Yes.'

'Where was it you went again?'

'Spain.'

'That's right, you said you'd hired a car and did some touring.'

'It was very nice. Bit warmer than here.'

'For sure. Did you get far?'

'Yes, I did a fair bit of travelling.'

'I did that once and went across the border. To Portugal, I think. I was surprised at how easy it was to get across. No border control at all. Did you do anything like that?'

'I think I did come across the border when I was

driving. It was a nice drive. It's good to be back though. Get back into the swing of things.'

Jane smiled and knew enough to know when the subject was being changed. 'What will happen about the deliveries to your house by the person who is doing these murders?'

'Now we know what's happening we'll be able to sort it. I would have thought he'd want to give me a wide berth now. After all he'd have to be really stupid to think we're not going to be watching the house for him.'

'You know that if you ever want to talk to anyone about it, you can always give me a ring.'

'Thanks. That's appreciated.'

'How are your sleep patterns now?'

'Well I haven't slept much these past few days but that's mainly because of work.'

Jane smiled. 'Perhaps I should let you get back to the real world then.'

'I didn't mean to be rude when I said that.'

'I know, don't worry, I won't get too upset about it.' Jane's smile was returned to her and for the first time in this session Jet was not feeling threatened.

'I wondered.' Jet was searching for words. 'How do you think things are going?'

'You worried about what I'm writing?'

'A bit I suppose.'

'These sessions are here to help you. The organisation

does have a responsibility to make sure that all of its employees are fit to be at work and after what you've been through it would be irresponsible for us not to make sure you are being taken good care of. But I've no doubt you are coping well and are certainly fit for duty. So there is no need for you to be worried, I'm not writing anything for you to be concerned about.'

'Thanks.'

'Don't worry. We need to be totally honest with each other. If we don't have that trust then there'd be no point in any of this.'

'I suppose you're right. It would be pointless.'

'I believe I'll be seeing you early next week. If there is anything in the meantime please just give me a ring.'

'Thanks, I will.'

Jet got up and made his way back into the gloominess of the corridor. He walked the short distance through the square building of the occupational health unit and was relieved when he was out in the dull daylight. As he walked towards the car, his tired mind spun around the detail of the conversation he had just had.

Soon he sat at the steering wheel of the Fiesta and spoke to himself. 'It would be pointless if we weren't being totally honest with each other.' Jet was still muttering to himself as he turned the ignition key. 'Pleased we're not wasting each other's time.'

Journal - Murder Three

Norman said he was just out for a drive and saw me in the archway that runs underneath the railway line just next to the Central Station. Said he thought I looked cold and might just need a lift. So he stopped his car and asked if I wanted to get in. He's probably done that a hundred times before and used the same old lines. It's what queers do, pretend to each other they lead normal lives. That they are not perverts. He looked a sad old man underneath his beige suite. He said he'd retired from his job. Used to draw plans for people's house extensions. Sounded to me like I did him a favour. If you can draw plans for years and then get bored when you stop doing it then you might as well be dead. He asked me if I would like a drive to the quayside and he smiled when I said what a nice idea and soon we were parked by the Royal Marine Reserve Centre near St Peter's Basin. Such a quiet spot. We walked on the riverside for a few yards into the dark shadows where queers belong. It was easy to get his trousers off him. He was all excited right up to the time I smashed the hammer through the back of his skull. If he has a family they might like to know his last words were 'that feels good'. So it wasn't all that bad for him.

Strange he had a nice new car but no watch. Never mind I took the two souvenirs I wanted. Three pricks in my collection now. I wonder how many more I will have time to collect.

Day Three - Morning (9.00am)

Ormond sat on his office chair and looked at his desk. In the centre was a pile of telephone messages containing various scribbled notes left for him by the incident room staff. He thumbed them; by the quantity he could tell the press office were particularly keen to speak to him. He pushed them aside. He pulled the handle of his desk drawer, lifted out the current case file he was using and opened it out in front of him. He drew another blank piece of paper towards himself and started to make notes. He needed to review how quickly the list of potential suspects was growing and make certain there was enough staff to talk to the new names being added. He also made a note to check where they were with finance and to see how they were getting on trying to trace the Ford Mondeo. Then there were the promised days off - why did people have to stick their noses in? When Ormond was a young detective constable everyone knew you did what detective inspector said without question. He was God! - how things had deteriorated.

He was just about to stand up to walk to the incident room when Superintendent York opened the office door then without saying anything closed the door behind him and sat down.

'I was looking for you earlier to have a chat to see how

things were getting on, did you have a lie-in?'

'No. We were keeping observations on Jet's house to see if the murderer turned up.'

'Any luck?'

'Nothing.'

'What sort of observations?'

'He's had two deliveries in two days, I was hoping he might get another one.'

'I don't remember authorising any observations.'

'I thought the less people who knew about it the better.'

'You don't trust me to keep a secret?'

'Of course I do Sir. We didn't have time to discuss it and I didn't want to leave notes about in case others started to read them.'

'What about the Regulation of Investigative Procedure Act?'

'I didn't have time to fill in an eight page form to watch one of our own officer's homes. Especially with him being there helping us.'

'Then it's a good job no one turned up, because the observations wouldn't have been legitimate.' York was getting angry.

'I'm just trying to catch a serial murderer.'

'Presumably we intend to put him in front of a court as well then?'

'Of course.'

'Then how are we going to present evidence if we don't follow the rules?'

'It's just a surveillance form.'

'If the Surveillance Commissioner comes along and finds out we've been keeping observations without the proper authority then there'll be hell to pay.'

'I'll fill it in now.'

'I can't authorise this retrospectively, you know that. The whole thing was illegal. Christ Nigel!'

'Don't you find it ridiculous that we have to fill in a form to watch a colleague's house to catch a murderer?'

'Of course, we all find it ridiculous, it is ridiculous, but they are the current rules and until they change we have to play inside them. Otherwise we lose. You've been in this game long enough to know that.'

'It never seemed this difficult. There was a time when we just had to worry about the bad guys. Now we have to worry about all the rules that people keep inventing to keep themselves in a job, while making life harder and harder for poor sods like us.'

'Nevertheless Nigel. It will do us no favours to catch this person and then see them walk because we didn't fill in a form.'

'OK, if we have to do it again I will have the forms done.'

'How are you managing with the Chief's instruction that the staff get two days off each?'

'I've told them they'll have to wait until we can do it.'

'Well, you're in charge of the staff. Let's make sure the Chief doesn't find out we've gone back on his promise though.'

'We just couldn't manage if the staff went home.'

'You heard the Chief. It was his instruction. As far as I'm concerned we're following it.'

'OK.'

'Anything on this Mondeo yet?'

'Nothing overnight. I'm just going to get a round-up. There have been no incidents overnight so maybe we're going to get some time to catch up.'

'Let's hope so.' York got back to his feet. 'If there are any developments make sure to let me know.'

Ormond did not reply as he watched York's back disappear out the door.

He pushed himself up on the arms of his chair and walked across the corridor to the incident room. The large space had desks scattered all around, half of which were occupied by people beavering away with their allotted tasks.

'How are we getting along with that list of suspects?' Ormond looked at the two intelligence officers who were tapping at their keyboards.

'Fine.' Lenny Jessop was the senior of the two intelligence officers who had been seconded to the team from headquarters. Max Drummond seemed quite happy that Lenny was spokesman. 'We've got the first batch out and they're being checked.'

'Where's Rosie?'

'She was here until late last night. I don't think they're used to quick shift changes at the university. Said she'd be here about ten.'

'Is her input of use?'

'Very interesting. We are pulling off those who fit the overall profile and she's going through them to see what she thinks and we're prioritising them from there. I've never worked with an outsider like this before, but it seems to be working. I guess time will tell.'

'Have any of the names you've come up with so far really jumped out at you?'

'Not really. It is surprising how many perverts there are around, we've come up with a lot of good names, it's prioritising them that's the problem.'

'That's good work, thanks.'

The incident room door opened and a figure familiar to Ormond walked in.

'Kevin, good to see you.' Ormond allowed himself a smile.

DS Kevin Butler was an experienced incident room supervisor and had been working at the central headquarters crime department for several years. He was used to being sent to various incident rooms to add his expertise. Ormond had worked with him on enough murders to know he could be trusted.

'Good to see you boss.'

'Are you here for the duration?'

'I'll be here until you tell me to piss off.'

'You could be here a while then. You can use that desk. The next briefing is at twelve. If there is anything you need let me know. Hillary and Tom over there are putting the information into the HOLMES computer system.' Ormond pointed to the two figures who were focused on tapping at their keyboards. 'Lenny and Max you know. They'll fill you in.'

'Good stuff.'

As Butler spoke the door moved again and a flustered Debbie McQueen came in. She was oblivious to the others in the room and carried several bags to her desk. Once there she pulled at her jacket making the studs that fastened it pop open, making a noise like a row of dull toy gun caps going off. She looked up at Ormond and Butler. Ormond eyed the bags on her desk.

'Moving house?'

'Had a dreadful morning, I couldn't find my Charlie.'

'Nothing worse.' Butler looked confused.

'Charlie's the cat.' Ormond said without thought.

'One of them; the other one, Dinah, was where she always is when I woke up, on my pillow.'

'And where was your Charlie?'

'I found him in the back of the wardrobe eventually.'

'Good.' Ormond did not sound overly concerned. 'Debbie this is Kevin Butler, he's taking the role of office supervisor.' Ormond turned to Butler. 'Debbie is the finance manager; she's keeping control of the budget.'

'Good luck with that one.' Butler smiled with the experience of an officer who had seen many others attempt it and fail dismally. Had he been asked he would have said he'd not seen anything to make him believe Debbie McQueen was going to fare any better.

'Kevin has just arrived; can you see he settles in all right?'

'Sure.' Debbie looked at Ormond. 'No problem.'

Ormond walked out of the incident room and did not hear Debbie follow him. He had just turned at his desk when he saw her walk in his office and close the door behind her.

'You look tired.'

'It's been a long few days.'

'Have you been home?'

'Just a few hours last night, I was out again by three this morning.'

'Have you decided what you're going to do?'

'I want to tell her but you know how it is.'

'She wouldn't be thinking about you.'

'I know but I'm not sure how she'll take it.'

'After the way she's behaved I don't know why it matters to you so much.'

'We've been married a long time. There was a time she cared for her family more than alcohol.'

'That's a long time ago.'

'I know, I will do it. But we have a lot to do here.'

'OK. But when you're ready.'

'Thanks Debbie, it means a lot.'

Jet pulled on the handbrake of the Fiesta and made his way up his garden path. He stopped at the sound of his mobile phone humming and pulled it from his pocket. 'DC Whittle.'

'Mark Donaldson here, we met the other day at Derek Thompson's office.'

'Oh yes, from the sports company. Hello Mr Donaldson, what can I do for you?'

'I just thought I'd tell you something strange has occurred.'

'Really, what's that?'

'We were checking the accounts Derek ran and things don't seem to add up.'

'Yes?' Jet was stationary on his garden path.

'Five thousand pounds is missing. We don't know for sure where it's gone, we'll have to do a full audit, but some odd cheques that Derek signed have been cashed.'

'You think Derek has been stealing from the company?'

'It's difficult to say without the full audit. But I thought I'd better tell you now just in case it's important.'

'When will you know for sure what the situation is?'

'I've called for a full audit of every account from this office. It could take a few days to do.'

'Thanks Mr Donaldson. Will you let me know as soon as you have the detail?'

'Sure.'

Jet put the mobile phone back into his jacket pocket and became aware again that he was on his garden path. He looked at the fence posts that were awaiting the attachment of fencing boards and hoped earlier events would not delay it. He would understand if it did.

He knew he was in for another long day and was going to have a quick shower, something to eat and change his shirt. He was confident this detour from headquarters would not be noticed.

He pushed the front door open and felt his heart leap as he saw a white envelope lying inside the door. He picked it up and recognised the handwriting.

'Bollocks.' The envelope felt bulkier than before. He took the envelope to his dining room and slowly opened the end. He carefully poured the contents onto the table. A mobile phone slid out and then a buff card which was folded down the centre. Jet touched the edge of the card to open and read it. 'This one saw his last seconds ticking away on his phone. Time is up for him as well now.'

Jet picked his own mobile phone out of his pocket and scrolled to Groom's number.

'All right Jet?' Groom sounded jovial.

'Not really. I've had another delivery. Must have come when we left.'

'Someone knew we were there?'

'I don't know. But it's the same handwriting. This time it's a mobile phone, not a watch.'

'Is it still working?'

'Doesn't look broken.'

'Have you touched it?'

'Only to see what it was.'

'Hang up and ring my mobile with it. I'll get the number and we'll try to find out who it belongs to. Once you've done that best to leave it where it is and we'll get forensics to come to you. Better check your front door out again, just in case they left any marks.'

'Will do.'

Jet felt he was touching hot coals, frightened he was smudging vital forensic evidence no matter how delicate he was trying to be. Carefully he programmed Groom's number in and then saw the word 'calling' come up on the screen. He waited until the number was connected and then he disconnected. He left the phone lying on the table, relieved that he did not have to touch it any more.

He went into his kitchen and had only taken one sip

of the coffee he'd made when there was a knock on the door. He recognised Paul Stimpson who came straight in when Jet pulled the door open. Stimpson carried a bulky metal case which he opened on Jet's dining room table and started to examine the phone.

Jet removed his front door key from his key ring and held it out for Stimpson. 'If I leave you this, can you lock up if I get back to the nick?'

'No problem Jet. I'll finish this and then do the front door, I'll not be long.'

'Will you leave the key on my desk when you get back to the nick. I gave the only spare to Groom this morning when we were doing the observations.'

'Cheeky of our man to make a delivery after you'd packed up.'

'Cheeky all right.'

Jet left Stimpson and got into the Fiesta. Jet barely noticed the journey as he turned over in his mind details of the most recent delivery to his house and the unusual interest Jane Metcalf had shown towards his holiday. The traffic had been kind but as Jet was walking into the station from the car park Groom walked swiftly out.

'You took your time. Come on, we've got an address for the phone.'

Groom looked impatient as he reached the passenger door of the Fiesta. Soon they were both sitting in the car and Jet again started the engine.

'Where are we going?'

'Near my old stomping ground. The address is Stocksfield in Northumberland. Head towards Prudhoe.'

Jet pointed the Fiesta towards the A69, the road which took traffic west out of Newcastle and drove.

'I take it we've found nothing overnight?' Jet was manoeuvring the Fiesta into the city centre traffic as he spoke.

'Nothing. No bodies that's for sure.'

'I had a call from Derek Thompson's boss. He thinks there might be some money missing from the company.'

'How much?'

'Five thousand. They're doing an audit to get to the bottom of it.'

'Don't think he was murdered for stealing a few thousand from his company do you?'

'Seems unlikely. His company are going to ring me when they know for sure what's happened. Do we know anything about the owner of the phone?'

'Name Norman Straughan. 25 Chesterfield Road, Stocksfield. That's it so far.'

'It was brave of our man to make the delivery this morning.' As Jet spoke he crunched the gearbox of the Fiesta as he moved from second to third.

'Brave or he has some really good inside knowledge.' Groom ignored the noises of the troubled gearbox and Jet could see his mind was elsewhere.

'You thinking of Manson again?'

'Can you remember what he said when we were in the toilets with the last victim?'

'What's bothering you?'

'He said "I think his time's up" remember that?'

'It did seem odd.'

'There are a lot of odd things going on here. This isn't just some random act. This person is really twisted.'

'A hatred of all things gay that's for sure.'

'And a knowledge of police procedure.'

'How would Manson know about our observations last night?'

'Not hard to work out. Even if it wasn't well known in the nick he would know the routine. Our cars, the way we work. He would also know when we would pack it in as well.'

'I don't know Mark, it's just a big accusation. From copper to serial murderer. I know nightshift can make you do funny things, but murder?'

The traffic on the A69 was light and soon Jet was manoeuvring the Fiesta down the minor road that twisted its way towards Stocksfield, a small town seventeen miles from Newcastle city centre. Groom swore as the car jolted while Jet braked to avoid a wild rabbit who could not decide which side of the road to escape to.

25 Chesterfield Road was in a small estate tucked in

the corner of a cul-de-sac. A blue soft-top sports car stood on the driveway of the house. Jet and Groom made their way up the drive and Groom tripped on a loose block paving stone that jutted out of the uneven surface. He placed his heavy hand on the roof of the car and it sank into the fabric. Jet heard a tearing sound and he widened his eyes when he looked at Groom. Groom steadied himself and shrugged his shoulders.

The door was promptly answered by a woman who Jet guessed was in her sixties. She looked frail and wore cream-coloured trousers pulled tight around her narrow waist, holding in a silk blouse which also looked too large. Her dyed blonde hair was short and carefully arranged, it looked fragile, a result of years of maintenance to attempt to keep it looking the same. The pale skin of her face was lined.

'We're from the police,' Jet produced his warrant card, 'nothing to worry about but we'd like to have a quick word with Norman Straughan if we could please.'

'He's not here.'

'Could you tell us where he is? It's important we talk to him.'

'I don't know where he is.'

'Are you Mrs Straughan?'

'Yes.'

'Could we come in and have a quick chat?'

Mrs Straughan released her grip of the front door and

Jet and Groom followed her through a short hall into the front room of the house. Two white leather sofas sat at right angles on the wooden floor and they took up the invitation to sit. The sofa felt hard. A flat screen television stood in the corner of the room but was flat against one wall. Its position restricted the view and struck Jet as a case of neatness over practicality. Jet thought the house felt sterile and unhomely.

Jet smiled as Mrs Straughan sat on the opposite sofa he and Groom had elected to sit on. Groom sat back and seemed quite content to allow Jet to continue the conversation unaided. 'When did you last see your husband?'

'Last night, he went to the golf club for a drink.'

'He hasn't come back yet?'

'No.'

'Were you not worried when he didn't come back at closing time?'

'He sometimes likes to go for a drive and he can be a bit late. He's retired now so he's no work to get up early for. I went to bed, I thought he'd be back when I woke up.'

'Is that something he often does?'

'He doesn't normally stay out as long as this. I wasn't sure what to do. Why do you want him?'

'We think we might have found his mobile phone. Do you have his number?'

'Yes.' She stood up to reach for a handbag lying on a sideboard and took her mobile phone out then scrolled through the numbers. 'I just rang it before but it went straight through to the answering service.'

She read out the number which corresponded to the one Groom had written down in his notebook.

'That's the same number. Do you know where your husband might have driven to?'

'He never says, he just enjoys driving.'

'Is that his car in the drive?'

'Yes, but he took mine. A black Honda, I've not had it long and he likes to drive it.'

'Do you have the registration number?'

'Yes, you're worrying me, what's happened?'

'I'm sorry Mrs Straughan. We don't mean to alarm you. But we'd like to find your husband as soon as we can. We don't think he's done anything wrong, we would just really like to make sure he's safe.'

'Why wouldn't he be safe?'

'Look, we really don't know very much ourselves. We just want to find him. If he's driving your car we could circulate the number.'

'I see.' Mrs Straughan disappeared through the open door to the dining room and after rustling in a drawer came back with a registration document in her hand. 'The car's new, the details are here.'

Her hand shook as she gave the document to Jet. He

recorded the vehicle's particulars in his notebook. 'Thanks, we'll circulate this now. Let's hope we find your husband soon and we'll have worried you for nothing.'

'Where did you find his phone?'

Jet looked at Groom and then forced a smile as he turned to Mrs Straughan. 'We're currently investigating two murders in Newcastle. The watches of both victims were delivered to the police. Your husband's phone was delivered in the same way. But listen, we don't know what's happened yet. We just need to do everything we can now to find him and that's exactly what we'll do. Do you have any idea where he might have gone for his drive?'

'No, he usually says he's just been driving around Newcastle, he just likes driving.'

'Mrs Straughan, I know this must be distressing, is there anyone we could call, a relative or friend, how about a neighbour?'

'No, Norman doesn't speak to the neighbours. Keeps himself to himself. I've a daughter who lives around the corner. I was just about to give her a ring anyway.'

'That's a good idea,' Groom made his first contribution to the conversation. 'I think it would be helpful if we got a police officer to stay with you for a while as well, just to make sure everything is all right for you.'

'If you think it's necessary.'

Groom stood up, 'Yes I think that would be a good idea and then you'll know as soon as we've found him. As my colleague says he could walk through the door at any minute.'

'We'll wait here if you want to ring your daughter.' Jet was finding maintaining the smile on his face a challenge.

Jet stood as Mrs Straughan went to her house phone and after punching the number pad for a few seconds Jet overheard the brief conversation with her daughter. 'Yes it's dad, the police are here, he didn't come back last night, I don't know, can you come round? Thanks.'

'She'll be here in a few moments, she's just up the street.'

'Do you have a photo of your husband we could borrow?'

'Of course.' Mrs Straughan walked to the windowsill and picked up a silver frame. 'This one was taken on our last holiday, in Mauritius.'

Jet looked at the plump tanned face that squinted from the photograph. 'We'll look after it. We'll have an officer here soon. Please try not to upset yourself, we still don't know what's happened. I'll leave my mobile number, if there is anything. I will let you know as soon as there is anything to tell you.'

Mrs Straughan looked bewildered. She sat down again and as she did Groom's phone rang. It took a few seconds and one 'yes' before it was back in his pocket. 'We need to go Jet.'

'OK. Mrs Straughan, will you be all right until your daughter arrives?'

'Yes, you will let me know if there is anything?'

'Of course.'

Within a few minutes Jet was back at the wheel of the Fiesta reversing out of the cul-de-sac away from the blue Porsche Boxster sports car.

'That's a strange car for an elderly plan drawer.' Groom nodded towards the drive.

'Wonder how having a hole in the roof will affect the resale value?'

'I barely touched it.'

'Looks like a midlife crisis buy to me. Aren't those the one's thirty-bob millionaires buy who can't afford the real thing?'

'Yeah, not the sort of car you take to pick up men in the gay areas.'

'The thought had crossed my mind as well.'

'I'd be surprised if we see Mr Straughan alive.'

'Better get a family liaison officer to Mrs Straughan.'

'I'll arrange it now.'

'Where are we going?'

'Point your car towards Kingston Park. The Mondeo has turned up.' Groom was pressing the buttons on his phone as he spoke. 'Oh and Jet.'

'Yes?'

189

Groom pointed a finger out of the windscreen. 'Don't spare the horses.'

The Fiesta roared as loud as its ageing components allowed as it headed back to the A69 towards Newcastle. Jet could feel the car acting more sluggishly as a result of Groom's additional weight but did not share this. It took Groom a few minutes on his mobile to arrange an officer to go to the Straughans' house.

Groom put his phone back in his pocket as the Fiesta headed along the slip road onto the A69.

'Is this as fast as it goes?'

'Yes.'

'Ever thought about buying a new one?'

'Nothing wrong with this.'

'Think I might be able to get you a deal on a blue sports car soon.'

'Not my style.'

Groom eyed the interior of the Fiesta. 'True.'

'Where is the Mondeo?' Jet was keen to move the attention away from his vehicle to another one.

'It's parked up on Tudor Way; the false plates are still on it. Uniform are keeping an eye on it.'

'If something has happened to Straughan that knocks out the link with Manson and the nightshift.'

'Could be the reason a body hasn't turned up in the city centre is because he's changed his pattern, he's gone to another area. Could be more evidence not less.'

'I just think it is so unlikely, a cop doing this.'

'You forgot about Harris?'

'Forget about the man who killed Julia?'

'Sorry Jet. That was stupid. I just meant, well I worked with him and I didn't know what he was doing.'

'Harris was doing it for the money. He made pots of it. Whoever is doing this is doing it for another reason.'

'You're too logical to be a murderer Jet. It requires passion.'

'To get away with murder you have to take the passion out of it.'

'What do you mean?'

'Passion gets you caught. You leave evidence, witnesses.'

Groom looked at Jet who was fixed on the road ahead. 'Maybe you could be a murderer after all.'

'If I was going to do it I would do my best not to get caught that's for sure. If Manson is doing this he must know sooner or later he'll get caught.'

'Not all murderers want to avoid being caught.'

'Not all murderers think about it, that's all. If they did they would act differently.'

'Well let's not assume that a man cutting people's dicks off is thinking things through as clearly as you.'

'Why would he be targeting gays?'

'He hates them. Classic motive. You heard him in the toilets. He's homophobic.'

Groom's phone hummed and he picked it out of his pocket. 'Yeah?.... Which way..... I'll go onto airwaves.'

Groom turned to Jet. 'It's mobile. Heading onto the A1.'

'We're coming to the A1 soon.'

Groom opened the glove compartment and rummaged about to fish out a police radio. 'Do you ever tidy this thing?'

Jet ignored the comment as Groom turned on the radio.

'Vehicle left, left, left. South on A1.' The voice on the radio was calm.

Jet pulled the Fiesta onto the roundabout which joins the A69 and A1 and parked on the flyover so he could see traffic coming towards them.

'Tango fifty-one.' The voice of the pursuing traffic officer contained no emotion. 'We have visual. Suspect vehicle, one male occupant heading south A1. What are instructions?'

'Stand by.' There was a calm bordering on indifference in the control room operator's tone.

'This is Zulu seventy-three.' Groom was talking into the radio. 'Suspect's vehicle is wanted in connection with murder enquiry. Vehicle to be stopped and occupant detained. We are mobile in area and will assist.'

'Tango fifty-one. That is understood, will stop vehicle now. A1 lay-by.'

'If Manson is driving this car it could settle it.' Groom was holding the radio close to his head in anticipation.

'Tango fifty-one. Vehicle has accelerated. Eighty, south on A1.'

'Bollocks.' Groom was still holding the radio.

'Tango fifty-one. Vehicle still accelerating, ignoring our indications. Hundred, south A1.'

'We'll be able to see it in a minute, it's heading our way.' Jet was looking out of the passenger window, north up the A1.

'We'll be able to wave at it but we'll never catch it at a hundred in this.' Groom sounded disappointed. 'If we follow it, we'll be close if it gets stopped.'

'Let's wait for a few minutes and see what happens. Don't see much point in zooming around Newcastle when there's no need.' Jet's adrenalin was clearly not pumping as fast as Groom's.

'Come on man, this is a murder suspect.'

'And this is a Ford Fiesta. Let the traffic cops do their bit now and we'll do our bit when he's caught.'

The sound of a siren grew from the left of the Fiesta as lights of the speeding vehicle came into sight, hurtling down the carriageway. It quickly passed underneath the flyover and was soon speeding away from the Fiesta, down the A1 towards the south.

'Tango fifty-one. Vehicle pulling left into A695 slip road. Still hundred MPH.'

'He's heading back into the city. He's going to do a runner. Quick Jet head down West Road and at least we'll get close when he does abandon the car.'

Jet reluctantly accelerated over the flyover and headed down the West Road.

'Tango fifty-one. Vehicle is a left, left, left, on Denton Road.'

'Turn right here, they're coming towards us.'

Jet was starting to feel his heart thumping as he drove south down Denton Road. They came to a small roundabout.

'Stop here.' Groom was shouting and sounded excited.

'What are we doing?' Jet looked worried.

'Just pull around the roundabout and we can stop the traffic.'

'Isn't that dangerous?'

'Not really - this is a murder enquiry.'

The sound of a siren could be heard getting closer. Jet stopped before entering the roundabout, knowing that the Mondeo and the pursuing police traffic car were speeding towards them from the opposite direction.

'Get on the roundabout man, stop the traffic.'

'It's too dangerous, what if we cause a crash?'

'We won't, they'll have to stop. Quick now man, I can see them.'

Jet pulled on to the roundabout very slowly. 'I'll let

them get past and we can turn around and follow.'

The Fiesta drove straight over the roundabout as the Mondeo approached from the other side. Groom suddenly grabbed at the steering wheel pushing it clockwise, causing the Fiesta to turn right on the roundabout and roll across the path of oncoming traffic. The Mondeo was now just yards away and heading straight for the passenger side of the Fiesta.

'Fucking hell!' Jet could see the Mondeo now tearing directly towards the side of their vehicle and instinctively hit the brakes which left the Fiesta broadside oncoming traffic.

The Mondeo was now heading straight at Groom as he stared out of the passenger window of the Fiesta. The Mondeo lurched to its left, mounted the pavement and then crashed through a garden wall. Jet sat frozen in the driver's seat as the Mondeo passed inches away from the front of his car. As the Mondeo hit the garden wall its front wheels were lifted from the ground and it slid across a front garden and then into another wall that divided two gardens. Groom reacted instantly, he jumped from the stationary Fiesta and went straight to the driver's door of the Mondeo. Jet could feel his heart thumping like an old traction engine and held onto the steering wheel as he tried to recover his composure. Groom pulled at the driver's door of the Mondeo and grabbed the arm of the driver. He pulled the figure back and looked at the face which appeared dazed but uninjured.

'Come on bonny lad, you're coming with me.' Groom reached over and released the driver's seat belt and then guided the driver out of the car. Two officers from the traffic car ran towards Groom as he guided the compliant figure towards the Fiesta.

'It's all right we've got him. We'll take him to the station.' Groom watched as the two officers slowed down, realising that the prisoner's escape was unlikely from Groom's sturdy grip. Groom opened the rear door of the Fiesta and bundled his prisoner inside.

'Keep an eye on him Jet.' Groom spoke to a still dazed Jet, who had got out of the driver's seat and was now standing by the driver's door, searching for equanimity.

As Jet guarded their prisoner Groom walked over to the two traffic officers.

'Good work that lads, if we get him to the station can you sort the vehicle out? Get forensics to examine it first before anyone starts rutting about inside it.'

The two officers surveyed the Mondeo, the front end of which had concertinaed against the second wall it had hit. The first wall was destroyed and thick black skid marks scarred the garden lawn across its entire length to where the Mondeo now rested.

'We'll look after it. I don't think it's going anywhere.' The older of the two officers looked like he was going to take the lead.

'Thanks. You might want to speak to the owners of these gardens and sort out an accident report while you're waiting.'

'Are you sure it was an accident?' The traffic cop looked at the Fiesta which was still stationary blocking the road.

'Yeah, what else, there's no damage done to any other vehicle, he just veered off the road trying to escape you.'

'Is the driver all right?'

'Yeah, he's fine. The police surgeon can check him over.'

'That's probably the most dangerous manoeuvre I've seen a police vehicle make.'

Groom looked at Jet who was standing by the passenger door overseeing their suspect and was out of earshot, as Groom spoke. 'He just gets a bit excited when he's driving. I'll have a word.'

'OK.'

'No real harm done though and we do have a murder suspect in custody.'

'Suppose.' The traffic cop did not look convinced.

Groom left the officers surveying the wreckage and walked to the Fiesta. He opened the rear door and slid in next to his prisoner. Jet then got into the driving seat and started the Fiesta

Groom's smile was broad. 'Good bit of work that Jet. Come on let's get back to the nick.'

Day Three – Afternoon

'Yes Sir. Just thought you'd like to know. We've got a suspect in for the murders. He was arrested after a bit of a car chase. The owner of that Mondeo we found on the CCTV with the false plates.' York had rang the Chief Constable in the hope the news might be welcome.

'Has he said anything yet?'

'No. We don't even have all his details yet, I just wanted you to know in case you heard something in the media and thought you weren't being kept up to date.'

'Good man.' The Chief did not sound as excited as York had hoped. 'Whilst you're on. I took a call from the witness protection people. They've sent someone to Portugal to liaise with the police there. Harris has disappeared off the face of the earth. His wife is distraught. She said he went to a bar he often visits for a drink one night and didn't come back.'

'Portugal?'

'Yes. Do you know who else has been to Portugal recently?'

'No.'

'Your man Whittle.'

'Are you sure?'

'It's from a confidential source but it's good information.'

'It must just be a coincidence. Whittle's not the vigilante type.'

'Harris murdered his wife.'

'I've known Whittle for years. He's a good cop.'

'Well let's see what the enquiry turns up. If Whittle is involved we will find out. He's not the Scarlet Pimpernel.'

'Harris could have just done a runner.'

'Left his family? His liaison seems to think it very unlikely. He still had plenty of money apparently and was quite happy that the future was sun, sand and sangria.'

'Is there anything you want me to do?'

'Nothing to do. Witness protection will do the enquiries here and liaise with the Portuguese authorities.'

'OK.'

'Keep me updated with the murderer.'

York felt depressed when he put the phone down. The news of the arrest had not had the impact he'd hoped for.

The interview rooms in the custody suite of the police station have a device that not only records interviews but transmits them live to a speaker located in another room across the corridor. By the time Jet got to this interview monitoring room Ormond was already there, his papers spread in front of him, looking like he had set up camp. Ormond had Rosie Shepherd with him and both sat facing the door on the same side of the square table that filled most of the small room. As Jet entered he guessed Ormond would feel uneasy with Shepherd alongside as an interview advisor and wondered to what extent he was just gritting his teeth and playing the game. Groom and Jet pulled out two hard chairs and sat next to each other opposite Ormond and Shepherd. Jet brought his own bundle of documents which he placed on the table in front of him.

'So what have we got?' Ormond clearly wanted to get straight down to business.

Jet lifted up the top edge of his papers. 'Adam Savage, thirty-five years old. Home address in Kenton. Various convictions for theft, handling, assault, burglary. He was arrested for indecency in a public toilet a few years ago.'

'What about the Mondeo?'

'Stolen plates. He's run up quite a few speeding tickets. Forensics are still with the vehicle. There were some tools in it and a baseball bat, they haven't been touched yet until they're checked for prints.'

'Has he said anything?'

'Only his name. He's got the duty solicitor with him.'

'OK. Groom, you and Jet interview him. Suspect agenda only. Just get his story and we'll see where that takes us.' Ormond was looking at his file of notes as he scratched his chin. 'I'll get Kevin Butler to start doing some background.'

Groom and Jet walked out of the monitoring room into the corridor. Jet was carrying his notes and blank paper neatly arranged on his clipboard. Groom turned and spoke. 'Jet, I'll do the first bit and we'll save you for when we need some diplomacy. All right?'

'Why can't I be bad cop?'

Groom eyed Jet who was not a small man but at least six inches shorter than Groom and at least that number of inches narrower. The two men had stopped outside the closed door of the suspect interview room and Groom gently ran his fingers down the outside of the lapel of Jet's suit jacket as he spoke. 'Because you look like a good cop, Jet. You look like you wouldn't hurt a soul.' Groom's face cracked a smile as his hand left Jet's lapel. 'Good job they don't know you as well as I do.'

Jet felt the hair on his neck stand up. Groom grabbed the handle of the interview room and pushed the door, his face straightened.

Savage looked up as they entered. Jet was surprised at how relaxed he appeared.

Jet put his clipboard on the table in front of him as he sat down. Groom pulled the chair from underneath the table and sat opposite Savage's solicitor, smiling at the young face as he did.

Jet pressed the buttons on the tape machine causing a high pitched whining. When it stopped Groom spoke. 'I'm DS Mark Groom, with me is DC Frank Whittle and

Adam Savage with his solicitor....' Groom searched for a name.

'I'm Clive Proctor, I'm Mr Savage's legal representative.'

'Not a solicitor?'

'I am a qualified legal representative.'

'A runner?'

'Legal representative.'

'Your firm does know Savage has been arrested for murder?'

'I am well aware of that and more than capable of advising Mr Savage.' Proctor looked offended at Groom's questioning and Jet realised that was the intention.

'Well, as long as Mr Savage is happy.' Groom looked Savage in the eye. 'Are you happy?'

'Look you've got nothing on me so why should I care?' Jet could see Savage was not going to be as easily rattled as Proctor.

'You were arrested driving a Ford Mondeo. Is that your car?'

'Thinking of selling it now the front end's missing. You interested?'

'How long have you owned the car?'

'Not really sure.'

'Who did you buy it from?'

'Don't remember.'

'Did you buy it from a garage?'

'A man I met in a pub said he wanted to get rid of it so I bought it off him. I gave him the money and he did say he would come back with the log book. I think I paid him too much and I haven't seen him since. I haven't done anything about it yet. Generous to a fault that's my problem. People take advantage.'

'The registration plates on the car are false. Why did you put false plates on the vehicle?'

'They were the plates on when I bought it. Looked all right to me. Never really checked. Hope I've not been swindled. You will look after me if you find I have been, won't you?'

Groom smiled. 'Okay, Mr Savage, tell me what you do for a living.'

'I'm resting between jobs at the moment.'

'What was the last job you did?'

'Security at the Energy Factory.'

'The night club in the Bigg Market?'

'That's the one.'

'Why did you leave?'

'I'd had enough of all the late work, wanted a career change.'

'You live at Kenton?'

'Yes.'

'Why park your car at Kingston Park?'

'It's a better area. Less likely to get stolen or damaged there. You never see a copper where I live, it's just not safe.'

'Are you sure you didn't leave it there so no one would know you were using that car?'

'No. Too suspicious for your own good you lot. I never did anything I'd need to keep a secret.'

'What do you carry the baseball bat in the car for?'

'It was in the car when I bought it. I just never got around to clearing it out.'

'So it won't have your prints on it?'

'How would I know, I might have touched it. I haven't played baseball with it.'

'Not many people do play baseball in Newcastle, but that doesn't stop them from using the bats to assault people. Do you use it as a weapon?'

'Why would I want to hurt anyone?'

'I was hoping you might tell me that.'

'Nothing to tell.'

Groom smiled as he collected his thoughts. 'How do you make money?'

'I don't at the moment. Dependent on the state.'

'Really.' Groom reached over to Jet and pulled the clipboard towards him. 'You have quite a lot of previous convictions.'

'I've been dealt with for those. Turned over a new whatsit.'

'The Energy Factory; that's known as a gay club isn't it?'

'I'm as open minded as the next man. Live and let live.'

'Are you gay?'

'I really don't see what that has to do with anything.' Clive Proctor straightened up in his chair as he spoke.

'Really? A qualified solicitor might, if you want to go and consult one.' Groom moved his gaze from Savage to Proctor as he spoke. He returned it to Savage. 'You were arrested a little while ago for indecency in a public toilet, can you tell me what that was about?'

'That would be a matter of record and I do not see what questioning my client about his previous convictions is going to achieve. If you pursue this line any further then I will have to advise my client to make no comment. He wishes to co-operate, as he has nothing to hide and he wants to help you with your enquiries as much as he can, but really you cannot seek to persecute him on the grounds of previous convictions.' Jet thought he could see a vein throbbing in Proctor's neck as he spoke.

Groom sat back in his seat. 'Your car was seen at two o'clock yesterday morning next to the toilets in the Bigg Market. What were you doing in the toilets at that time?'

'I don't know what you're talking about. I do quite a bit of travelling about, plenty of time now I don't work, I don't remember going to the toilets in the Bigg Market.'

'Your car was caught on CCTV outside the toilets.'

'Really.'

'So?'

'So what? I may or may not have gone to the toilet. Do you keep a note every time you take a piss?'

'There was a mutilated body in the toilet at the time you were in it. Did you take a note of that?'

'I never saw any body, mutilated or not.'

'Think hard about where you were at that time. You must remember going to a public toilet yesterday.'

'Don't remember.'

'Why didn't you stop for the police car today?'

'Didn't want the hassle – it's only ever bad news when you lot get involved.'

'Why were you running away?'

'Not running away, just avoiding trouble.'

'So you have nothing to hide?'

'Nothing.'

'Where were you last night?'

'Here and there, just driving around the town, enjoying the sights.'

'Did you speak to anybody?'

'I spoke to a lot of people.'

'Did you call into the Energy Factory?'

'I popped in to see the doormen I used to work with, just to say hello and have a bit crack.'

'Did you meet a man called Norman Straughan last

night?'

'Not that I remember.'

'He was driving a black Honda Accord.'

'No, never saw anyone driving a Honda.'

'Did you speak to many strangers?'

'I was out speaking to mates and had a drink at a few of the pubs; spoke to a lot of people.'

'I think that's all for the moment Mr Savage. Just relax and we'll make some more enquiries and talk again soon.'

'How long are you going to keep me here? You've got nothing on me.'

'If you've done nothing wrong then there's no need for you to worry. Just relax.'

'I would like a private consultation with my client now.' Proctor looked up and watched Groom who was rising from the table.

'No problem. We'll not be too long, just need to check some things out and we'll let you know when we're ready to conduct the next interview.'

Groom and Jet left the interview room and walked towards the monitoring room.

'What do you think?' Groom had slowed down at the door of the monitoring room.

'He couldn't lie straight in bed.'

'It's going to be like drawing eyeteeth that's for sure.'

'Listen, this might be nothing, but did you notice the last time he was arrested?' Jet's face twisted in thought.

'What about it?'

'Assault, while he was working as a doorman, a few months ago.'

'Probably why he was sacked. So what?'

'Did you notice who the arresting officer was?'

'No.'

'I think this is Manson's number on the conviction sheet.'

Groom pulled at Jet's clipboard. 'Really?'

'It doesn't necessarily mean anything.'

'There's something not right Jet.'

Groom pushed the door of the monitoring room. Jet put the clipboard on the table as the rustle of chairs dominated while he and Groom sat down.

Ormond eyed Groom as he made himself comfortable. 'Mark, do you have to wind the legal representatives up quite as much?'

'Just keeping him on his toes boss.'

'Well try not to piss him off too much, we're better off with him there than a solicitor.'

'Don't worry boss, he sees it as a personal challenge now, he's not going to bow out.'

'What do you think of Savage's story?'

'Cock and bull.'

'Jet, what do you think?'

'He's a cool customer. It's going to take some work to get him to tell the truth.'

'He's never been programmed to tell the truth. He wouldn't admit to us he was breathing in and out on a regular basis.' Groom rubbed the bottom of his chin with his thumb as he spoke. 'I think we need to start gathering the facts and give him a real good run for his money.'

'Agreed.' Ormond was looking at his ever growing file of papers. 'The car is still being examined, I'll try and get something from forensics for the next interview.'

'I'll visit the club and see what I can get from there.' Groom was now rubbing his shirt sleeve over an old scar on his left arm. It was an unconscious act.

'Good idea, you and Jet go and see if you can find out who Savage was speaking to last night.'

'I was thinking I might go there on my own. I know the owner of the club from my drug squad days, it might help if I speak to him alone.'

Ormond looked up from his notes. 'Mark, I want nothing shady going on.'

'Shady? Me? Come on boss, I just know him of old and he doesn't like strangers. Plus I think there is something better Jet could be doing.'

'What?'

'The video we found last night of our friend the Priest and the first victim. Might be they did know each other, needs checking out. Jet's on good terms with the church.'

'OK, Jet speak to the Priest, but no pissing around. Savage is our priority and the clock is ticking. I want all the evidence we can get on him now.'

'One last thing boss.'

Ormond looked wearily at Groom. 'What?'

'The two people we know were at the toilet before the body was discovered were Savage and PC Manson. Manson arrested Savage a few months ago.' Groom paused, eyes focused on Ormond, who did not respond. 'I think I should speak to Manson.'

'Why?'

'Well, we could find out what happened when he dealt with Savage, ask him about the circumstances and see if he has any information that might help us.'

Ormond stared at Groom. 'You want to see the whites of his eyes?'

'Never hurts.'

'You think he's involved?'

'As ever, I have an open mind.'

'Yeah, all right, but when you speak to him make sure Jet is with you.'

'Second opinion?'

'Witness!'

The Energy Factory was a tall solid stone building which stood on the corner of the Bigg Market. Most of the buildings in that part of Newcastle were centuries old and stood as majestic reminders of the past. Groom did not know what the building's original purpose was but felt sure it was not the night club its substantial construction, tall windows and high ceilings now accommodated. The front doors stood on the corner of the smooth stone building. Two huge mahogany doors protected the glass doors behind them. Although clearly not open for business, Groom could see the doors were not locked and with a push moved a wooden door and then walked through one of the glass doors which was also ajar.

'We're closed.' The voice belonged to a heavy-set man in a thick black coat. His hair was cropped short and nose squashed out of shape. Groom guessed he hadn't quite mastered the art of ducking. He walked urgently towards Groom who stood inside the glass door.

'I'm here to see Gary Hobson.'

'Do you have an appointment?'

'Just tell him Mark Groom wants to see him.'

'He's not available.'

'Tell him Detective Sergeant Mark Groom is here to see him.'

'He's still not available.'

'He will be if you just deliver the message. Do you think you can manage that?'

'I told you, he's not available and I'm going to have to ask you to leave now.'

The shaven-headed man lifted his right hand and cupped it around the top of Groom's right arm. Groom stood solidly looking at him straight in the eye. Quickly the man increased the force to push Groom out of the door. As he leaned forward to add his weight to shove Groom out of the building, Groom side-stepped and at the same time using his left arm pushed him and with this addition to his own momentum the man propelled himself through the open glass door. Groom gave him a last push and then clicked the Yale lock on the door locking the man outside. The shaven-headed man frantically pulled at the brass handles but could do little more than rattle the substantial door and look on helplessly at Groom who stood inside smiling out. Groom shrugged his shoulders and then turned to walk inside the club. A door at the rear of the dance floor with 'private' written on it was open and Groom followed a corridor to an office door which he opened.

'I told you I didn't want to be bothered.' The man did not look up from behind his desk and continued to scribble on the large notebook he had opened in front of him.

'Cooking the books?' Groom walked towards the desk and as he did pulled a chair which he turned to sit on to face Hobson.

'How did you get in?'

'Your man let me through, I think he's gone to make us coffee.'

'That's good of him.' Hobson closed the ledger in

front of him and sat back in his chair. 'Detective Sergeant Groom, I thought you were in prison?'

'No, it was a case of mistaken identity. Everything is back to normal now.'

'That's good to hear. What can I do for you?'

'We have an employee of yours, Adam Savage, in custody, for murder.'

'I don't recall an employee called Adam Savage.'

'Look Hobson, this is a once only offer. You tell me about Savage and in return I will leave you and your club alone. If I find out you're holding things back I'll be all over you like a cheap suit.'

'Even cheaper than the one you're wearing now?' Hobson smiled and for a second both men stared considering each other, until Hobson again spoke. 'Savage was a doorman here who I had to let go. He became over-zealous with a customer and was done for assault.'

'Had he worked for you long?'

'A few years, he was a good doorman. People tended not to mess with him, if you know what I mean.'

'Violent?'

'Firm but fair.'

Hobson's mobile phone vibrated on his desk and he looked at the screen. 'Ah, it's our Wilf; he must be having trouble finding the milk.' He put the phone to his ear and after a second spoke. 'Yes, no thanks to you. Where are you?' Hobson smiled at Groom as he listened for a few more seconds. 'Just stay there and maybe he'll let you back in when he leaves.' Hobson put the phone back on the table.

Groom continued. 'Have you seen much of Savage since he was done for the assault?'

'He still comes in now and again. He keeps in touch with the lads on the door. I help him out occasionally with the odd freelance job.'

'Doing what?'

'Running errands, a bit of collection work, that sort of thing.'

'Debt collecting?'

'Nothing as crude as that. Occasionally people might run up a large tab which they can't settle on the night and I just get one of the lads to pick the money up for me the following day.'

'You still lending money?'

'No, that would be illegal. On occasion to help a good client I might lend them some money to tide them over but nothing that need trouble the law. It's all friends helping friends.'

'Is Savage gay?'

'How would I know that? I don't ever recall seeing him with a girlfriend but it's not my business.'

'Do you have the names and addresses of the people who Savage has visited for you?'

'No. It would have just been an informal job. No records kept. Savage is a good man, someone I can trust.'

'Then why did you let him go?'

'He lost his licence to be a doorman.'

'Don't you normally put them out of the way for a while, say they're just looking after the cashbox or something until the heat is off?'

'There can be ways around these things but to be honest Savage was attracting the wrong sort of attention.'

'What do you mean?'

'I put him back on the door when he was on bail and could still work but that copper of yours kept calling in to see him. Every night it was; it was giving the place a bad name, getting the customers nervous, so I had to do something.'

'Which copper?'

'The one that arrested him, Manson. Being a real pain he was. Savage said he kept trying to get information out of him. Wasting his time with Savage.'

Groom rose. 'Thanks, that's all for now, I trust you'll make sure you're available if I need to come back.'

'If you tell Wilf to come in and see me I'll make sure he's briefed.'

Jet was struck by the silence of St Stephen's. Even the noise of the traffic could not pierce the sacred serenity. It unnerved him. He did not know why. He walked to the front of the church and again surveyed the altar. It was clean. He looked up and could see dust particles dance in shafts of light that forced their way in the high windows. The words, 'sun comprehending glass', crossed his mind and he smiled at another quotation Julia had shared with him, which he now could not place. With every day that passed she became slightly more faint, he found it hard to bear, he knew he needed to implement his plan to stop the erosion. But he still had things he needed to do. It had been the thought of Ray Harris that had driven him before, at the moment it was a serial murderer, but soon the murderer would be caught and Jet could get back to his plan.

Jet sat in the front pew and lifted his notebook from his inside jacket pocket. He had resisted using the mobile number the Priest had given him, preferring to give him little chance to prepare or make himself scarce, but he was now reviewing that strategy in the solemn silence, surrounded by many well-polished symbols. Expensive earthly trinkets buying hope of better things to come. Good money after bad Jet thought.

Jet looked up to one of the recesses in the church which seemed to hide a passageway to a private part of the building but felt too uncomfortable to explore it.

The sound that came from the door in the recess was so faint it could have been a mouse out for a stroll, but for want of competition the noise was clearly audible and the figure of the Priest emerged.

Jet did not think the Priest had noticed him as he approached and Jet spoke. 'I was just about to give you a ring.'

The Priest looked up. 'I didn't hear anyone coming in.'

'The door was open.'

'Is there something I can do for you?'

Jet could see that the Priest would have preferred the church to be empty. 'I just want to clarify a few things with you.'

'Yes?'

'You told us that you did not know Derek Thompson.'

'You said he was someone who came to the church and I did not recognise him. Yes.'

'I think you do know him.'

'What are you talking about?'

'You met him at the George and Dragon the night before he died.'

'I don't know what you're talking about.'

'Were you at the George and Dragon pub three nights ago?'

'I often call in there, that's not a problem is it?'

'I spoke to people who worked with Derek Thompson. They told me he had a friend at this church called Paddy. That's your name isn't it?'

'On odd occasions friends will call me that. It's not a rare name.'

'You were caught on CCTV at the George and Dragon talking to Derek Thompson on the night he was murdered.'

'I have told you I was there. I met a lot of people, part of what I do is to socialise, I often speak to people in the area. I might have spoken to him, I might not. Some people who come to this church do use that pub, it's quite nice and a good place to meet. I don't know what you're driving at.'

'It's important that we find out everything there is about the victim of this murder. We need to find out what happened. You've told us you don't know him but there you are talking to him the night he was killed. Surely you can see how that looks.'

'You're wasting your time. I can see that my comments have angered the police, but really stooping to this sort of behaviour is beyond contempt. I fear that this is getting very close to harassment and perhaps I should speak to a solicitor.'

Jet got to his feet. 'You must do what your conscience predicts.'

'I don't think you are in a position to preach to me about following my conscience.'

'Perhaps not.' Jet did not think the Priest could

imagine how much he agreed. 'Thank you for your help.'

It had taken just a few moments for Jet to get to the Fiesta and then find Groom who was waiting outside Newcastle's Central Railway Station. Jet ignored the din of car horns as he pulled over in the taxi rank and Groom slid into the passenger seat.

'I hope you had better luck with Gary Hobson than I had with the Priest.'

'Hobson's not someone who's going to show you all his cards but he did tell me that Savage is still working for him.'

'On the doors of the club?'

'No. He had to take him off the doors because Manson kept visiting him, which is interesting.'

'So what was he doing?'

'Reading between the lines I think he was collecting debts for Hobson.'

'Debts?'

'Yeah, Hobson reckons he's been lending cash to friends but he's been suspected of loan-sharking for years. No one can get close enough to get evidence. He lends to people who aren't going to tell the police when they get charged a hundred percent interest and then get roughed up if they can't pay. He's probably been using the contacts in the club to lend to vulnerable people, he lets the payments slip and then sends out someone like Savage to recover the debt and a mountain of interest.'

'Sounds like a job Savage would excel at.'

'Yeah. A sadistic bastard like that starts frightening people and gets to enjoy it more and more and before you know it he's smashing their skulls in.'

'Let's hope it's that simple. One question though.'

'Yeah.'

'Where's Straughan?'

'My money's on dead.'

'The body would have turned up by now.'

'Maybe. Savage will know where he is, if he's still alive we might have a chance of finding him.'

'Savage is not going to be easy to break down.'

'We just need to know how to push his buttons.'

Jet drove the Fiesta onto Jesmond Dene Road. 'I think it's the next left - here it is.'

Jesmond is one of the leafier suburbs of Newcastle. Jet guessed most of the grand old houses would have started their lives as homes to rich industrialists but over recent years most had been converted to apartments for the more affluent residents of the city. It was a place Julia had often expressed the wish to live, convenient for her mother who lived close-by in the equally pricey area of Gosforth. Julia would often cite the existence of Jesmond Tennis Club as proof positive of the exclusiveness of the neighbourhood. She was never sympathetic to Jet's observation that as it was a game neither of them had any interest in playing, buying an expensive house because of its proximity seemed rather a waste.

The estate was quiet as they pulled up outside Manson's first floor flat. There was a small garden which was paved and two metal chairs leaned against a round table; a touch of the Mediterranean in the north east chill.

Groom knocked on the door and Manson looked surprised to see him and Jet at his door.

'Everything all right?' Jet thought Manson less than welcoming.

'Yeah, can we come in for a few moments? We just need to pick your brains.' Groom was moving forward which limited Manson's response. He pulled the door and led the way down a short hall into the living room.

'Nice place you have here.'

'Yeah, what can I do for you?'

'We have a man called Adam Savage in custody for these murders and you were the last to arrest him, just wanted to know if you had any information that might help us.'

'Savage; the doorman from the Energy Factory?'

'Aye. You locked him up a few months ago.'

'Yeah, he assaulted one of the punters. Two gay-boys were having a bit of a spat and he sorted them out. He punched one of them and before he knew it they had kissed and made up then made a complaint of assault against him.'

'Do you know who the two boys were?'

'Not offhand. It'll all be in the crime report. Just a couple of puffs from Gosforth. Don't think they'll ever go back to the club.'

'You don't seem to like the gay community much.' Groom's eyes fixed upon Manson's.

'What's that to do with anything?'

'I don't know; it's an observation that's all. I'm just curious.'

'It's unnatural. Blokes kiss each other in public now, my dad will be turning in his grave. You should see some of the things I've seen them get up to in the Gardens or in the back lanes. Disgusting.'

'I forgot about your dad,' Jet had clearly just dusted off something on the shelf of his memory bank. 'He was a cop when I was a probationer.'

'Yeah, good old-fashioned copper. People looked up to him. Staunch catholic, would have had plenty to say about the way things are going now.'

'Times do change you know.' Groom had maintained his stare at Manson.

'Not always for the better. It shouldn't be allowed.'

'Did you speak much to Savage after his arrest?'

'Yeah, tried.'

'The owner of the club said you were becoming a

regular down there.'

'I did wonder whether I could get any information from Savage, in return for a good word at court but got nowhere.'

'What were you hoping he might tell you?' Groom persisted.

'He's the sort who knows everybody's business.'

'Quite a violent man.'

'He can handle himself that's for sure, but I don't think he's got too much form.'

'A queer basher, do you think?'

'Not especially, I don't think he discriminates, he'll bash anyone.'

'The night the second body was found in the toilet, did you see him in the Bigg Market?'

'No. Why?'

'A video turned up of his car parked near the toilet at the time of the murder, at the same time you walked past.'

Jet thought Manson looked startled at Groom's enquiry. 'I didn't know he had a car, never saw him.'

'On the morning we met you in the toilet you made a remark about time being up for the victim, what did you mean?' Groom was still focused.

'Don't remember saying it, but I would have thought it was obvious under the circumstances.' Manson looked agitated. 'What odds does it make what I said to you at the scene, no one is going to complain are they? Listen, what's this about?'

'We're just making enquiries into a serious matter and the more information we have the better.'

'Well I've told you everything I know and I've got to be making tracks now. It's my day off and there're things I need to do.'

'Right.' Groom turned to look at Jet. 'Well thanks for your help, we'll leave you to enjoy the rest of your day off.'

Groom turned and walked back towards the hall. Jet followed and his eye caught a crucifix hanging on the wall, red paint ran from the crown of thorns on the head of the effigy.

The door was quickly closed behind them and soon Jet was turning the ignition of the Fiesta. 'Would never have put Manson down as the religious sort.'

'Me neither, what was his dad like?'

'One of the old guard. A lot of cops who were coming to the end of their service at that time were like him, joined the police after a stint in the army. Regimental sorts. I remember his dad was famous for dispensing his own brand of summary justice.'

'Cuffs around the ear?'

'That and a bit more, those were the days when you could get away with it.'

'Those were the days.' Groom grinned.

'Aye, I think you would've enjoyed it.'

'Yes York, Chief here, has the murderer said anything yet?'

York immediately felt uneasy when he heard the Chief Constable's voice. 'No Sir, they're still interviewing him. I just spoke to DI Ormond, they've just finished the suspect agenda and he's come up with a cock and bull story. They're now breaking it down. Looks like we're in for the long haul.'

'I need to speak to you about Ormond.'

'Really?'

'Yes, I told the staff to expect two days off and when I left he countermanded it.'

'Perhaps he just misunderstood?'

'I won't have junior staff pissing me around York. When I say it, I mean it, and it's not for some poxy DI to ignore.'

'I think it's most likely he thought you meant the staff could get a few well-earned days off when the pressure was off.'

'Just needed a bit of modern thinking and better management to change the staff around, better results all round.'

'Well Ormond is old school, but he's very thorough.'

'Past his sell-by-date. I won't forget this. I'll have his

bollocks.'

'He's co-ordinating the interview at the moment, what do you want me to do?'

'Nothing whilst they are dealing with the prisoner. I'll get him up here when the case is finished.'

'I'm sure he didn't mean to undermine your authority.'

'Did he speak to you about it?'

York swallowed hard. 'No, first I've heard about it, it's been so busy since these murders started to happen and now we have this crazy Priest acting himself.'

'I've had a briefing from the witness protection people. They still can't find any trace of Harris. Disappeared from the face of the earth.'

York realised the sudden change of subject meant the Chief was not interested in hearing excuses. York was pleased to move onto something else. 'Are the Portuguese police involved?'

'For what it's worth. They have a missing person report and we are liaising with them. I don't think they are terribly interested if the truth's known but our people are trying to work with them.'

'Anything I can do?'

'No. Keep it under your hat for the moment until we decide what to do. Turns out Harris's wife had been in touch with her mother. They get briefed about it but every time there's a leak it's someone talking to their mother.'

'Is the mother involved in his disappearance?'

'She said a few weeks ago she had a visit from someone from the probation service who said they were there to see if there were any welfare issues to resolve. She didn't think anything of it, but turns out an address book went missing at the same time. Of course probation know nothing about it, why would they, they wouldn't send anyone out to see his mother-in-law.'

'Any idea who it was?'

'All we have is someone in a suit with thick glasses.'

'And Harris's address was in the book?'

'Telephone number and a town. Enough for someone with a bit of nous to find them.'

'Any leads on who it was?'

'Who do you think?'

'I still don't think Whittle could be involved.'

'Well if he is, it'll all come out in the wash. I think we'll have enough to arrest him soon. Who else could it be?'

'What about the criminals Harris gave evidence against?'

'Whoever did this knows the system and is subtle. Don't you think it's a huge coincidence that Whittle was in Portugal at the same time Harris went missing?'

'We have no evidence.'

'Not yet but we're getting close. Keep it under your

hat and don't forget to let me know when these murders are sorted.'

The phone clicked before York could reply. He dialled an extension number. 'Is DI Ormond there?' York felt impatient. 'Well get him.' A few seconds passed and then York barked. 'Yes it's Superintendent York, I've just been briefing the Chief about the prisoner. He's well informed and I thought you should know that someone from your staff is speaking directly to him, just wanted you to know. The first bit of news you get on this prisoner, let me know. We better get a result or traffic duty in Berwick is beckoning us both!'

Ormond was on his own in the monitoring room when Jet and Groom returned. Ormond scribbled on his file papers and looked up as the door opened.

'What have you got?'

'It looks like Savage was debt collecting for the club owner, I think he probably just got to like the power and the violence.'

'I've got Rosie coming down in a few moments perhaps she can help us with how best to approach Savage now.'

Groom frowned. 'We just need to keep pressing him; he'll crack when the evidence is firmed up.'

'Maybe.' Ormond looked like he had other things on

his mind. 'Mr York seems to think we have a mole in the camp. Someone has been reporting our progress, or lack of it, straight to the Chief Constable. I don't suppose either of you are friends of the Chief?'

'I'm his love child but he abandoned me at birth, won't even pay maintenance. So I'm not speaking to him. Jet probably goes to his house for Sunday lunch every week, if you get Jet in a headlock I'll punch him in the stomach and we'll soon get the truth.'

Ormond's frown grew. 'Can you take anything seriously?'

'I just don't think it's worth worrying about. One thing I know for sure is there are no secrets.' Groom turned his gaze from Ormond to Jet as he spoke. 'No matter how you try to keep things tight, someone else always knows.' He then turned back to Ormond. 'Savage is our man. We've already got his car at the scene of one of the murders, he's got form for violence and looks like he was employed to frighten gays to extort money and just got the taste for it. There must be a mountain of evidence. I don't think we've got anything to worry about.'

'I wonder if Mrs Straughan would agree.' Jet interjected.

'Let's get into his bones and get to the bottom of this.' Groom flashed his ocean-blue eyes, levity quickly replaced with steely determination.

Ormond took a deep breath. 'OK, let's see what we've got.'

A rustling came from the door, it stuttered as Rosie Shepherd wrestled with competing demands - the handle, her notes and a mug of mint tea, the string of the tea bag resting over the edge of the cup. She put her things on the table and straightened her sweater which looked bulky over the top of her black jeans. Jet wondered if only he was thinking 'fish out of water'.

'Ian Davison is coming down the corridor and I passed the message for Paul Stimpson to come.' Rosie did not make eye-contact as she spoke but sat down at the table, opening a wire ring-bound notebook.

Davison and Stimpson were both twice the size of Rosie but made much less noise when they entered and joined the gathering around the table.

Ormond had his file open in front of him. 'Right, Ian, what did the search of Savage's house turn up?'

'House is neat and pretty sparse, not what I was expecting, he lives there by himself. Neighbour says he's been there a couple of years. Says there is a woman who visits every now and again who they think is his sister. No known current partner. He's got a Mazda sports car outside, which is also clean as a whistle. He doesn't own a computer. The only thing we found of any interest are these magazines, which were under his bed.' Davison placed five magazines which were contained in a clear polythene bag. Naked torsos looked through the plastic. 'Gay porn, all men. Nothing too unpleasant if you like that sort of thing.'

'Jesus wept.' Groom shook his head. 'Is there anybody in this enquiry that's not a puff?'

'I'm not.' Stimpson made his first comment of the meeting.

'I know the boss and Jet are straight as well so at least that's four of us.' Groom looked at Davison who summoned a weak smile.

'Thanks Mark,' Ormond clearly wasn't in the mood for levity. 'Was there nothing at all in the sports car?'

'Looks like his pride and joy, washed every Sunday according to his neighbour. A few CDs in it, otherwise clean as a whistle.'

'So the Mondeo is the one he keeps for murders. It makes sense.' Groom had his determined head on again.

'Does he socialise with his neighbours or anyone in the street?' Ormond looked at Davison as he spoke.

'No. By all accounts he's a loner. Just his sister, who we have an address for. But I don't expect a great deal from her.'

'Thanks Ian, will you try and speak to his sister and just see what she has to say?'

Davison was looking at a notepad he had pulled from his jacket pocket as Ormond was speaking to him. 'Will do. Oh, the neighbour did say they weren't sure whether

Savage was turning to God recently, because he had seen a vicar there a few times.'

'A vicar?' Groom spluttered.

'Yeah, it does seem odd. That's why his neighbour was surprised, Savage doesn't seem the religious sort.'

'Maybe the sister could shed some light on that, track her down as soon as you can, Ian.' Ormond sounded peeved.

'Before that's done do you think it might be an idea if Davison goes back to see the neighbour and takes a photo of our friend the Priest. Just to see?' As Groom spoke Jet wondered if he too was surprised that Davison had not realised the significance of this sighting.

'Good idea, Ian, can you sort that?' Ormond's mood wasn't improving.

Davison frowned. 'Sure.'

Jet thought he could detect a sigh from Ormond as he looked back to his heap of notes.

'Paul.' Ormond seemed keen to move on. 'Anything from the Mondeo?'

'We've taken the tools for a full exam at the lab, that'll take time. We used the crime lights in the boot and there does seem to be a lot of blood on the tools. Seems likely that it'll be more than one person's.'

'What makes you say that?'

'There's a bat, pliers, pipe wrench, and a hammer, they all have blood stains on them. I don't think he'd carry them all. I think he selects his weapon of choice, which means he's probably used each of them at least once.'

'Good God.' Rosie's comment seemed to slip unguarded from her mouth.

'Yeah, I think he's quite a forceful character.' Stimpson continued. 'We'll know more once the lab's had a look at it all. I'll get them to take samples from the victims and if we're lucky we might get a match.'

'Thanks Paul.' Ormond sounded more contented with this brand of professionalism. 'I think that's all we need from you for the interview, could you let me know straight away when you get a result.' Stimpson got up to leave and Ormond looked at Davison. 'Ian, same for you, can you get on and let us know what the neighbour says about the photo of the Priest? It's important.'

Davison straightened his jacket as he stood and left the room behind Stimpson.

Groom looked at Ormond. 'Is it me or could that piece of information about the Priest being at Savage's house be quite important?'

'At least we know about it now.' Ormond was back to shuffling through his notes. 'Rosie; Savage is clearly a violent man. The most likely explanation seems to be that he's just got more and more violent and moved into murder, any observations?'

'He does seem to fit the profile. He's a loner, violent,

dominant and judging by his attitude from the first interview his conscience doesn't seem to be bothering him at all. He's remote and it's possible he doesn't see what he's doing is wrong. His lack of meaningful relationships and lack of feelings of guilt do point towards a sociopathic disorder.'

'Sociopathic.' Ormond repeated.

'Violent bastard with a slate off.' Groom added.

'So I guess we aren't going to be able to appeal to his gentle side during the interview?' Ormond enquired.

'Not likely he has one. Sociopaths tend to feel no guilt for what they do nor have a sense of moral responsibility.'

'It's just as I thought boss, we need to hit him with evidence, he's going to lie and wriggle and we just have to nail the bastard.' Jet could see Groom was growing impatient.

Rosie's face twisted. 'In essence, I suppose.'

'What about the gay porn?' Ormond stared at the polythene bag that seemed to soil the table in front of him.

'Repressed homosexual, not as rare as you men might like to think. Not a required quality of a sociopath but it doesn't preclude it.'

'Is it possible that he's working with someone else?'

'Not impossible but not likely. Sociopaths are very antisocial.'

'What about the watches and the notes? Why is he

doing that?'

'I've looked closely at them. He's cocking a snoot. It fits with the lack of guilt or moral conscience. He's showing off.'

'Why Jet's house?'

'My guess would be that it's a convenient place to deliver. He doesn't want to get caught. He thinks he's being clever and he's having fun. He's taunting you.'

'If he has Straughan and he's not at his house, then he must have another place elsewhere. Maybe the sister could help with that.' Jet had remained silent until now.

'Yes, maybe.' Ormond didn't sound convinced.

'Can I suggest that we get someone to make enquiries around where the Mondeo was found?'

'What you got in mind Jet?' Groom knew when Jet's mind was racing ahead it was always worth finding out where it was.

'If he had a second car, why not a second house, rented perhaps, or even a lock-up garage where Straughan and his car might be.'

Groom smiled and looked at Ormond, 'That's an interesting thought.'

'I'll get someone to co-ordinate a search.' Ormond scribbled on his notes again.

'I hear what you say about sociopaths working alone but what about the Priest?' Groom again rubbed the deep scar on his elbow as he spoke, as if the wound of many years ago still itched.

'We don't know if that is the Priest yet.'

'Hell of a coincidence if it's not.'

'Let's not get ahead of ourselves Mark.'

'If Straughan is still alive and Savage does have an accomplice then we need to get a move on.' Jet thought Groom was growing more anxious.

'One step at a time.' Ormond had finished scribbling and closed his file. 'We need to be methodical. Get in there and let's start putting facts to Savage and see if we can start to shake him.'

'You got it.' Groom rose. 'Come on Jet let's go and talk to Savage.'

As they walked across the corridor Groom spoke. 'Same as last time. I'll lead.'

Jet shrugged, resigned to being good cop for the duration.

Jet thought he could feel the smugness still projecting from Savage as they pulled up the chairs to sit opposite him and Clive Proctor. Jet pressed the tape recorder and it howled for a few seconds so no one could be in doubt that their words could now become evidence.

'Adam. Let's get this out in the open now. If Norman Straughan is still alive, it will be much better for you in the long run to do the right thing and tell us where he is.' The directness of Groom's opening statement took even Jet by surprise.

Savage smiled; Jet wondered if it were designed to annoy Groom. 'I don't know anyone called Straughan.'

Groom smiled back at Savage. 'You know Adam you're a bit of an enigma.'

'Really.'

'Yeah, you keep your home and sports car very tidy but your working car, the Mondeo, that's very messy.'

'You could give it a valet whilst I'm in here if you like.'

'Well we are looking at it. Forensics tell us there is a lot of blood in it, especially on the tools.'

'I don't know how that happened.'

'I think I do.'

'Really.'

'I spoke to your employer Gary Hobson. He tells me that he employs you to collect debts. Are you good at collecting money?'

'I'm just a messenger. Gary tells me to go somewhere and meet someone and they give me money and I take it back to him.'

'I think you're being a bit modest there Adam. I think you're very talented at extracting things from people. What do you do when they can't pay?'

'I just arrange to go back and see them when they have the money.'

'You don't threaten or use violence?'

'That would be illegal.'

'Did Derek Thompson, Justin Gallagher and Norman

Straughan owe money or did you just see them at the club and decide to meet up with them later to kill them?'

'Don't know those people and I certainly never killed anyone.'

'You think you've been clever with the notes and the watches, but there are always forensics. Blood, hair, fibres, DNA, there's always something that'll give you away.'

'I haven't done anything.'

'Did you have a sexual relationship with Derek Thompson or any of the other people you killed?'

'I don't know any of the people you're talking about.'

'But you admit you are gay?'

'I admit nothing.'

'There was gay porn under your bed.'

'I'm keeping that for someone from the club. There are a lot of punters go there who are married and can't keep that sort of stuff at their own places so I do them the odd favour.'

'You're just the regular Good Samaritan, aren't you? Who is this friend that you're doing a favour for?'

'I don't know his name. I'll return it to him when I see him on the door of the club again.'

'You were arrested for indecency in a public toilet. You got a caution for that. Were you doing someone a favour then as well?'

'Fitted up by you bastards, that's what happened

there. I went for a piss and was approached by someone in the toilet, before I could tell them where to go they produced a warrant card and I was nicked. Fitted up well and truly.'

'So why accept a caution?'

'Easiest way out wasn't it? I didn't want the hassle of going to court and having it in the papers, once you are tarred with that brush you've had it.'

Groom leaned back on his chair. 'You know you have an excuse for everything. I don't think you know how to tell the truth.'

Proctor interjected. 'Officer I don't see how your ill-considered opinions have any relevance at all. My client is answering your questions, can you stick to the facts otherwise I might need to speak to him and reconsider the full co-operation that is being given. All my client wants to do is help, that's all.'

Groom maintained his focus on Savage. 'Do you keep any record of who you collect debts from?'

'No need. Gary tells me where to go and I pick the money up.'

'So you could have spoken to Thompson, Gallagher and Straughan?'

'I don't remember their names and I certainly didn't hurt anyone.'

'Hobson keeps records. Soon I'll have them and once they link you to the murder victims then the noose will start to tighten even more.'

'Officer, this is no way to conduct an interview.'

Groom continued to stare at Savage apparently oblivious to Proctor's remark, then continued. 'And one more thing for you to think about Adam. Your friend the Priest. He's had quite a bit to say.'

'What Priest?'

'Oh, I think you know, Father Patrick O'Brian, from St Stephen's. He's being very co-operative.'

'I don't know what you're talking about.' Savage snarled.

'Officer I think I would like a private consultation with my client now please.'

'That's fine by me. We'll terminate the interview now for Mr Savage to have his amateur legal advice. But just before we turn the tape off why don't you tell us why you go to the bother of smashing your victims' watches after you've killed them?'

'Officer I think that's enough now.' Proctor's face was red and his head shook slightly as he spoke.

Jet pressed the stop button on the machine and removed both tapes. He then followed Groom out of the room and across the hall to the monitoring room.

'Well that's put a cat amongst the pigeons.' Ormond was looking at Groom as he sat down, Jet following quickly.

'I did think I would try to unsettle him.' Groom

grinned.

'Well you've definitely unsettled his solicitor.' Ormond did not return the smile.

'Runner.' Groom corrected.

Jet was content to remain silent and observe the exchange between the two.

'Runner.' Ormond conceded.

'I have an idea.' Groom's grin broadened.

'I have an ulcer.' Ormond remained straight-faced.

'If we let him go he might lead us to Straughan. Even if Straughan is dead he might want to get rid of evidence, they always go back to the scene.'

'Far too risky.'

'What is there to lose?'

'Our prisoner.'

'We keep him under surveillance.'

'We had Jet's letter box under surveillance this morning and we lost that. And it's attached to Jet's door.'

'We might find Straughan alive. I don't think we can afford not to try it.'

'Bollocks!'

It had taken fifteen minutes for Davison to secure a search warrant for the Energy Factory. A few minutes later Davison and Townsend were driving to the arranged rendezvous point where Groom and Jet stood next to an unmarked van which contained an eight-man task force they had managed to co-opt for the search.

'We did well to get this team at this short notice.' Jet was casually leaning against the wall of St Nicholas Cathedral as he spoke.

'Apparently they were doing some observations in the east end which was coming to nothing. They were happy to drop it when a murder enquiry was mentioned.'

'Lucky for us.'

'Yeah, they're all search-trained as well so we'll be able to give the club a thorough going over.'

'Do you really think Hobson is going to keep records?'

'He's a businessman. He has to.'

'Seems unlikely he'll keep anything incriminating.'

'Hobson isn't a thug, he employs thugs. He needs to keep records so he knows who it is he needs to terrorise. He has to be efficient, can't let anyone slip under his radar. If he let anyone get away with not paying then his reputation would slide and when you make your living from being an evil bastard then reputation is everything. Somewhere he will have records.'

Davison pulled his car onto the broad pavement beside the cathedral and walked over to Groom, warrant in hand.

'Any problems?' Groom did not look directly at the approaching Davison as he spoke.

'None.'

'We had better make progress then, the quicker we go the less likely Hobson is going to be prepared for our visit.'

'How could he possibly know we're coming?' Davison frowned.

'Hobson pays market price for good information.'

'Are you suggesting one of us would tell him?'

'I'm saying let's go.' Groom plucked the warrant from Davison's hand. 'Better if I do the talking, I met his minder a little while ago and worked hard to build a rapport with him.' Groom peered into the open window of the van's front passenger door. 'Tell the lads we're going now.'

Groom and Jet walked around the corner into the Bigg Market, and within a few more yards they were in sight of the front door of the Energy Factory. They headed to the front door. The search team followed, all of them dressed in blue boiler suits, the leader carried a thick metal door ram.

The front mahogany door was open and Groom entered and pulled at the heavy glass door. It would not budge. Groom looked through the glass as he rattled the door and saw a dark figure appear. A familiar shaven head peered out; wearing the same thick black overcoat he had on when Groom had pushed him out of the club.

'Hello Wilf, it's the police again. We need to come in.'

Wilf looked at Groom through the glass and shook his

head gently. Groom stared back and nodded his head. Wilf shook his head with more vigour.

'OK lads.' Groom turned his head as he spoke and within a second the door ram hit the wooden edge of the door sending the lock flying into the club and the door crashing open. The team of officers ran past Groom into the club. Two officers stood by Wilf to make sure he was unable to do anything. Realising he was hopelessly outnumbered he stood still. The rest of the officers made their way into the club, two of them headed straight to the office Groom had told them was Hobson's.

Groom walked through the shattered door and stopped to look Wilf in the eye. 'Not doing much of a job guarding this door Wilf.'

Wilf's top lip curled but he made no sound.

'You just wait here and we'll go and see Mr Hobson. Don't worry about making us tea; we'll not be staying too long.' Groom smiled at Wilf.

Jet thought he could feel a chill coming from Wilf's expression as he glared at Groom and spoke for the first time. 'We'll meet again.'

Groom's smile broadened further. 'If that's your Vera Lynn impression it's only marginally better than your talent for looking after doors.'

Wilf moved forward but stopped when one of the boiler-suited officers beside him placed a hand on his chest. 'Now now Vera, you just relax and we'll go and speak to your employer. Don't worry, I'll put in a good word.'

Groom moved inside the club and as Jet caught up to walk alongside him he spoke. 'You make friends so easily.'

'It's a talent.'

Groom pushed the door into Hobson's office and Jet followed. Hobson was sitting at his desk, one of the boiler-suited officers was standing next to him and another had already started to go through a filing cabinet.

'Mark,' Hobson smiled as Groom walked in. 'Twice in one day, how nice to see you again so soon.'

'We have a warrant to search the place.'

'Feel free. What are you looking for? I might be able to help.'

'Your loan-sharking records.' Jet looked around the large office as Groom spoke. A row of filing cabinets stood against one wall. There was another door which led to a small shower room, Hobson's personal dressing room. It surprised Jet how tidy the office was. Jet was a man who liked organisation and efficiency, but it did not sit well with him that he had this in common with Hobson. Criminals should be slobs. What furniture existed in the office looked expensive, the colours matched the finely polished wooden floor. It reminded Jet of York's office.

'Can't help you with that, see I just don't do that sort of thing, it would be illegal.'

'It's not that we don't trust you Gary, but we've got the warrant so we might as well have a look for ourselves.'

'Help yourselves.' Hobson's grin was accompanied by a regal wave. Jet knew the aura of a man confident there was nothing to find. Hobson remained seated behind his large mahogany desk, the thick drawer pedestals at either end held up the large desk surface and Hobson leaned back in his leather chair, exuding an air of superior opulence.

Jet walked over to the filing cabinets and began looking in the drawers at the opposite end to where the other officer had started. The drawers were all open, keys were in the locks but it looked to Jet as if that was the permanent position.

Jet thumbed the files. Membership records, stock sheets and invoices.

'If you lift things out will you make sure they're kept in order please. Don't want to have the taxman on my back. How could you provide this excellent service if hard working people like me weren't organised enough to pay their taxes?' Jet kept his back towards Hobson. The smugness was irritating him.

Groom pulled up a chair and sat at the other side of the desk and looked at Hobson.

'We've still got your man Savage in custody. He tells us that he collects debts for you.'

'He's not my man – just someone who does a little bit

of work for me when the occasion arises. As I told you before, I'm just a soft touch. People run up debts and sometimes I just need to get the money they owe collected. It's nothing out of the ordinary really. I'm sure people will owe you money and you will owe money. It's how the modern world operates. Look at the financial crisis the world found itself in recently when the banks had lent too much.'

'I'll bet the banks aren't charging your level of interest.'

'I don't charge interest. People sometimes run up debts in the club and they pay it back. Since the banks went bust it's happened more and more.'

'So where are the records of the people who owe you money?'

'I keep telling you, I don't need records. It's just a favour for the odd punter.'

Jet thumbed all the records needed in the filing cabinets to realise they were not going to yield any evidence. 'Mr Hobson.'

Hobson turned his head to Jet. 'Yes?'

'Where do you keep your cash? Where's the safe?'

'There's a small room next door. Let me show you.'

Hobson removed a bunch of keys from the top drawer of his desk and rose to his feet. Jet followed him into the corridor and Hobson unlocked a smooth heavy door of a small strongroom, in which sat a very substantial metal safe.

'We keep a bit of cash in here. A float for the club.'

Hobson unlocked the safe door then pulled it open a few inches and stood back to allow Jet to pull the thick metal door fully open. Two till cash drawers were on the top shelf and a small cash box was on the bottom. Hobson gave Jet the key to the cash box and he opened it to survey the contents.

'Just petty cash. For buying light bulbs and paying some of the casual workers. That sort of thing.'

'There seems quite a bit in here to be petty cash.'

'About a thousand I would've thought. We have a few door staff to pay, it's all above board.'

Jet closed the cash box and replaced it in the safe. He quickly ran his hands over the shelves in the hope that it might yield something else but it was forlorn.

He handed the keys back to Hobson and Jet led as they returned to the office where Hobson slid himself back into the comfort of his executive swivel chair. The officer at the filing cabinets had finished going through each one and stood idly beside them. The team sergeant then pushed his head through the office door and fixing Groom's gaze shook his head.

Hobson recognised the indications and smiled at Groom. 'It's as I told you all along. There's nothing here. Now if you don't mind I have a lot of business to attend to.'

Groom stood up. 'OK Gary.'

Hobson's already wide smile seemed to broaden further.

'Before I go Gary, I don't think we checked your desk.'

'Help yourself. Hobson rolled gently away from his desk on the castors of his leather chair. Groom walked around to Hobson's side of the desk and pulled at the drawers. They glided open to reveal neatly arranged contents – several marketing letters which Groom realised were mainly from breweries as he thumbed through them and stationery which included a gold pen. In the second drawer Groom pulled out a novel and looked at the cover.

'*The Myth of Justice,*' Groom read out the title to Hobson.' I didn't take you as a literary man.'

'Only quality material. You can borrow it if you like; it's a really good read. I think the bloke who wrote it used to be one of your lot.'

Groom put the book back in the drawer and then opened the larger bottom drawer. Two bottles, one brandy, one whiskey and four crystal glasses clinked as it opened.

'For important visitors. I'd offer you one but I know you're on duty.'

Groom smiled at Hobson as he closed the drawer. 'It's too early for me Gary.'

'Well if there's nothing else I can help with.'

'No Gary, thanks for your help, you've been very patient.' The grin still played around Groom's lips as he spoke. 'Just one more thing, if you don't mind.'

'Yeah.'

'Every time I come in here I always admire this desk. The thought always crossed my mind that if I was going to hide something I might take advantage of these big drawers.' Groom lifted the end of the desk and slid it along the floor. Underneath where it had stood was a hatch in the floorboards. A brass handle was inset in the polished floorboards. Groom reached down and opened the hatch and inside the deep recess was a neat pile of ledgers.

The smile disappeared from Hobson's face. 'I think I should speak to my solicitor.'

'Yes,' Groom clutched the ledgers. 'I think you'd better. Do it at the station.'

Groom and Jet took their position on the opposite side of the table from Rosie Shepherd and Ormond in the monitoring room. Five ledgers rested on the table.

'The top one looks like the current one, it's going to take a bit of deciphering, looks like all his underhanded deals for a lot of years. I bet the taxman would like to see them.' Groom looked pleased as he spoke about his find.

'Is Savage mentioned?'

'I couldn't see his name, but I did find Thompson's details.'

'The first victim?'

'Aye. Look at this.' Groom thumbed back through the pages and pointed to an entry. 'Looks like he owed Hobson five thousand pounds.'

'What about Norman Straughan, our missing man?'

'Can't find his name, or Justin Gallagher.' Jet thought Groom's tone changed to one of slight disappointment. 'But there are a lot of entries that seem in some sort of shorthand or code. We need time to go through it all in detail. Someone from the fraud squad might be useful.'

'Yeah. But interviewing him about Thompson will be a good start. He's owed money and his debtor turns up dead. It should get things going.'

'What about Savage?'

Ormond looked apprehensive as he replied to Groom's question. 'It's a hell of a risk!'

Groom pushed open the door of the interview room and a weary looking Savage cringed. Jet sat down next to Groom, opposite Savage and Clive Proctor, who Jet thought was also currently looking a little dog-eared.

'We have your employer in custody now.' Groom got straight to the point.

'I don't have an employer.'

'Really, well Mr Hobson thinks differently.'

Savage grunted.

'Think about it Adam. Hobson's as bent as a nine-bob note, but he's not going to be associated with murder. He's going to get his clever legal people to cut a deal, so he gives every bit of information to us about you and in return we leave him alone.' Groom looked at Proctor, 'And Hobson can afford a real solicitor.'

Jet thought Proctor was trying to smile but conflicting emotions made it difficult, the result was a painful grimace.

'Look, I've done nothing wrong.'

'Have you driven around Wallsend recently?'

'No. Why?'

'Your car was seen in Station Road, Wallsend during the early hours over these last few days. I was wondering what you were doing there?'

'I wasn't at Wallsend.'

'Really. So there is no chance that you're going to appear on any CCTV down there, or a witness is going to say you were there?'

'No chance.'

'You know that every lie you tell we're eventually going to be able to disprove, don't you? You think you're being clever but they are all nails in your coffin. Hobson, the Priest and Straughan, they're all going to add up together and build a case you won't be able to get out of.'

'I don't even know who Straughan is.'

'The man you met last night. The one that's still missing.' Groom's eyes fixed Savage's as he spoke. 'Even if it's just a body, it'll have enough evidence to bring you down.'

'I didn't meet anyone last night.'

'Even if that's not his blood on the tools in your car, we will find the evidence eventually.'

Clive Proctor raised his head from his scribbled notes. 'Then why don't you go and do that officer, instead of this pointless speculating. My client has told you he's not involved in the matter you're investigating. If you have evidence then I suggest you produce it. If not, then this doesn't appear to be getting us anywhere.'

Groom banged the table, shot to his feet and growled. 'I'm going to find Straughan and when I do, it'll be the last nail in your coffin.'

Jet stood up next to Groom and put his hand on his arm as if trying to prevent Groom from further aggression.

'This interview is now terminated,' Jet spoke for the first time during the exchange and switched the tape off. He pulled at Groom's arm and headed to the door. Jet used his arm to guide Groom out of the room then close the door behind them as they halted in the corridor.

Groom cracked a smile at Jet as they stood on the

outside of the closed interview room door. They remained still in silence for a couple of minutes then Groom spoke quietly. 'Well go and do your nice cop bit.'

Jet pushed the door and interrupted Savage and Proctor in conversation. Both looked at Jet as he returned to the table and sat down.

'I'm sorry about my colleague. He's anxious about the missing person, that's all.'

'It's no way to conduct an interview.' Proctor was stern-faced.

'I've had a word with the Detective Inspector and at this stage of the enquiry we think it best if we bail Mr Savage to come back to the police station in a couple of days. By that time we'll have concluded our enquiries.'

'You mean you have no evidence and this fishing trip you've been on has got you nowhere?' A faint smile materialised on Proctor's face.

'We don't go on fishing trips, we pursue reasonable enquiries.'

'What is he talking about?' Savage looked at Proctor.

'They clearly have no evidence, so they're letting you go. If they really thought you were involved they would have kept you and put you in front of the court but my guess is even they think you didn't do it.'

Savage smiled. 'About time.'

Jet got back to his feet. 'If you could just wait here for a moment an officer will be along soon. He'll take you to the custody sergeant who will go through the procedure, to bail you to come back to the police station in a few days.'

'Thank you officer.' Proctor looked at Jet, 'At last a bit of common sense prevails. I'll use the time to speak to my client.'

'We have eyeball.'

Groom held the radio as it spoke. He was in the front passenger seat with Jet who was in the driving seat of the Fiesta which was still parked in the police station car park.

'How many surveillance cops did Ormond get?' Jet held the steering wheel.

'Two teams of three. It'll be enough.'

'I hope so. I'm surprised York went along with it.'

'I'm not sure he knows.'

'That's brave.'

'Suppose Ormond could always blame me if it goes tits up.'

'Well at least Mr York won't be directing traffic in Berwick.'

'The sea air will do us good.'

'Left, left, left.' The radio's voice was calm and clear.

'He's heading towards the station.' Groom arched his eyebrows as he spoke to Jet.

'What if he goes mobile?'

'They've got a mobile team on standby.'

'Right, right, right. High Bridge Road.' The radio voice was steady.

'Perhaps to the Bigg Market to the club or for a drink?' Jet pondered.

'Let's get moving so we're close.'

Jet drove the car out of the car park and immediately joined a queue of traffic. 'Brilliant.'

'Don't worry Jet, there's no hurry. We don't want to be too close and get in the way.'

'Right, right, right.' The radio commentary continued.

'Not the Bigg Market either.'

'Left, left, left.'

'Is he heading to the club?'

'Might be Jet, but he must know no one's there.'

'Right, right, right.'

'Not the club.' Jet added as he followed the crawling traffic ahead.

'Subject, eyeball, St Stephen's Church.' The commentary was still perfectly calm.

'He's going to see the Priest. I knew he was in on it. Let's get over there.' Groom smiled.

Jet crunched the Fiesta into second gear. Groom looked down at the pedals. 'Are you using the clutch?'

'It's just a bit temperamental.' The engine roared as

they pulled out to overtake the line of traffic ahead and shot off in the middle of the road in the direction of the church, ignoring several disgusted looks in addition to the sound of car horns as oncoming traffic swerved to their nearside.

'Echo two. Eyeball disturbance at church. Awaiting further instruction.'

'Echo two.' Ormond's voice burst on the radio. 'Further detail on disturbance.'

'Target and male. Verbal altercation inside church. Escalating.'

'Groom, how close are you?' Ormond's voice was not as calm as the surveillance officer.

'Just seconds away.'

'Echo two. Stand off. Do not risk blowing cover. Maintain eyeball. Assistance will be there soon.'

'Come on Jet.' The Fiesta lurched forward as Groom spoke. 'I did say we were only seconds away.'

'I heard!'

Jet mounted the kerb, weaving around vehicles waiting for a set of traffic lights to turn green, ignoring more irate sounding of car horns and one pedestrian who almost reached a canter whilst shaking a fist. The Fiesta accelerated away from the angry motorists but soon screeched to a halt outside the church. As Jet hurried up the steps he could hear loud voices.

'I didn't tell them anything.'

'Lying twat! They told me.'

Savage held handfuls of the Priest's shirt as he stared into his face.

'Spit it out now before I rearrange your face.'

'I haven't said anything.'

Savage jerked his head back and then violently forward, head-butting the Priest on the nose. Jet saw blood splatter across the pews and the stunned Priest slumped backwards like a rag doll. Neither heard Jet and Groom approach.

'That's enough.' Savage looked around. He had taken another firm grip of the Priest, raising him up, but realising Jet was now just yards away, he let go and the Priest collapsed backwards onto the pew.

'What are you bastards doing here?'

Jet took Savage's arm. 'That's enough. You're being arrested for assault.'

Savage looked angry but did not resist Jet's grip.

Groom took hold of Savage's free arm. 'You get the Priest Jet. Let's get them both back to the station.'

The Priest looked dazed. He rubbed his right hand across the bottom of his nose, spreading the blood across his top lip.

'Come on Father.' Jet raised him slowly to his feet. 'You're under arrest on suspicion of assault.'

'That's ridiculous. He attacked me.'

'We saw him make the last blow but it can't have been

for nothing. It'll all come out in the wash. We'll sort it at the station.'

'I understand you've refused legal representation?' Jet was facing the Priest over the interview table. Only the two of them in the room.

'I don't need it, I've done nothing wrong.'

'Then explain what happened at your church.'

'I was assaulted.' The Priest brushed his hand on his nose and flinched.

'Why were you arguing with Savage?'

'Does it really matter? Surely the important thing is he came in and assaulted me.'

'When we came in you were trying to convince Savage that you hadn't said anything?'

'He did seem under the impression that I had betrayed a confidence, which I had not.'

'What was it about?'

'I had not betrayed the confidence then and I have no intention of doing it now.'

'This is a murder enquiry. Don't you think it's about time you started to tell us what's going on?'

'I know nothing that will help you with your enquiry.'

'What was Savage referring to in the church?'

'That is none of your business.'

'If you've done nothing then why won't you help us

260

with our enquiries?'

'I can't. I don't know anything.'

'Why are you protecting an animal like Savage? If we hadn't got there when we did it would have gotten far worse.'

'Well at least some good has come from your enquiry.'

'We'll need to keep you here whilst we interview Savage and see what he has to say.'

'This is ridiculous. I am innocent of any wrongdoing.'

'If that's so, then I'm sure the truth will prevail. But we need to speak to Savage.'

'Well whilst you do so you can tell him I will not be pressing charges for the assault against me.'

'It's a common misconception.'

'What is?'

'Pressing charges. It's an American thing. Here we prosecute on behalf of the crown, you don't decide if he gets charged, we do. We saw him hitting you, so we have enough evidence to charge him with assault, without a statement from you.'

'You seem determined to prove something.'

'Why are you protecting him? What does he know to have such a hold on you?'

'I'm not protecting him.'

Jet rose from the table. He pushed the door and was back in the monitoring room within a few seconds.

Groom smiled as Jet took his seat and Ormond

continued to stare at his notes. The thought 'fish out of water' returned to Jet as he watched Rosie Shepherd craning her neck to peer at Ormond's writing.

'Well he's not going to be any help.' Ormond still did not look up.

'He knows what's going on though.' Groom's smile had straightened slightly.

'Look, I think we're in for the long haul now. I'm not letting Savage go anymore. As it is, I'll probably end up directing traffic in Berwick for letting him out to chin the Priest in the first place.'

'It was a good call. We have the Priest and we know he's involved.'

'We have a vague link between the first victim and Savage. A possible link with the Priest. We have no idea where the second victim fits into this and we have fuck all idea about the third one. We don't even know where the poor fucker is!' Ormond's frustration seemed to startle Shepherd.

The door stuttered and Stimpson poked his head in, his eyes quickly circled the room until they made contact with Ormond. 'Boss, just had the lab on. Early confirmation that there was a lot of different blood on the tools found in the Mondeo. But one of them is definitely Thompson's. They're still working on the other samples.'

Ormond's face cracked a rare smile and he relaxed

back into his chair. 'Halle-fucken-lujah!'

'We've enough to charge him with the murder and the assault on the Priest, I think that's the beginning of a result boss.' Jet could see visible signs of relief on Ormond's face as Groom spoke.

'It's a start but it's still the long haul. We need to break down every part of his story and link in the records kept by Hobson.'

'We might get a charge on Hobson yet.'

'We might consider a deal if he can finger Savage for the murders. If he can give us a link it's worth a thought.' Ormond was scribbling more notes as he spoke.

'Hobson will do anything to save his own skin but those books will be enough to put him away for a long time. Not sure I would be thinking of a deal yet.' Jet could tell Groom was finding it hard to keep his personal dislike of Hobson under the surface.

'Don't worry Mark. Let's break it all down and see what we can prove and disprove. We still haven't got forensics back on the second murder yet, so you never know. These books of Hobson's might lead to a charge of incitement to murder.'

Ormond's mobile phone rang and he swiftly plucked it from the table. 'Ormond.'

The room went quiet as he listened and as he did he lifted his eyes towards Groom and then Jet. 'Yeah, tell them not to touch anything yet. I've got two people with me here I will send down now.' Ormond put his phone back on the table beside his file. 'The Honda has turned up at Fenkle Street multi-storey. You and Jet get down there and take a look.'

Groom and Jet moved towards the door.

'Give me a ring when you get there and let me know what we've got. We'll make a start on an interview plan for our prisoners.'

Fenkle Street Car Park is an unlovable construction of concrete slabs resting on thick concrete pillars. Tucked around the corner from Westgate Road, it is only a short distance from the city centre. It was a place Jet avoided using whenever he visited this side of town, preferring a slightly longer walk after leaving the Fiesta in a less hostile looking place further out of town. The concrete shelter was a gathering place for winos when the weather drove them to look for cover. The Fiesta's engine seemed to labour as they encountered the slight incline to the car park entrance. Jet felt relieved when they turned from the road onto the slope which led down to the underground level.

'Are you going to get that clutch seen to?'

'When I get a chance.' Jet did not attempt to hide his irritation.

Two officers stood talking to each other behind their

vehicle and the sound of the Fiesta's racing engine did not attract their attention. Hands in pockets with backs to approaching traffic; neither wore hats but had short fluorescent jackets flapping open.

'It's a wonder we ever catch criminals.' Groom scowled as he pulled the Fiesta door handle and walked up behind the two who were engrossed in each other's words.

'Sorry to interrupt the diligent pursuit of your duties.' The two officers looked at Groom who eyed the black Honda parked neatly in a bay facing the concrete wall. 'What do you know about this car?'

'A car park warden called it in. A family liaison officer dropped off a spare key just a few minutes ago. They must be with the owner for some reason.'

'The husband of the owner is missing.' Jet's voice was calm and sounded more forgiving as he put out his hand and took the key. 'Have you had a look in it?'

'No, we were told to wait for you.'

Jet pulled at the driver's door and realised it was locked. The interior looked tidy and clean. Jet pressed a button on the ignition key and heard the locks pop open. He opened the driver's door and the new-car smell struck him. He eyed the interior, careful not to touch anything. Black leather and vinyl gave a dull shine where slivers of the car park's fluorescent light hit it. He thought it would not have been out of place in a showroom. He lifted his head briefly and looked at the dirt that edged up the side of the Fiesta, hoping that Groom might spare him all of the witty comparisons he knew he would be aching to share. Jet's eyes returned to the pristine interior when he heard a loud voice.

'Is that your car?' A uniformed car park attendant marched towards them.

'No.' Groom was at the rear of the Honda as the Warden approached. 'We're with the police.'

'It'll still have to be paid you know.'

'What will?' Jet moved towards the Warden to prevent him from getting too close to the car.

'The fixed penalty ticket. It's been here all day and no one's paid to park it.'

'Well we don't know what's happening to the car yet. Perhaps you could leave it with us for the moment.'

'It's all lost revenue. Someone's got to pay.'

'Leave it with us and when we know what's happening, we'll let you know.'

As Jet was talking to the Warden he heard Groom open the boot and quickly close it.

'As long as the owner knows it's got to be paid. It doesn't matter who you are, everyone's got to pay for the parking.'

'We'll be sure to tell the owner when we find him.' Jet gave a diplomatic smile as the words 'just go away' danced across the stage of his mind.

266

'Jet.' Groom still had his hand on the Honda's boot as Jet looked over his shoulder to look at him. 'I think I just found the owner. Tell Hitler there he's not going to give a fuck about paying for the ticket.'

Jet and Groom stood five metres behind Paul Stimpson who was dressed in his white forensic coverall and looked into the boot of the Honda. Stimpson gently pulled at various bits of clothing, making an early examination of the corpse which was curled in a foetal position. He knew many hours of painstaking examination, sample taking and photographs lay ahead before the body could be removed.

'You know a body in the boot will cripple the re-sale value of that car. You might get yourself a bargain if you get in quick.' Groom's face was straight as he spoke to Jet.

'Yeah. I could press home my advantage by negotiating a price whilst we are telling Mrs Straughan she's a widow.'

'Got to make hay whilst the sun shines.'

'Not much sun shining on the Straughan's at the moment. I think I'll settle for a new clutch in the Fiesta.'

Stimpson pointed to one of his colleagues who was carrying a camera and left him taking pictures of the contents of the boot of the Honda. Jet looked on at the repeated white flash of the camera and thought it somehow irreverent; the last undignified pose. Jet knew when his own body was found there would be no doubt about what had happened. No need for photographs.

Stimpson walked over and spoke to Groom. 'It's going to take us a long time to sort this. We'll have to cover every inch of the car so we don't miss anything.'

'Is it the same as the other two?'

'Looks like the penis has been cut off and the head has been crushed.'

'I wonder if he was killed in the car.' Jet interjected.

Stimpson slowly shook his head as he considered the possibility. 'It's really difficult to say. My guess would be no, because of the lack of blood in the boot and there is no blood on the outside of the car. I think he's probably been clubbed and then put in the boot and driven here. But we'll not really know until we've had everything examined and had a full post-mortem.'

'Are his trousers in there?'

'Around his ankles. Just like the others.'

'So chances are we have another scene somewhere?'

'I would think so, with lots of blood.'

'Well, I better go and make a start.' Stimpson turned to walk back to the Honda.

'Better you than me.' Groom spoke to the back of Stimpson's head and then turned to Jet. 'What do you think the link is between Straughan and Savage?'

'I wonder how many names in Hobson's records are

pseudonyms.'

'I was wondering how many were false myself.'

Jet smiled. 'There must be a code of some sort.'

'Why?' Groom stroked the scar on his left arm over his jacket. 'Why would Hobson keep records but include just some of the real names?'

'It's hard to make sense of it.'

'In the immortal words of Toyah - it's a mystery.' Groom still did not smile.

'Do you think we missed something in the club?'

'Maybe. Why don't you swing by there whilst we still have people at the place and have another look.'

'Where you going?'

'I have an itch I can't scratch.'

'Manson?'

'Something's not right.'

'Three bodies and four suspects in custody. Don't you think we have enough to be doing just at the moment?'

'We're just around the corner from Thompson's apartment. I thought if you go to the club, I'll go and speak to his neighbour again and see if she's seen the Priest or Manson at his place. It's worth a visit.'

Jet looked Groom in the eye. 'So you go and see the attractive brown-eyed woman in her home and I get to rummage around a gay club.'

'My motives are entirely professional.'

'If you say so Sarge. Suppose there might be worse

places for you to get your itches scratched.'

Groom pushed the button to apartment 7c and soon the intercom vacillated a greeting.

'It's DS Mark Groom, I was just wondering if I could have a quick word.'

'Come up.'

The door buzzed and Groom climbed the stairs to find the door opening as he approached.

'I'm sorry to disturb you.' Groom smiled broadly. 'I won't take up much of your time.'

'No problem. You did well to catch me. I've just got in from work, I was just going to get something to eat. Would you like coffee?'

'If it's no trouble.'

Sarah disappeared into the kitchen as Groom sat in the same spot on the cream leather sofa as his previous visit.

'It's been really odd since the last time you were here.'

'Odd?'

Groom could hear the faint humming of an electric kettle as Sarah returned from the kitchen. 'Yes, odd. Quiet as the grave.' Sarah shivered, 'Sorry I didn't mean to be ghoulish. I meant it's been silent. I can't help thinking about poor Derek. I used to hear him coming and going but it's desperately quiet now.'

'Did Derek have many visitors that you noticed?'

Sarah returned to the kitchen. 'How do you like your coffee?'

'Just milk please.'

'I didn't hear many people going to Derek's, he was a pretty quiet neighbour.'

'Hobbies, friends? Anything you know about his background might be useful.'

'I often saw him with his camera; he was a great one for photography.'

'I suppose his pictures would be on his computer?'

'Yes, we could go and have a look at them if you like.'

'Don't you need a password or something?'

'Not if he's like me, we won't.'

Sarah grabbed the key from a bookshelf and soon she was disarming the alarm in Thompson's flat.

'Do we need a warrant for this?'

Groom was slightly distracted as she stretched to reach the keypad on the hall wall, watching as her silk blouse rose slightly from the waistband of her neat skirt, catching a subtle whiff of scent as she lifted her arm. He shook his head as his attention returned. 'No, Derek is the victim, we're trying to find information he might have to help identify suspects.'

Sarah led the way through a door off the hall. The spare room had a desk on which a computer sat, she switched it on and within seconds was manoeuvring the mouse along the desk.

'This looks like the most recent file.'

Sarah flicked the keyboard and photos flitted across the screen. Grey's Monument with the sun sitting low in the sky and other buildings Groom recognised in the city centre.

'He really was a happy snapper.' Sarah's voice had a warmth Groom found pleasing. 'He had a few cameras, my guess would be that this is the small one he often used to carry in his pocket, the bigger cameras were too large to carry all the time.' She nodded towards the small camera sitting on the dock next to the computer. 'They're probably on that camera, he must have just put it on the dock when he came home, some of the photos on it are from just a few nights ago.'

The screen changed from street scenes to a number of figures inside what looked like a pub. A group of four people sitting together facing forward. They were smiling at the camera. Groom recognised the Priest.

'Stop there a second.' Groom examined the screen closely.

'Someone you recognise?'

'Yes. I think he's a priest from the local church.'

'Oh yes, I think they knew each other quite well.'

'Had you seen them together?'

'The Priest came here a few times. I think Derek was quite religious.'

Groom examined the other three faces in the picture

and recognised one of the faces next to the Priest. 'Manson.'

'You know him as well?' Sarah was still smiling.

'Yes, have you seen him visiting Derek?'

Sarah looked closely at the screen. 'Don't think so. Doesn't look familiar.'

'I don't suppose we could take a print of this?'

'No reason why not. Let's just figure this out.'

Within a few seconds Sarah was deftly pressing buttons and the printer burst into life.

'You're very adept at this.'

'I use computers a lot.'

'I never really got into the technological revolution myself.'

'Does your wife do all of the online stuff?'

'Not married.'

'Girlfriend then?'

'Not one of those either, at the moment.'

'It's easy enough to find your way around a computer. Perhaps I could show you some time.'

'I can't think of a better way to learn.'

'Should we have that coffee now?'

'I suppose I really ought to get back, we have suspects in custody and the clock is ticking. But perhaps I could call you soon and we could have a drink?'

Sarah lifted the photograph from the printer tray and handed it to Groom. He felt the soft skin of her hand as he took the photograph from her. The thought occurred to him to make an excuse and accept the coffee, but the notion quickly passed as he realised he would be missed.

She smiled. 'I would like that.'

They locked up Thompson's apartment, walking in silence to her door. She turned as she opened it and Groom again smiled at her. For another second they stood in silence.

'Soon then?'

'Soon.' Sarah returned the smile as she spoke while Groom moved away slowly and he turned to walk out the apartment block.

Groom felt his spirits lifted as the fresh air hit his face. Photo in hand, he started the short walk back to the police station.

John Dawkin stood in the doorway of the Energy Factory. He did not seem pleased to be there. Then as far as Jet could recall, Dawkin never seemed happy being anywhere, doing anything. That was why he had stood for election as the police federation representative. He had been appointed unopposed. No one else could summon the energy to stand for the position. Jet heard that York had even approached a few people himself to try and interest them in the post. He understood York's desire to have a more balanced and active mind in the position of staff representative but it had backfired, being seen as underhanded management interference in the politics of the federated rank. When Dawkin got wind of York's interventions, he had quite liked the thought of his appointment being opposed by management, and had used it to market himself as the choice of the rank and file. A man of the people. A thorn in the side of those who wished to run rampant on the rights of the hard working constable. The reality was somewhat different and Jet thought it was succinctly summed up by Groom after he had endured some of Dawkin's post-appointment rhetoric. 'Not so much William Wallace as William Wally.' Jet thought that even if the historical reference was a little suspect the sentiment was spot on.

'All right John?' Jet approached the door.

'I will be, in about an hour when the shift's over.'

'You shouldn't wish your life away.' Jet's response had been instinctive and he immediately wished he had not said it.

'It's not like I'm on overtime. You know they're using duty officers for this which means the rest of the staff are run off their feet doing all of the jobs that are coming in. I offered to stay here on overtime to help the late shift out but they turned me down.'

'I thought you wanted to be home?'

'Just trying to help my colleagues out.'

'At time and a half?'

'Effective policing doesn't come free.'

'Yeah. I'm just going in to check something. I'll just be a few minutes.'

Jet went straight to Hobson's office. He eyed the room. Then he started to examine the pictures on the walls to make sure nothing was hidden, a safe, a document, anything. Nothing. He lifted the desk and opened the secret compartment they had found and used his knuckles to knock on each surface, hoping this clandestine place might itself reveal another secret. But it was solid. He checked the small room which Hobson had taken him to and knocked on all the walls. Nothing. It had always been a long shot, was the thought he consoled himself with, as he made his way empty-handed, back to the door and the fresh air.

'Thanks John, see you later.'

Dawkin's summoned a grunt as Jet walked back to the Fiesta. Before he reached his car he made a quick detour to the small chemist shop off Neville Street. His plan was coming along.

'Jet!' Groom had caught sight of him heading to the CID office.

Jet turned. 'You were quick. Was she not keen to help you with your enquiries?'

'On the contrary Jet. Look at this.' Groom thrust the

photograph towards Jet and he eyed it for a few seconds.

'Bloody hell.'

'My thought exactly. Let's go and see Ormond.'

Groom peered into Ormond's office and saw him sifting through his notes.

'Can we have a second?'

Ormond looked up. 'Yeah, I was just about to head to the monitoring room. We need to work on our interview strategy.'

Groom put the photograph down on Ormond's desk. 'I found this on Derek Thompson's computer. It was taken the night he died. It looks like it was taken by him and it's the Priest and our own PC Manson.'

Ormond examined the photograph closely for a few seconds and then sat back in his chair. 'It's interesting but what does it prove?'

'Nothing on its own but something stinks.'

'What do you propose?'

'We have enough to arrest Manson. I think we should do it now.'

'Arrest a police officer. For what?'

'He's at the scene of every murder. He's an associate of our main suspect. He's constantly making homophobic comments. He's had his photograph taken by the first murder victim, who we know was gay, on the night of his death.'

'But what is it evidence of Mark?'

'That's why we need to bring him in now. Then we'll have all of the suspects here and we can get to the bottom of it.'

Ormond scratched at his chin for a few seconds then looked up at Groom. 'Look, I hear what you say. But we currently have four people in custody and the detention clock's ticking. We need to interview them now. If there's any further implication of Manson we know where he is.'

'What if he's out there now disposing of evidence, or murdering some other poor sod?'

'Mark,' Ormond was getting angry, 'before we start bringing in cops let's make sure we have the evidence and we're not doing it on a wing and a prayer. If we arrest a cop and it turns out he's done nothing, there will be hell on. Surely you can see that? In any case we have more than enough to do at the moment. Now drop this for the moment and let's do the interviews for the people we do have evidence against.'

It looked to Jet as if Groom was about to make further comment but bit his tongue.

Ormond gathered up the notes in his file and stood up. He was first to leave his office and head towards the monitoring room in the custody suite. Rosie Shepherd was already waiting in the room with another cup of mint tea standing in front of her releasing steam into the air. Ormond sat next to her on the seat that had clearly now become his. Jet and Groom sat down at the table and just as the door had closed Ian Davison pushed it open and peered in. 'You wanted to see me Inspector?'

Ormond looked up. 'Yes, sit down. I was waiting for Paul Stimpson as well.'

'Yeah, he's just behind.'

Stimpson hurried in and the six people in the monitoring room made it feel crowded.

'Paul,' Ormond was note shuffling, 'what does the scene at Fenkle Street look like?'

'My people are still there. The pathologist has had a look at the body and we should be able to do the post-mortem soon.'

'Is cause of death the same?'

'It looks the same. Head smashed in and penis cut off.'

'Anything that would help us with the interview of Savage?'

'No, we'll check to see if there is a match with Straughan's blood with anything we found in Savage's car but the results will take a while.'

'Let me know as soon as possible.'

'Ian, can you take a team down to Fenkle Street and cover all of the CCTV? I want any footage of the car going in or anyone that may have been seen leaving it. Get on it now.'

'Certainly Sir.' Davison scribbled a note for himself and Groom rolled his eyes at Jet as he watched Davison write down CCTV. 'Just one small point, Sir.'

'Yes.'

'Some of the officers were querying the Chief's promise of a couple of days off and were wondering what the score was.'

'Jesus Christ, Ian.' Ormond's face turned a shade of crimson Jet thought rare even for him. 'We have a third murder victim, four suspects and you want the day off.'

'It's just the Chief said....'

'Fuck what the Chief said. We need to get this case sorted and if you don't realise that then maybe you need to have a think if CID is the job for you. Now will you just fuck off and do what I've told you to do.'

Groom smiled at Davison as he rose to his feet.

Ormond went back to note shuffling as the redness started to drain from his face. Jet scanned the rest of the table and could see Rosie Shepherd was nervously scribbling on her notepad. Jet wondered how many meetings at the university ended with the chairman telling someone to fuck off and do what they were told. He guessed not many.

The door closed behind Davison and Ormond took a deep breath. 'Right. We have Hobson, Savage, the Priest and Wilf Stone. I don't think there is any doubt that Savage is our man, so no more letting him go.' Ormond eyed Groom as he spoke. 'Instead let's just pull him apart and get him charged. The other three can be witnesses as long as we get the three murders cleared up.'

'We're not thinking of deals are we?'

'We're not ruling it out. At the moment I would settle for the evidence to charge Savage with the murders. But let's see what we get. Groom, you and Jet go and talk to the Priest again then Hobson and Stone. We'll see what we have after that.'

As Groom and Jet walked across the corridor Jet spoke gently. 'Good cop?'

'You know the Priest well enough. I think it's too late for you to be the bad cop.'

Jet nodded at Groom as they stopped for a second at the interview room door. Jet then looked up the corridor where Ian Davison's back was in clear view. They could see he had his ear to his mobile phone, but were not close enough to hear what he was saying

Groom smiled. 'He's probably ringing his mam.'

Jet pushed the door open and thought the Priest looked pathetic as he sat behind the interview desk, all former righteousness evaporated.

Jet smiled as he pulled out and then sat on the chair opposite. Groom's expression was gruff as he sat on the chair beside Jet.

Jet pushed the button on the tape machine which made it howl for a few seconds. Jet spoke when the machine went silent.

'Father O'Brian, how long have you been the priest at St Stephen's?'

'Five years.'

'How do you know Adam Savage?'

'Adam Savage?'

'Yes,' Groom interjected, 'the man who was trying to rearrange your face.'

'I wouldn't say I know him.'

'Then what?'

'I've told you, he thought I was breaching a confidence and attacked me at the church. I've come across him as a result of my work as parish priest and I'm not able to say any more than that.'

'What about Derek Thompson?' Jet placed the photograph of Thompson which he had already shown him at the church, in front of him again.

'What about him?'

'Look, we know you knew him. You were even seen at his apartment at the Old Engineering Works, we have witnesses. So why don't you just tell us what's going on?'

'There is nothing going on. I come across a lot of people through my work at the church. They come to me with their problems and I do my best to help. If they thought there was any risk I would betray their trust it would compromise my work. I will not do it. All I can tell you is I know a lot of people who come to the church. Even police officers come to the church.'

'Yes I've heard. One of my colleagues, Steve Manson, he's told me he goes to your church.' Groom's interruption took Jet by surprise.

'Yes, he does.'

Groom continued. 'Do you know Steve well?'

'Yes, he comes regularly to the church, what has that to do with this?'

'Nothing, I was just curious.'

'I know a lot of people but I don't know anything that will help you to find your murderer.'

'Unless you are the murderer.' Groom stared at the Priest.

'That's ridiculous, even for you.'

Jet wondered if the Priest was deliberately trying to push Groom's buttons and thought if so, he was doing a reasonable job.

Groom's body tensed as he leant forward over the table. 'Listen. You're under arrest. You've been telling us lies. It's not a good position to be in. Now if I were you, I would start to do the sensible thing and tell us what's going on. If you don't, you'll find yourself on a charge sheet. Now you're either a witness or an offender. Which one?'

'I have done nothing wrong.'

'Well let's see then.' Groom stood up angrily and Jet realised that the interview was over for the moment and turned the tape off. They left the Priest sitting at the table and Jet followed Groom out of the room.

In the corridor Groom turned towards Jet. 'He's not

going to budge is he?'

'Doesn't look like it.'

'Why all of the secrecy?'

'He's a catholic priest, guess it's second nature.'

'You've got to have a slate off to believe in all this religious crap. He dresses up for a living. He could be our man.'

'As balanced as that argument might be Mark, I don't think the Crown Prosecution Service are going to authorise a charge of murder without evidence.'

Groom reflected on this for a second. 'What is he hiding?'

'I don't know Mark,' Jet rubbed his chin hard with the back of his hand, 'what were you hoping to get out of him about Manson?'

'I had a feeling that at some stage in the future the Priest might have wanted to deny knowing Manson as well.'

'Manson is a cop, and Ormond is right, there's no reason to think he has anything to do with this.'

'Maybe Jet. But something is wrong.'

'Look we better go and speak to your friend Hobson.'

'Yeah. I'll take the lead. Let's go and listen to what he has to say.'

Groom led the way into the next interview room where Hobson sat. Next to him was a man whose suit, Jet thought, had a value greater than his Fiesta. Groom and

Jet were just pulling their seats up when the man in the expensive suit spoke. 'I'm Oliver Lackenby, Mr Hobson's solicitor. I want you to know Mr Hobson is going to co-operate as far as he can in this serious enquiry.'

Jet pushed the button on the tape recorder and when the familiar shrill stopped Groom spoke. 'That's good to know.' Groom's gaze turned to Hobson. 'You can start your co-operating by telling us about the ledgers we found hidden in the floor under your desk.'

Lackenby spoke first. 'Those records might be of some use to you but they are simply business transactions. Mr Hobson is a businessman and he has unwisely allowed people to take advantage of his good nature.'

'Good nature?' Groom sneered.

'Yes, officer. You see, in these tough financial times, some of Mr Hobson's clients from the club have approached him to borrow money, to tide them over. Mr Hobson has done his best to help these unfortunate people. The books simply record these transactions.'

'How much interest has Mr Hobson charged these unfortunate people?'

'That is surely irrelevant to your enquiry. Suffice it to say that Mr Hobson has to approach this in a business-like way or he would himself go bankrupt. These people are not the sort who were in a position to go to their banks for money and would be in a hopeless plight, were it not for Mr Hobson.'

'And what about the plight of these people when Mr Hobson wanted his money back and they couldn't pay?'

'This is where, I think, fortunately for you, we will be able to assist in your enquiry.'

'Really?'

'Yes. Of late Mr Hobson has employed, in good faith, a Mr Savage, who I believe you have in custody on suspicion of murder.'

'And?'

'The records in themselves may not be of any real value to you but with a full statement from Mr Hobson, you should be able to identify the links between Mr Savage and the victims, with Mr Hobson's full co-operation at court you will have removed a dangerous man from public harm.'

'That's very good of Mr Hobson. Why doesn't he explain it to us now?'

'He will be pleased to do so. But before that happens we need some assurances about action against Mr Hobson.'

'Go on?'

'Well Mr Hobson realises that his actions may, on the face of it, seem unorthodox and therefore we would want something in return for our good will, before we proceed.'

'What did Mr Hobson have in mind?'

'An assurance from the Crown Prosecution Service, in

writing, that he will not be prosecuted using information contained in the documents you now have or the evidence he will give you in his statement.'

'How about we just go through the books ourselves and prosecute Mr Hobson for being a loan shark? With luck he'll get ten years. We'll also get enough evidence to get the other murdering bastard off the street. Who's to say that Mr Hobson hasn't been arranging the murders of these people?'

'Really officer. We do not think there is any doubt about who the murderer is in these circumstances and I would have thought your priority would be to resolve that issue. There is no reason to think Mr Hobson had any actual involvement, it was an unfortunate accident that your suspect was in the employ of my client and that is how he met with his wretched victims. With my client's evidence, you get to put away a murderer and my client has learned a valuable lesson and in the future will be careful not to do anything that could be considered as a transgression of the law. It seems to me to be the ideal solution.'

'As an act of good faith then, please ask your client to tell us what the link is between Savage and all three victims. We have Thompson's name in the ledgers but we cannot find the name, Straughan or Gallagher, the other two victims.'

'All in good time officer. Perhaps you should go and

consult your superiors and once we have written assurance then I am sure we will be able to proceed.'

'I'm sure you will appreciate time is ticking and it would be useful if we could hear what Mr Hobson has to say now.'

'I don't think it would take long for you to get the appropriate assurance to us. Minutes if you hurry. As soon as it is here you will have our fullest co-operation.'

Groom leaned back in his chair and folded his arms. He stared at Hobson as he did. 'You must really be worried about what's in those books if you're prepared to go to court and give evidence for the police. That's not going to do your reputation much good in the Newcastle underworld.'

'Just doing my civic duty.' Hobson spoke his first words of this encounter.

'Well Gary, that brings a lump to my throat. I suppose it has nothing to do with saving your own skin?'

'I'd be lying if I didn't say I'd prefer not to go to prison. After all, I heard what it did to you when you were inside. You know, your wife getting shagged by another bloke and losing your kid. It's a lesson to us all.'

Groom moved quickly forward and Jet instinctively placed a hand on his shoulder, oblivious to the fact that he could not have stopped a determined Groom if he was intent on assaulting Hobson. Lackenby flinched away whilst Hobson moved forward as if goading Groom.

Groom stopped as he placed both his hands on the table, his knuckles white as he clenched the edge.

'I think this is a good time to terminate the interview.' Jet turned off the tape recorder as he spoke. He pulled his hand which was still on Groom's shoulder in an attempt to guide him out of his chair. Groom was reluctant to move but after a few seconds' hesitation he stood up and Jet followed him out of the room. As they left the smile returned to Lackenby's face, joining the smirk that had never left Hobson's.

Jet shut the door of the interview room and spoke to Groom. 'You all right?'

'Yeah, thanks Jet. Sorry about that I just …. Well you know.'

'Yes I know.'

They stood in silence for a few seconds as Groom composed himself. As he took deep breaths Jet spoke again. 'His solicitor has really thought this through.'

'Doesn't seem like much of a deal to me. Letting a chance of getting Hobson put away go begging. He's been a thorn in the side for a long time.'

'Yeah. I think Ormond might see it differently. His priority is getting three murders solved. I think getting Hobson would have been a nice bonus but that's all.'

'Bastard.'

'Well put Mark.' Jet smiled at Groom and gradually a smile formed around Groom's lips. Jet continued. 'You know, it's odd when you think about it.'

'What?'

'Well, we have a priest who won't speak to us in case he breaches a confidence and a criminal who wants to sing like a choirboy.'

'I'm not sure I want to watch Hobson wriggle out of this.'

'Should we go and have a word with Stone before we go in and see Ormond?'

'After you.' Groom gestured Jet ahead and followed as they headed towards Wilf Stone's interview room.

Jet turned the door handle and Groom followed him into the room.

'Hello Vera. You were right. We will meet again.' Jet rolled his eyes as Groom spoke even though he felt impressed at the speed it had taken Groom to recover his composure.

Stone remained expressionless. 'I've got nowt to say to you.'

Groom and Jet sat down in the monitoring room. It looked like Ormond had not moved since they had left. He did not look at them as they sat and Rosie Shepherd looked similarly static, contemplating deeply the words of the interviews just conducted.

'The way you make friends Mark, you should be in

public relations or show business or something.' Ormond was looking at his notes as he spoke.

'It's a gift.'

'We've nothing on the Priest and it looks like Stone is going to say nothing.' Ormond still had his eyes fixed on his file.

'I doubt Stone knows anything. He's just Hobson's minder.' Groom spoke to the top of Ormond's head.

'There's no rush to do anything with the Priest and Stone now, we'll keep them for a while until we sort out Savage.' Ormond's eyes were firmly set on his notes.

'What about Hobson?' Jet thought Groom was trying not to sound anxious but it wasn't working.

'I'm waiting for someone from the Crown Prosecution Service to come down. If it takes his evidence to get Savage on a murder charge then we'll see if the CPS will sanction a deal.' Ormond seemed reluctant to lift his head.

'What!' Groom's anger grew quickly. 'Not yet surely. You know the CPS will go along with what you want to do. If they see a deal with three convictions for murder attached they'll go for it. But this is a gilt-edged chance of getting Hobson put away as well. For all we know he could be behind the murders.'

Ormond finally raised his eyes to look at Groom. 'Mark, you're letting your personal feelings get in the way. This is about evidence, about getting the result at court. All we know for sure is Savage has the murder weapons and been doing the killing. He's a sadistic bastard. If we go after everyone then we run the risk of getting nobody. That's stupid. If we get Hobson's evidence to link Savage into all three and we charge him with murder, that's a good result.'

'But we don't even know what Hobson's going to say. We have his ledgers, we've got a good case already.'

'Even if Hobson's evidence just guarantees us a conviction for the first murder, it'll be worthwhile. But we could get all three cleared up. I know it's got a bad taste, but it's worth it. If we go after everyone we could easily end up empty-handed. It's too risky. You know that Mark.'

Jet could see the veins of Groom's neck throbbing. He looked close to exploding, but remained silent.

'Look Mark,' Ormond continued, 'go and talk to Savage and see what he has to say now, he might change his story when you put the new facts to him. Don't worry about Hobson. We didn't get into this to catch him lending money. He'll come again, once we have this sorted we'll give him another look and see what we can do about him.'

'He's been involved in serious crime in this area for years and we've looked at him dozens of times. I spent months in the drug squad chasing him but got nowhere. Those ledgers are a real find. This is the first time we've had evidence.'

'You did well finding them Mark and it's not a waste. We'll get three murders detected because of it. That's a result.'

Groom shook his head and Jet thought he had the look of resignation about him. He looked at Jet. 'Come on then, let's go and speak to Savage again.'

The telephone rang on York's desk. He pressed it to his ear.

'Superintendent York.'

'Chief here.'

York's heart sank. 'Nice to hear from you Sir.' More lies.

'Any news about the murders?'

'Nothing new. They're still interviewing. I think we'll have a charge before the day's out though. Looks like the murderer is one of Gary Hobson's goons who he's been setting onto people. Think he just got over-zealous and started to kill.'

'At least someone has staff who are over-zealous.'

'We're trying our best and it looks like we'll have a result soon.'

'Your DI Ormond told a briefing to fuck what the Chief said. Is that what you're teaching your staff?'

'I don't know what you're talking about Sir, I'm sure

DI Ormond wasn't being disrespectful.'

'York, don't make things bad for yourself as well. I know what the fucking idiot said and I'll have his bollocks for it.'

'Any news from Portugal?' York was hoping the change of subject might help.

'Still no sign of Harris. They'll carry on with enquiries where he went missing and something's bound to turn up. As soon as we can put your man Whittle in the area we'll arrest him and start things rolling from there.'

'I still find it hard to believe.'

'York; you don't even know what your DI is saying to his staff. It doesn't surprise me that you are literally letting them get away with murder. Get a fucking grip soon, or I will.'

'Yes Sir.' York did not know whether the Chief had heard his last words as the sound of the disconnected tone purring began as soon as he had stopped speaking.

He put the receiver back onto its cradle and spoke to himself. 'Bollocks.'

Savage gave a shudder as he saw the huge unmistakable figure of Groom walk into the interview room behind Jet. They sat. Groom carried a plastic bag containing a large pipe wrench and placed it on the floor next to his chair.

Clive Proctor, pen and folder in front of him, looked

as weary as Savage.

The tape recorder squealed and when it silenced Groom spoke. 'Mr Savage, you were arrested attacking a priest in St Stephen's church. Would you like to explain why you did that?'

'It's between me and him.'

'It will become a matter for the court soon. Do you not want to explain what was happening?'

'Look, you told me he'd been accusing me of things and I wanted to know why he was saying it. The discussion got a bit heated that's all. It was nothing.'

'I don't think the court is going to think attacking a priest in a church is nothing.'

'Officer,' Proctor was scribbling notes as he interrupted. 'I don't see how your guesswork on what the court may or may not like is relevant.'

'OK then let's talk about something very relevant.' Groom lifted the plastic bag from the floor. 'This is one of the tools from the boot of your car. For the purpose of the tape I am showing Mr Savage and his solicitor, pardon me, legal representative, exhibit MG1. A large heavy plumber's wrench. Do you recognise this Mr Savage?'

'No.'

'It was in the boot of your car. It has your fingerprints on it.'

'Told you, there were a few tools in the boot of the car

when I bought it. I don't really remember what was in it.'

'You don't look like the DIY type and there was no toolbox in your flat. Do you do many plumbing jobs?'

'No.'

'So why do you keep heavy tools like this in the boot of your car?'

'Told you, they were in there when I bought it and I just haven't got around to clearing it out.'

'When was the last time you used this wrench?'

'I never used it.'

'So why does it have your prints on it?'

'I must have just moved it about when I was using the car.'

'The wrench has your fingerprints on one end and Derek Thompson's blood on the other end.'

Clive Proctor's eyes moved up from his notepad for the first time and he looked at Savage. Savage remained poker-faced.

Groom continued. 'Derek Thompson had his skull smashed in with this wrench. It has his blood all over one end of it and your fingerprints at the other. What do you have to say about that?'

'I didn't kill anyone.'

'I think you'll have to do better than that now, don't you Mr Savage?'

'You can't prove I killed anyone.'

'I think we can and will. You have the murder weapon

in your car. It has your prints on it. You keep a boot full of tools that might look innocent enough if you're stopped by the police, but they're your arsenal of nasty weapons. When the police tried to stop your car you made a dash for it. Your tools have blood on them.' Groom paused for a second and stared at Savage who stared back hard. 'You were given instructions by Gary Hobson to go and extort money from these poor sods. Then what happened? Did you start to enjoy the power, did the threat of violence stop exciting you? So you had to start using more violence and then before you knew it you were smashing people's brains in?' Savage's eyes bore into Groom. 'I warned you that Hobson would sell you out and that's exactly what he's doing now. He's making a statement that links you to the three murders and he's making a sweet deal for himself, so he just walks away scot-free.'

'I didn't murder anyone.'

'Yes you did. The question is whether you are going to let everybody else involved in it walk away. They're all signing statements at the moment dropping you in it. It's sacrificial lamb time now Adam. Are you going to let that happen? What's in it for you now to protect everyone else? Why don't you do yourself a favour and just tell us what Hobson's part was in this and what Father O'Brian did? Why don't you just tell us the truth?'

'You'd like that wouldn't you, you stupid cunt!'

Savage's outburst was loud, raw aggression exuding from every word. 'You want me to grass everyone up on the strength of your bullshit. Go fuck yourself and take this prick with you.' Savage looked at Jet as he spat his words. 'You can't prove a thing and no one is grassing on me.'

'That sounds like a threat Adam.'

'It's reality. I've nothing else to say to you.'

'Perhaps it would be a good time for me to speak alone with my client.' Jet thought that Clive Proctor looked shaken and sounded nervous.

'That sounds like a good idea.' Groom stood up as Jet reached over and stopped the tape machine, removing the tapes.

Groom pushed the door of the monitoring room open and Jet followed. Jet recognised the face of the woman who looked out of place sitting next to Ormond in the room's cramped confines. Ormond spoke 'You know Abbi Peters from the CPS?'

Groom attempted a smile as he sat down and Jet nodded to the round face that smiled back at them. Jet knew Abbi Peters as one of the local Crown Prosecution Service solicitors and had often seen her presenting cases at Newcastle Magistrates Court. A task which primarily involved constant thumbing through the day's mound of files and trying to make light work of the many cases brought daily to the court. 'Heavy on paper, light on justice' was the thought that often fleeted across Jet's mind when he witnessed the performance. A woman in her mid-thirties, she wore lawyers' clothes, formal and expensive, she seemed relaxed sitting next to Ormond.

'I've brought Abbi up to speed and she's just listened to what Savage has said in interview. She's agreed the priority has got to be the murder charge against Savage. There's no doubt now he's our man. So we do what we need to do to get Hobson to give evidence and nail him.'

'I suppose we'll send Hobson a letter of commendation for being a fine upstanding citizen?' The venom in Groom's words was undiluted.

'I think you summed up the case against Savage quite well when you were speaking to him.' Abbi Peters voice was without a hint of accent. 'DI Ormond has told me of your reservations. I realise it's not the most palatable of compromises but it is the best outcome given the evidence. I've spoken to Hobson's solicitor and he has agreed the full co-operation of his client once we have given him written assurance we will not use the ledgers you found in the club as evidence against him. My decision is we now charge Savage with the murder of Derek Thompson and we apply to the court for a three-day remand whilst we gather the evidence to charge him with the other murders. It will give you time to go through Hobson's records and get a full statement so we can prove the other two murders.'

'That sounds like a sensible plan to me.' Jet thought Ormond looked more relaxed than he had for some time.

Jet could see that Groom was aching to speak but had seemingly resigned himself to watching Hobson walk.

'Look Mark, it's been a long day. Why don't you and Jet get some rest? We can bed down the prisoners for their statutory rest as well. I'll get Jardine to take Hobson's statement and we can go through the ledgers and sift as much of the evidence out as possible. We can come back fresh in eight hours or so. You and Jet can interview Savage again and put all of the evidence to him. You can have the pleasure of charging him when it's all done.'

'OK.' Groom picked up the ledgers. 'I'll go through the ledgers thoroughly before the interview. What about the Priest and Stone?'

'There's no hurry for them. It's a murder enquiry so let's keep them until we know we have everything we need. I think we've had enough of letting prisoners go today and then finding out we need them back.' Ormond attempted a rare smile at Groom.

'OK.' Groom's expression remained grim.

Groom got to his feet. Jet pushed the door open with his arm and allowed Groom to leave the room first.

Outside the monitoring room Groom turned to Jet. 'I suppose we can at least go home and have a bit of rest before we get back to it.'

'Yeah.'

'I'll follow you home if you like. I don't want the clutch failing you and leaving you stranded.'

'I'm sure it'll get me home.'

'It's not far out of the way.'

'Well, if you don't mind.'

They walked down the corridor. Groom held the five ledgers under his right arm and reached his left hand out allowing his fingertips to brush the corridor walls. 'Why do they insist on painting everything magnolia?'

'Suppose it's just easier to maintain.'

'The easy option.' Groom grinned at Jet as they walked. 'You know Jet everyone goes for the easy option. I think there's only me and you trying around here.'

'If you say so Sarge.'

The Fiesta engine seemed to be crying more than ever as Jet pressed the accelerator as he approached his house on Station Road, Wallsend. He pulled onto the drive of his home. Groom pulled his Audi sports car up outside the house and then got out of the vehicle to stand with Jet looking at the bonnet of the Fiesta.

'You'll have to get that seen to soon.' Groom nodded to the Fiesta, as if further clarification were required about what needed attention.

'Won't be cheap. It never seems to stop.'

'Why don't you think about just trading it in for something newer?'

'There's lots of life left in it yet.'

'Are you sure?'

'Yes.'

'It's only a car you know.'

'I know.' Jet smiled. 'Julia didn't like it very much. Too basic, she said.'

'She had a point.'

'It'll do me for a while yet.'

It occurred to Jet that it must have sounded like he was defending an old friend. He felt as if he was. Although Julia had never cared for the Fiesta, he could still imagine her in it. Their journeys. Her using the mirror behind the sun visor. Him watching out of the corner of his eye as she applied lipstick. Him swerving the car slightly, claiming he was avoiding a pothole. He adored that strained look of disapproval at his childish behaviour.

Groom looked at the new fence that enclosed Jet's front garden. 'It looks good.'

Jet cast his eye over it. 'Yeah, finished on time as well.'

'See, chasing him down the street and assaulting him was good motivation. No complaints made. Maybe you should try it with all of your contractors.'

'Don't speak yet. He might be waiting until I've paid him until he makes a complaint against us. He'll get more in compensation than I'm going to give him for the fence.'

As they spoke Jet could see the figure of Terry Luton walking up the street toward them.

'We were just talking about you.' Jet smiled at Luton as he got within hearing distance.

'You're not going to set your friend on me again, are you?'

'Don't worry I was just going.' Groom walked to his sports car. 'Should I pick you up to go back to the nick?'

'If you don't mind.'

'What time?'

'I don't even know what time it is now.' Jet turned to Luton, 'Terry, you got the time?'

Luton shrugged. 'No, don't have a watch. It'll be about nine o'clock judging by the light.'

Groom pulled his mobile phone out of his pocket. 'Good guess, it's five past.' He returned his phone to his jacket. 'So how do you know when it's knocking off time?' Groom's eyes scanned Luton's evenly tanned arms.

Luton grinned. 'No need for watches when you work outside all of the time, I work by the daylight. In any case when you work for yourself there is no knocking off time. I'm done when I'm finished or it's dark. Thought you cops would need them though?'

Sensing a trace of hostility remained in the air Jet smiled at Luton and interjected. 'We've been interviewing suspects most of the day, when we do that we take our watches off and go by the same clock in the interview room. It can be confusing if you have too many things telling you the time as they never seem to say the same.'

'Don't suppose it would do to tell the judge that you hit a suspect at five past, when your friend's watch here says it's ten to.' Luton did not smile and Groom grimaced.

'Something like that.' Jet smiled weakly as he spoke, realising he was never going to preside over any conciliatory words between Groom and Luton.

Groom turned to Jet. 'Suppose we better get in early, pick you up at six?'

Jet sighed at the thought of the alarm going off at five. 'OK.'

Groom was almost at his car when he spoke again. 'That reminds me I still have your door key.' Groom patted his jacket pocket again. 'I think I must have left it in my desk drawer with the watches.'

'You haven't lost it have you?' Jet was trying not to show the sense of panic that occurred with the wish he'd tried harder to remove Julia's fob from the key ring before he had handed it to Groom.

Groom sensed he had unintentionally hit a nerve. 'Don't worry, I'm sure it'll be safe.'

A weak smile grew on Jet's face. 'Sure. Sorry Mark.

You will find it tomorrow though?'

'I must have put it in my desk, as soon as I get it I'll return it to you.'

Jet tried to raise a smile but as hard as he tried he could not conceal the pain on his face. She had been taken from him and now even her memory was fading. Piece by piece she seemed to be disappearing. Jet knew that if it was happening to someone else he would be able to be more rational about it. But it wasn't someone else.

Groom got into his Audi and pulled it out into the street and soon disappeared from sight.

Luton turned to Jet. 'Sounds like it's been a long day?'

'Yes, it happens every now and again.' Jet looked at the fence. 'Looks like you've been working hard as well.'

'Yes, I thought I'd get it finished today. It's been a fine enough day and it's good to be working so close to home.'

'Don't suppose you saw that Mondeo any more?'

'No. Just the time I rang you about.'

'That's good to hear. We've a suspect in custody. If it had been back again it might have made things a little complicated.'

'No, I've been here most of the day off and on. Nothing at all.'

Jet looked straight in Luton's eyes. 'Listen Terry, it's been so busy that I've not had a chance to get to the cash machine. Don't suppose I could give you a cheque?'

'Yeah, that's all right. I'll be going to the bank tomorrow anyway.'

'Great. I'll just get my cheque book.'

Jet walked up the garden path, finding his keys in his jacket pocket as he did. He turned the Yale lock and opened the front door.

'Come on in, the cheque book's just in the dining room.'

Luton followed as Jet walked along the short hall to the dining room door. Jet had just moved through the dining room threshold when he felt a blow to the back of his head. The pain seemed to take a second to register, but when it did, everything became fuzzy and distant. He was only vaguely aware of his body falling face down onto the dining room table and then onto the floor. Then it was just black.

Water. Jet's next thought - water. He could feel it being poured over his face. Cold liquid, it felt good. Then the pain returned, the stinging on the back of his neck. He thought he could feel blood running down his back but could not be sure. He tried to touch but his hand could not move. His eyes started to focus and he saw his hands were handcuffed together in front of him. His own handcuffs from his jacket pocket. Jet tried to move his legs but realised they were tied together tightly. Jet looked up and saw Terry Luton. He held a claw hammer in his right hand and it swung gently by his leg. Jet's eyes blinked rapidly and soon fully focused he could see Luton staring at him.

'Time's up for everybody sometime.' Luton's words made Jet shiver. 'And now PC Whittle it's up for you.'

'Terry?'

'You're slow on the uptake today. Feeling dazed?'

'Yes.'

'Don't worry you won't feel any pain soon.'

'I don't understand.'

'Or remember, do you?'

'Remember what?'

'You arrested me PC Whittle, don't you remember?'

'You?'

'Indecent and Lewd behaviour, that's what you said.'

'Terry, I never....' Jet was confused. 'I don't know what you're talking about.'

'You don't remember chasing me from the Gardens? another copper chased my mate but didn't catch him, but you caught me. Bit more determined than your colleague. You thought it was funny. I smashed my watch in the struggle, not remember? You laughed, "Time's up for you" don't you remember your joke?'

'No.'

'Never missed a day's church after that. Confession every week. No chance of being indecent or lewd after that. No, my dad saw to that, thanks to you.'

'Are you sure Terry?'

'Sure?' Luton shouted. 'Am I sure! You ruined my life and you want to know if I'm sure!' Luton clenched the handle of the hammer tightly. Jet could see his knuckles whiten as his hand strained. 'I was fifteen years old. Fifteen, PC Whittle.' Luton shook his head and his voice lowered. 'Fifteen. My friend, who I was being indecent and lewd with, he said the Gardens was a safe place. The coppers were supposed to leave it alone. He said there was an agreement, if we went there, and nowhere else, we'd be all right. It was in the pink-press as a meeting place he said. It'll be all right. But it wasn't was it, cos you decided you wanted to arrest somebody that day.'

'Terry, I don't remember. Sometimes, in those days, when we had complaints from members of the public we would keep observations and arrest people who were committing offences there, but Terry, it must have been a long time ago.'

'All a very long time ago. Does that make it OK with you?'

'Terry I don't understand.'

'I bet you don't. Can you imagine how hard it is for a boy to realise as he goes through school he's different from the others? Hiding things. Not letting anyone know how you felt. Bottling it all up. Then you come along and next thing my secret's out. My dad never got over it. I wasn't allowed out after that. I was too disgusting to be allowed out, couldn't be trusted. The shame I'd brought on my family, how could my dad ever look at me like his son again? Unnatural, that's what he said I was. Unnatural, not fit for anything. Not fit to feel anything but shame.'

'I was just doing my job.'

'Buggery. That's what he shouted at me every day. A pervert who wanted to bugger people.'

"There is no shame being gay.'

Luton raised the hammer to his shoulder and Jet cowed as far as his restraints allowed.

'Don't you talk to me about shame. I know shame.'

'Killing me isn't going to help.'

'Trying to save your skin?'

'I just don't understand. You have a house, a business, a lot to live for, why this now?'

'I'm changing things forever. Making my mark. My protest to the world and what a way to go. A mass murderer. My dad will be spinning in his grave.' The hammer swung at Luton's side. 'I'll not amount to anything my dad said. I'll not be remembered for anything. Just the shame a pervert brings on his family, that's all.' Luton paused for a second, the hammer still swinging. 'But don't you worry PC Whittle, I'm going to put you out of your misery as well. You'll be famous for a while. Not remembered as long as me, but you will have your fifteen minutes. A martyr, a victim, but that's all. Not like me, I will be remembered for the protest.'

'But why gay people?'

'They will be martyrs as well. It's the only way for people to know. A small sacrifice.'

'Killing innocent people?'

'It'll be all worth it for the future, because it will free people.'

'But things are changing.'

'Changing? Did you hear what that Priest was saying? The church isn't going to change. Do you know what the priest said to me, the one my father made me go and see, he said I'd brought shame on the family and I was an abomination in the eyes of the Lord. An abomination, evil. I knew then, one day, I would show the world what evil really was and then the opportunity came along.' The hammer head swung gently past Luton's knee now as he spoke.

'I had to help your fence down, when the gale come along.' Luton smirked. 'What better tool to use than you, the man who started it all in the first place. I thought I recognised you when I saw your face in the paper after your wife died. I was at the funeral, just there at the graveside to see your face. All those people feeling sorry for you, but I didn't. So you can take your place in history now. Don't worry I'll make sure you're dead before I cut your cock off.' Luton was wild-eyed and Jet could see he was confident of his dominance. 'Nothing personal, you know, but what a way to make a point. They'll talk about me for generations. The man who saved the queers by killing them. Queers, that's what my dad called us. Queers, should be a way of identifying them at birth and drowning them.' Luton paused and then lifted the hammer again, now gently tapping its head on his palm. 'My dad might have made sure I wasn't a practising queer, but I'm going to go out with a bang now.'

Jet watched the gentle motion of the hammer as he spoke. 'I can tell you've suffered at the hands of others, but believe me I know about loss and the pain it brings. But can it be right to cause suffering to others?'

'Ah, your wife. At least you had a wife, a relationship, I was denied all of that.'

'Is revenge going to make things better?'

'It's not revenge. It's progress, are you so stupid? Can't you see what this is about? If it had been revenge I would have killed you by now. We're showing them all now. I'm going to be remembered forever. Killing you is just a bonus.'

'So this is about making you famous?'

'I was told every day I was a pervert, an unnatural thing. That brought disgrace. Well I'll be remembered for changing things for the better.'

'Is killing people making things better?'

'How small-minded you are.' Luton's eyes burned into Jet, the hammer now swinging gently by his side again. 'It's the casualties that make a war. My dad said the great war was called great because of all the blood that was shed.'

'You see this as a war?'

'Of course it's a war. How else? Hitler persecuted the Jews and we went to war with him. I've been persecuted all my life because I was different. Of course it's a war. People will see it in time. When the press tell everyone about the victims, people will ask why it happened. They will see it was necessary, the only way to make things better.'

'And you'll be the hero?'

'Hero is your word. I will show those who said I'd amount to nothing how wrong they were. People like that Priest will have to think, or there will be more people like me to fight.'

'There must be other ways. We've seen things change.'

'Change, what do you mean change? You mean perverts like me are tolerated as long as we're out of sight. Harmless puffs, given a pub so they can meet with all the other harmless perverts, out of sight of the real world.'

'Surely there must be another way?'

'There is no other way. I am a pervert, that's what my dad told me every day. I was his son and that's what he thought of me. You think I'm a pervert, you won't say it

312

but that's what you think. I'm going to change the way people think, even people like the Priest will have to think again, because when you and the Priest really think about it, you will realise you did this. You persecuted people like me and this is what happens when you force people against the wall. You did this.'

'I was just doing my job. I didn't think....'

'No you didn't think. Soon people will have to.'

Luton raised the hammer above his head. 'Don't worry it'll be quick, quicker than the torture I've put up with.'

'Then what happens?'

'What does it matter to you?'

'It matters to you. Isn't that why you haven't killed me yet? Didn't you want to torment me a bit?'

'I wanted you to know how stupid you'd been and to let you know why you were going to die. Doesn't it make you feel better you died for a good cause?'

'No.'

'It's taken a lot of careful planning to get here. The timing has been perfect. We've waited and planned for the right time. Then the conference came along. People coming from all over the country to talk about how to make things better for gay people. Well they're going to make things better all right. With their sacrifice.'

'You're going to kill more people?'

'I put enough explosives under that conference room

to blow every queer in it to kingdom come.'

'Explosives?'

'You're so stupid. I even had some of the makings of the bomb on the truck when I was outside your house. Ammonium Nitrate, the IRA used it for years, it comes in fertiliser. I've got tons of it. The tricky part was rigging the detonator, but once you know what to do and are as good as me with your hands; well it wasn't such a challenge. I got a job looking after the grounds there, nice big storeroom with loads of stuff in it.'

'You could kill hundreds.'

'I told you it was a war.'

Jet pulled at the handcuffs urgently. 'You can't do that.'

'It's pointless struggling. We've planned this thoroughly. You're not going to escape.' Jet tried to raise his body. Luton put the sole of his shoe on Jet's knee and straightened his leg. Jet's torso fell backwards under the weight; the thick bindings tying his ankles together held tight. Luton raised the hammer up. 'You know you were even stupid enough to fall for me telling you about the Mondeo.'

Jet could see Luton's arm was outstretched, the hammer in mid-air.

'PC Whittle, time's up for you.'

Luton thrust the hammer towards Jet's head. Jet instinctively jerked back as far as he could from the blow which was picking up speed. He pulled his shackled hands to his face. Jet felt the hammer hit the edge of the metal handcuff and bounce away from his head. Luton pulled the hammer back towards himself again to prepare for a second swipe. Jet's heart thumped in his chest as he realised he was helpless, death imminent. Jet closed his eyes and fell to his left hand side, as far away from Luton as his restrains allowed. He felt the leg of one of the dining room chairs against the back of his head and he quickly moved his manacled hands as far as he could to grab the leg. Before he could reach it he heard a loud thud, and then a crash. Jet looked up and saw Luton was falling face down onto the dining room table. His weight caused two of the legs to collapse as he fell helplessly upon it.

Jet squinted past the liquid his eyeballs had produced and could make out the figure of Mark Groom in the dining room doorway. He had a vase in his hand. He looked at Jet and then the vase.

'What's this made out of?'

Jet squinted again and he recognised the vase from the hall table. 'I think it's alabaster.'

'Fuck. I thought it was heavy. I hope I haven't killed him.'

'I don't care myself.'

Groom examined the vase closely. 'It doesn't look damaged, was it a present?'

315

'It was Julia's. Do you think you could get me out of these cuffs?'

Groom jingled the keys in his jacket pocket as he produced a small bunch and leaned down to grab Jet's wrists to release the cuffs. Once his hands were free Jet pulled at the blue nylon rope secured around his ankles.

'I thought you'd gone home?'

'He didn't have a watch when you asked him the time, it made me think. I told you he was shifty. Your front door is open as well.'

'You came back because he didn't have a watch on?'

'Didn't you think it was odd?'

'Frankly no.'

'I thought it odd, especially as you were getting messages about time being up.'

'It's a good job you did.'

'I also found Julia's key in my pocket. I thought it best to return it now.' Groom held out the door key attached to the leather fob which had the name 'Julia' looking a little worn on it.

'Thanks.' Jet smiled as he took the key and slid it in his trouser pocket. 'She's still looking after me.'

'You all right?'

'I think so, but he was going on about explosives at the conference. The one NEGRA are having. Said there were enough to blow everyone to kingdom come. Didn't someone say they were having a big function tonight to open the conference?'

'Aye, they did, but how would anyone get explosives there?'

'I don't know if he was serious but we better play it safe. I'll ring the nick and get the place evacuated until the bomb squad can have a look.'

'We'd better get an ambulance as well.' Groom looked at the motionless figure resting face down on the remains of Jet's dining room table. 'Last time I thought I'd killed a criminal I ended up right in the shit.'

'I remember.' Jet was on his feet now and his heart was beginning to slow down a bit.

'We better get a move on.' Groom looked at the unconscious body. 'I think it best if I stay with him.'

'OK. I'll use the phone and get down to the conference centre if you're staying with our friend here until help arrives.' Jet was rubbing his wrists as he spoke and then got his mobile phone out of his pocket. As he fumbled with the phone he looked up at his dining room. 'Look at the mess in here.'

'On the plus side, you have saved three hundred quid on your fence.'

'Is he still breathing?'

Groom got as close as he felt comfortable to Luton's motionless body. 'I think he'll survive. Ask the station to send some cops down as well so we can keep an eye on him at the hospital.' Groom stood up considering the unconscious body. 'I suppose this means we've been wasting our time with Savage.'

Jet's hands were shaking as he tried to find the right buttons to press on his mobile to get through to the station inspector. 'Maybe.'

'Do you want to take my car?'

'Mine will make it, it's not far.'

'If you're sure.'

'Yeah, you'll need the car yourself.'

'Sure.'

Jet's call was answered and after the conversation with the station he put his phone away and then lifted his head to speak to Groom again. 'Right. they'll be here soon, I'll head off to the conference hall.'

Groom could see that Jet was hesitating as he looked at the recumbent figure lying on his broken dining room table. 'What's the matter Jet?'

'He said we've been planning?'

'What?'

'Just before he tried to smash my head in he said we've been planning to do this.'

'Are you sure?'

'I think so.' Jet started to make his way out of the room. 'Then again I've had a serial murderer fixing my fence all week so what do I know?'

'Bollocks.' Jet sat in the driver's seat of the Fiesta and the screaming of the engine as he pressed the accelerator reminded him the extent of its current frailties. The thought occurred to him to return and ask Groom for the keys to his sports car, but now he had the Fiesta engine running, he felt committed, and in any case the conference centre was only a few miles away. He could be there in fifteen minutes. His mind raced as fast as the Fiesta engine as the events started to slip into place. The Inspector he had spoken to at the station sounded understandably alarmed when Jet had told him there may be explosives in the conference centre and he sent some of the local officers to evacuate the place immediately. The gathering was at a large conference room at the Community Centre on Westgate Road, near the city centre. Jet manoeuvred the Fiesta off the Coast Road heading into Newcastle to cut across the city to get there. He thought about all of the bomb calls he had been to over his service. They had become less popular in recent years, now that the IRA had ceased its campaign, but they still occasionally had bomb scares and they could cause a lot of panic. He thought about the things Luton had said during their conversation and he realised that even for a man of Luton's practical ability, it would be quite an undertaking for him to have constructed a bomb big enough to cause a lot of damage at the Community Centre. Especially under the noses of so many people. Jet knew from previous experience the materials needed to cause explosions were readily available, but the hard part was detonation. Luton would have to be very close himself, to ensure the explosives went off, or would have had to have been incredibly ingenious to ensure detonation, especially at his first attempt. It was some time since Jet had been on a bomb course but he remembered something about the requirement of chemicals which could be difficult to get if you wanted to make a really good job of it. It is not like Luton had the experience of the IRA to draw upon, where trial and error led to greater success. Jet knew they had been lucky with Luton tonight, at last fate had given him a break. He knew Groom would always now claim that it had been his nagging doubts about Luton not wearing a watch which had led to his detective radar being activated and his return, but Jet thought it more likely to be him feeling obliged to return Julia's key ring. Either way a lot of people could be grateful that fortune had smiled upon them and Luton was not now able to finalise his plan. Yes, they had been lucky. They would make sure the building was empty and to be on the safe side evacuate the adjacent buildings, just as the manual said and then get the bomb squad to check everything out and in a few hours everything would be wrapped up. As Jet turned into Westgate Road he could see the blue flashing lights of a police car outside the Community Centre and as he did he afforded himself a wry smile. Yes, they had been lucky. The smile had just formed around his lips when he heard the explosion. It sounded like the whole of Newcastle had been destroyed. 'Bollocks,' was the word that slipped out of his lips. He whispered it to himself as he felt the earth shake.

People were running down Westgate Hill. In suits and evening wear, people dressed to celebrate a landmark event now felt terror. Jet pulled the Fiesta over to the side of the road, turning the key to stop the engine's screams and then he ran towards the Community Centre. Every window in the building had blown out and glass showered those who had gathered outside. As Jet ran through the crowd he could see people examining cuts on themselves and others. Some had stopped running, perhaps they could go no further, and rested on low walls.

A cloud of black smoke billowed from the bottom of the building and engulfed the second storey. Rubble and wood had been thrust out of the ground floor windows.

Jet ran up the path towards the building, the crowd had thinned as he had moved off the main street and on the path was a lone uniformed figure. Jet recognised Stan Evans, a duty shift officer. He looked pale and shaken; his face was covered in black grime. He stood outside the shattered building and looked confused.

Jet took him by the shoulder and he startled as Jet turned him around. 'Stan, it's Jet, are you all right?' Stan looked like he could not breathe and gave Jet a vacant look. 'Stan,' Jet continued, 'are you hurt?'

Stan seemed to regain some awareness. 'Jet, I think the whole fucking first floor's come down.'

Jet looked up at the solid shell of the building but could see that some of the structure of the first floor had been forced out of the ground floor windows by the power of the explosion.

'Stan, do you know if there was anyone in there?'

'I don't know. We evacuated the function room just like we were told. Some people wouldn't leave at first, we had to force them.' Stan had panic in his voice. 'They wouldn't fucking leave Jet, we had to force them out.'

'So everyone's out?'

'No, someone said there were people still in the toilet, so Steve said he'd go back.'

'Steve?'

'Aye, Steve Manson, he told me to stay at the front door and keep people from coming back in and he'd go and check the toilets.'

'How long had Steve been in the building before the explosion?'

'I don't know Jet, a minute, maybe.'

'Listen Stan, help is on its way. But I need you to help me, can you do that Stan?'

'Aye Jet what?'

'Listen Stan, we need to think about a secondary device, another bomb, sometimes it happens that way Stan. To make sure, they plant a second or even a third device.'

Stan looked alarmed at this new thought, 'Fuck no Jet.'

'Stan, don't panic, we just need to make sure everyone that's outside here moves away from the building, as far as we can get them. Stan, get all the casualties to congregate at the car park down the street and get the ambulances to go there. Use that as a rendezvous point. Have you got that Stan?'

'Aye Jet.'

'Do you have a torch on you?'

Stan pulled a small cylinder torch from a leather pouch on his belt. 'Just this, the big one's in the car.'

Jet took the small torch and switched it on. "This'll do. Can you go and move people away now?' Stan looked breathless. Jet took a hold of the top of his arm and spoke gently. 'Stan, you'll be all right, just make sure everyone's away from here.' Jet looked in Stan's shocked eyes. 'Stan, can you do that now?'

'Aye, Jet, Aye.'

Stan ran away from the building down the path and started to shout directions at the people around him and shepherd them away down the hill.

Jet moved towards the main door of the building. The dust was beginning to settle as he peered in. A mass of rubble lay in front of him and it was hard to even try to fathom where the rooms of the building had lain before the explosion. He looked up at the ceiling and could see everything that had been held up by floor joists had come down and now lay in the mass of destruction where gravity had carelessly put it. Jet slowly edged his way inside. He lifted himself up on what appeared to have been a wall which was now lying on its side and he surveyed what he could.

'Steve, are you there!' Jet was shouting, 'Steve, it's Jet.'

A beam of light shot from behind Jet and he turned to see a fireman coming into the building, the reflective strip of his uniform glowing in the dullness.

'Are you all right?' The fireman shouted at Jet.

'Yes, I think there are still people in here. There was a policeman inside when the bomb went off.'

The fireman shone his torch ahead at the mass of rubble and devastation. 'Listen pal, I think you should get out.'

'I'm with the police; I'm looking for a colleague who was in here when the bomb went off.'

'Pal, it's just not safe. This whole building could come down at any time; there'll be mains gas and electrics. We need to get out. We'll get a search team in to look for casualties as soon as we can.'

Jet looked around at the debris. 'But he could be here.'

'Pal, there's nothing you can do now. Let us get on with it; if you get stuck in here you'll just make matters worse for us and your friend.'

Jet looked at the small torch he had been using to try and find his way around the rubble. He scanned the debris. 'Fuck!' A frustrated outburst at the reality of his helplessness. Then he climbed off the rubble and walked out of the building.

Outside he could see the path to the building was clear and Stan had managed to drive people a good way down the street next to the small car park. The wail of sirens now engulfed the atmosphere and a congregation of blue lights near the car park gave it the feel of a bizarre discotheque.

Jet made his way to the car park and saw the uniform Inspector getting out of his car, he appeared bewildered as he scanned the chaos. He saw Jet and the two made their way to each other.

'The building's been blown to smithereens. We don't know who was left in but Stan Evans says Steve Manson was in there when the blast happened. I had a look but it's just a mass of rubble.'

'I've had a radio check done and been told Steve Manson is the only officer not answering his radio.'

'I thought Steve was off today?'

'He'd come in to do an overtime shift.'

'If he was inside I don't see how he could have survived.'

'I better go and try to sort some things out, there's cops travelling from all over the force area, so we'll have plenty of people here soon.'

'If it's any consolation I think we have the crazy bastard who did this in custody.'

The Inspector eyed the surrounding pandemonium. 'It's not.'

Day Four – Morning

'York.' The Superintendent felt weary as he spoke into his phone. It had been a long night and he'd just returned to his office, hoping for a little respite.

'Chief Constable here.' Those three words did nothing to restore York's flagging morale. 'It's a total shambles from what I hear York.'

'It could have been a lot worse; the evacuation saved a lot of lives.'

'While Ormond was pissing around with the wrong suspects, the real murderer was planting a bomb. It shouldn't have happened. I've had the Home Secretary on to me this morning going ballistic. There's all sorts of rumours and stories going on in the press about terrorists and the police having lost total control of the area.'

'I've made arrangements for a press conference later this morning.'

'And what's this I'm told about a deal with one of our major criminals giving him immunity from prosecution?'

'Ormond spoke to the CPS and they thought it best to use him as a witness.'

'For what? He knows fuck all about the murders.'

York cringed as the Chief Constable spoke. His overriding emotion was to find out who was leaking information and strangle them. 'Well Ormond didn't know that last night. We thought we needed Hobson to tell us about the instructions he gave to Savage.'

'So to cap it all, you had the chance to take out one of the force's main criminals and instead of charging him you gave him complete immunity for fuck all reason!'

'With hindsight Sir….' York did not get the chance to finish his sentence.

'Hindsight, it's foresight you need to work on! Criminals will be queuing up to come to Newcastle now.'

'At the time it seemed….'

'No more excuses York,' The Chief was not in the mood to listen. 'I want Ormond out of there today.'

'But is that wise in the middle of….'

'You questioning my judgement York?'

'Not at all, I'm just saying….'

'Good, Ormond is being transferred to CID training today.'

'But the investigation is still….'

'You have a Detective Sergeant there called Davison. I'm told he's a good man. Put him in as temporary Detective Inspector and get him to clear the mess up. We'll sort out a full-time replacement after that. If Davison does well we'll make it permanent.'

'But….'

'Good, pleased that's sorted. What about PC Manson's family, how are they bearing up?'

'I broke the news to his mother this morning. We'll

make sure that everything is done to help. She's the only close relative. His father was an ex-cop, he died a few years ago.'

'Great shame. Keep me updated.'

The phone clicked and after a few second's silence York replaced the phone on its cradle and once it was back in its holder he shouted at it. 'Bastard!'

Sombre was the word that crossed Jet's mind as he looked around the briefing room. The customary jokes between colleagues were absent. Today was not a day for petty bickering or triviality. Thoughts of mortality were going to dominate the collective mood for quite a while. At 9.00am the last few staff entered the room for the arranged meeting. Ormond, file in hand, walked in and took his place at the front. He kept his eyes on the file he placed on the lectern.

'Right, I guess you'll all know what happened at Westgate Road last night. The good news is we have the person responsible in custody. He was released from hospital a few hours ago after treatment for a bump on his head. I've just been told the body of Steve Manson has been recovered from the rubble. Everyone else has been accounted for. Needless to say the press are here in their droves. So it's going to be a busy day. Groom and Whittle will continue the interviews with me and Rosie

Shepherd. Everyone else will be tasked by the incident room. There are a lot of people to speak to and statements to take. We need to get our main suspect charged and in front of the court as soon as possible. Any questions?'

A second's silence followed then Ormond lifted his head. 'Let's get on with it then.'

As chairs rumbled in protest of being dragged along the wooden floor the door opened and Sergeant Sharkie, the duty station sergeant, walked over to Ormond. 'Boss, Superintendent York asked if you'd go up to his office now to see him.'

'As if I didn't have enough to do.' Ormond grumbled.

Jet and Groom sat around the table in the monitoring room and looked at the list of suspects on the paper in the centre of the table. Savage, Stone, Hobson, Luton and O'Brian.

'Well it shouldn't be so hard to work out an interview plan now.' Jet had his clipboard in front of him as he spoke, the one he used for his interview notes. He was a person who liked order. He admired Groom's ability to 'wing it', but Jet always thought spontaneity was a risky strategy to rely on. Jet liked to have a plan.

'Now we have Luton in custody, I guess at least we can rip up that crazy agreement we had with Hobson. If anyone deserves throwing to the dogs it's him.' Groom almost wore a smile at the thought of this particular silver lining.

'I wonder if Hobson really thought Savage was going out and killing people who owed him money?'

'My guess is he didn't really give a shit. But I bet he's found it easier to collect his debts since.'

'Yes, nothing like a serial killer coming after you to focus the mind.' Jet remained poker-faced.

'Maybe the local authority could have a look at it. I'd bet their success rate for collecting the council tax would shoot up.'

The door of the room stuttered open and Rosie Shepherd shuffled in. Steam was being released from the cup she held out in front of her, the string from the teabag hanging over the edge of the cup.

'Is Ormond on his way? Not like him to be late.' Groom's eyes followed Shepherd around the room.

She spoke as she manoeuvred herself into her usual chair. 'I haven't seen him for a while. I got a message from the incident room to come here as the interviews were going to be started.'

After her comment everyone was quiet, the silence only broken by Rosie's shuffling into position. Jet thought she was collecting a file of a size to match that of Ormond's and he wondered what she was finding to write in it.

The door was thrust open and Ian Davison came in followed by Stuart Townsend.

Groom looked up. 'We're expecting some proper police officers in here soon and there's not much space. If you're looking for the canteen it's on the next floor down.'

Jet thought he could detect an unusual glint in Davison's eye as he sat down. Townsend sat next to him with his usual cheerless expression.

'As of this morning I am acting detective inspector in charge of the case.'

Groom's jaw dropped. 'What's happened to Ormond?'

'He's been seconded to the training department.' Davison's smug expression seemed to be growing.

'What? In the middle of an enquiry. Are they mad?' Groom could not hide anger in his voice.

'I'm sure we'll make a success of it.' Davison opened a neat file in front of him and removed a piece of paper. 'We have a revised prisoner list.'

Jet and Groom looked at the paper. It had the names of Luton and Savage on it.

'Where's Hobson, Stone and the Priest?'

'Stone and the Priest have been bailed. There's no reason to keep them for the moment, we can get them at anytime if we want.'

'And Hobson?'

'We signed an agreement with Hobson last night saying we wouldn't use the books we recovered from the club against him if he gave us a statement implicating Savage. Jardine is still dealing with him but we'll be ready to release him soon. No need to worry about him with regard to the murders, or devise an interview strategy.'

'Now we have Luton and we know the murderer isn't Savage, surely we should go back to the CPS and tell them we need to call the deal off?' Groom was earnest.

'I don't think we need to. We'll still use the evidence to charge Savage.'

'With what?'

'With assault on Thompson. The blood found on the tools in his car belong to the first victim. He must have assaulted him before he was murdered. We use Hobson's evidence to convict him.'

'But it was Hobson who arranged it. Savage is a thug, but Hobson's the man we want. As soon as we let him go he'll just hire some other goon to do his work. Those ledgers had enough evidence to put him out of business. Think of what the taxman alone could do with it.' Groom's voice rose.

'Listen, I've had to make some hard decisions to get a result out of this mess.' Davison was looking at the files in front of him as he spoke. 'We build a case against Savage and get him charged. We charge Luton with the murders. It's a good result all round.'

'Bollocks,' Groom banged the side of his fist on the table. 'We're letting a good chance go here to get one of the main criminals in Newcastle put away.'

'Ormond and the CPS brokered the deal, so it's done, not worth the effort to try and go back on it.'

'You mean you're frightened to take the risk and you can always just blame Ormond.'

'Thanks for your thoughts on that Mark, but this is my decision and we're going to let Hobson go after he's made a full statement. Mark can you speak to John Jardine? I've asked him to take the statement from Hobson. I want you to liaise with him and give him the information he needs. He'll need the ledgers you have belonging to Hobson.'

'What about the interview with Luton?'

'Stuart here is now acting detective sergeant, he'll lead the interview with Luton and Jet can assist him. Given that you nearly knocked his head off last night, it would be wiser to do it that way. Jet can help with any additional information we might need during the process.'

'So you're sidelining me?'

'As detective inspector I need to make sure I'm using my resources to their best effect. I trust as a detective sergeant under my command I'll have your total co-operation?'

Groom's face was growing an ever deeper shade of red.

He sat silently for a few seconds, then nodded and got to his feet. 'I might as well go and see Jardine now and see what I can do.' Jet was relieved to detect an air of resignation in Groom's voice. He could think of times when he'd been less amenable.

The door closed behind Groom. Davison looked up from the table and spoke to Townsend and Jet.

'We don't need to worry too much about Luton's co-operation. Let's just have a straightforward interview; give him the chance to say what he wants. The important thing is we don't leave him and a clever solicitor enough space to think up any great stories before he gets to court.'

Jet was feeling unsettled at the revelations of the last few minutes but decided not to pursue any of the questions circling around in his head. Townsend led the way out of the room. Jet followed. As they got to the interview room Townsend placed his hand on the door, stopped and turned toward Jet.

'I'll do the talking. Say nothing unless I ask for something.'

Jet looked at Townsend in the eye but did not speak, simply giving a slight nod.

Townsend pushed open the door and they both walked towards the table behind which Luton sat. Next to Luton was a middle-aged man in a grey suit. Jet thought he would not have looked out of place in an

Estate Agent's office. He had a blank A4 pad of paper in front of him which sat neatly in a brown leather folder. The thought crossed Jet's mind that the leather folder looked like it had been a Father's Day gift or birthday present. Jet often saw a variety of police officers carrying in new leather look briefcases after Christmas. Presents from relatives that rarely got used past Easter. Julia had once bought him a brown leather briefcase and in an absent moment whilst he had put his coat in the boot of the Fiesta he left the case on the ground. It was not until he felt the back wheel of the car bump up and down he remembered where he had left his case. The battered looking case was still in the loft.

Townsend pressed the button on the tape machine causing its customary howl for a few seconds and when it stopped he introduced himself and Jet for the benefit of the recording. The man in the grey suit announced himself as Eric Bell the duty solicitor who was here to represent Luton. Luton remained silent. Jet could see there was a large plaster dressing on the back of his neck where Groom had introduced him to his alabaster vase last night.

'Mr Luton.' Townsend started. 'I should tell you that since your arrest we have searched your house and found a number of items which I want to talk to you about.' Townsend removed a clear plastic bag from his folder which contained an A4 ring-bound notebook. The cover was green and had a hologram image of a spider on the front.

'We took this from your living room. This bag is sealed for forensic reasons but I do have a copy of the pages it contains. It is a journal. Can you confirm that this is your book and this is your handwriting?'

Luton looked straight forward and said nothing.

'I take it that you do not wish to confirm or deny this?' Townsend continued.

Bell looked at Luton. 'My client has no comment to make at this time.'

'But he does not deny the book we have is his?'

Luton continued to sit in silence.

'The book is a journal; it has your fingerprints all over it. It explains how you committed three murders that happened over the last four days, starting with the murder of Derek Thompson at The Gardens, then of Justin Gallagher in the toilets at the Bigg Market and then Norman Straughan who you killed on the Quayside and then put in the boot of his own car. Do you have anything to say about this?'

Luton said nothing.

Jet looked at Bell and thought he looked uncomfortable. He guessed that if he had had the choice of a client he would have chosen someone a little less repulsive.

'Are you sure they're my client's fingerprints?' Jet

thought Bell was struggling with his conscience and his desire to provide Luton with some form of defence.

'Yes, your client had his prints taken when he came into the station. There's no doubt they're his.'

'Are there any other fingerprints on the book?'

Townsend seemed irked at Bell's enquiry. 'Only the odd mark you would expect from the shop where he bought it. The vast majority are your client's. There is no doubt that he is the sole user of the book and he's written what's inside of it.'

Jet thought the smile Bell returned to Townsend was awkward before he silently lowered his head to scribble on his pad.

'We also found in your house a blue metal toolbox. I have a photograph of it here.' Townsend placed on the table a photograph of an innocent enough looking toolbox. 'In this toolbox we found what we believe to be the severed penises of the victims.' Townsend placed another photograph on the table. Luton did not look at it and Jet thought he could detect Bell trying hard not to cringe, but failing. 'The contents are currently being subjected to pathological examination but there seems little doubt what they are. Your journal describes how you cut them off and why you took them.'

Luton remained silent.

'In your journal you explain why you have killed these people. I'm giving you a chance to explain now, for the purpose of the court, why you did what you did. Do you wish to explain?'

Luton looked as if he was trying hard not to listen.

'When you attacked DC Whittle you told him about the bomb you had constructed and put in the Community Centre. That must have taken some time to build. How did you do that?'

Luton remained silent.

'OK, then, why did you do it?'

Bell looked at Luton and spoke. 'My client has no comment about that at this time.'

'Mr Luton,' Jet could see that Townsend was starting to enjoy the interview.' Why did you attack DC Whittle at his home last night?'

Luton did not move.

'Was it your intention to harm DC Whittle?'

Luton was silent.

'I understand that many years ago you were arrested for engaging in sex with another man in a public place. Is that right?' Townsend paused but there was still no response. 'DC Whittle was simply performing his duty as a police officer but clearly you held a grudge against him. Why would you do that for something so minor?'

'Minor!' Luton shouted his first word of the interview. 'My dad wouldn't speak to me again. I was dragged to church every day of my life after that. He even stopped me going to school.'

'So you felt you had been subject of an injustice?'

'All anyone had to do was leave us alone.'

'So for that sense of injustice you carried out these murders. To make a point?'

'It's his fucking fault; all he had to do was leave us alone.' Luton directed a finger towards Jet.

'So you decided to kill these people so you could make a point?'

Luton stuttered as if he was trying to summon further words but couldn't.

Bell looked at his client again. 'Listen officer, I think it would be wise if I have a private consultation with my client now.' He looked directly at Townsend. 'It also looks to me that, for whatever reason, the presence of DC Whittle is inflaming things, perhaps we both could do with a break and take further instruction.'

Townsend nodded. 'As you wish.' He stopped then removed the tapes. He got to his feet and Jet followed him out of the room and across the passage into the monitoring room.

Davison smiled as they sat down. 'Good interview that Stuart. I think we have everything we need to charge Luton. Nice result, a serial murderer and an act of terrorism. It'll not do your CV any harm at all.'

Jet felt his stomach muscles tighten as he heard Davison talk and knew he was thinking mainly about his own CV. The word 'prick' crossed his mind.

'Look Jet,' Davison was still smiling, 'you've had a rough few days, why don't you leave this to us now to sort out? Luton's solicitor might make some objection if you go back in.'

'What about Savage?' Jet thought he already knew the answer, but asked any way.

'Leave him to us. We'll get him charged in a short while.'

The word 'prick' crossed his mind again. But he did not speak.

'Why don't you go and see if there are any jobs that need to be tidied up for the incident room and once that's done get yourself away home.' Davison was still smiling but Jet did not reply, he just continued to think of the word 'prick' as he turned and left the monitoring room.

Jet walked into the incident room. It was a hive, buzzing with activity, everyone focused on their individual task. Jet strolled over to where Kevin Butler was sitting, punching at a computer keyboard.

Butler looked up. 'All right Jet?'

'Yeah,' Jet lied. 'Seen Mark Groom about?'

'He was in here a while ago. He popped out to do a job to help John Jardine.'

'What about Ormond?'

Butler looked around as if he was frightened someone might overhear. 'He went to see York first thing and he only came back to pick up his coat. Rumour is he's been transferred out.'

'Where to?'

'God knows; don't suppose it really matters. Wherever it is, it's under a cloud.'

Jet looked at Debbie McQueen's empty desk. 'Is Debbie away today as well?'

'She went not long after Ormond. I don't know where to and to be honest, I don't care. I'm not going to ask.'

'That sounds like a wise policy.'

'Are you finished the interview with Luton already?'

'His brief took exception to me being there.'

'I thought it was Groom who tried to knock his brains out?'

'Aye, it was, but he used my vase.' Butler smiled and Jet rubbed his chin and then changed the subject. 'It looks full tilt in here.'

'Yeah, we're expecting the Chief down. After Steve Manson's death there's going to be a lot of attention, we better make sure we're up to date.' Butler paused and it was his turn to change the subject. 'Could you do me a favour and take these phone records to Davison? They're for Luton's mobile phone, all the calls made and received, they might be useful during the interview. That bomb must have been detonated somehow.'

'I don't think it was with a mobile phone.'

'How's that?'

'Because when the bomb went off he was lying face down on what's left of my dining room table.'

'I suppose if you're clever enough to make a bomb that big, then making a timing device to set it off would be easy enough.'

'Suppose.' Jet pondered for a second and he tapped the phone records in his hands. He then jerked back into action. 'No bother, I'll be heading past the monitoring room soon; I'll drop these off to our new detective inspector.'

'Thanks Jet. Don't suppose it's urgent.'

Jet flicked through the several pieces of paper, which were held together with a bulldog clip, then put them under his arm. He had just done so when Groom came into the incident room. Groom spotted Jet and moved towards him. 'Jet, finished interviewing?'

'Been sidelined as well.'

'I wondered how long that would take. Never mind, you can help me with a job.'

'What?'

'Just a quick job at the Energy Factory to help John Jardine out with his enquiry.'

Jet's mobile phone rang and he fumbled in his jacket pocket to pull it out, leaving the pocket gaping open, looking like the hungry mouth his wife Julia had often complained about.

'Whittle.' He paused, 'Yes Father O'Brian, should we say about five o'clock? Good, see you then.'

'The Priest?' Groom looked puzzled.

'Yes, he asked to speak to me. Wants me to go to the church later on this afternoon.'

'He'll be trying to convert you Jet.'

'Maybe.'

'Yes, well at least he's trying. Let's go and help Jardine.'

Jet felt uncomfortable in the front seat of Groom's Audi. The gears seemed to move smoothly as Groom spoke. 'Which garage did the AA tow your Fiesta to?'

'One near my place in Wallsend.'

'Are they going to fix it or should we go down and give it a minute's silence as a mark of respect before we put it out its misery?'

Jet looked offended. 'I just burned the clutch out.'

'How much they charging you?'

'Thick end of four hundred quid.'

'Never mind, use the money you saved on the fence.'

'I'll have to ring my house insurance people about the dining room table as well.'

'Do they have a clause for a mass murderer trying to club you with a claw hammer?'

'Knowing my luck they'll have some way of getting out of it.'

'If they try to claim it's an act of God you can always send them to your mate the Priest. He'll tell them God wants nothing at all to do with puffs.'

Jet remained silent but smiled to himself as he considered Groom's political incorrectness.

Groom held onto the steering wheel of the Audi and leaned forward. He pulled a new packet of paracetamol tablets from a small compartment shelf on the dashboard. He handed them to Jet. 'I found them on the floor after you left the house. They must have fallen from your pocket when you were struggling with Luton.'

Jet took hold of the tablets. 'Thanks.'

'You've never struck me as someone who takes tablets. Been having headaches?'

'No, just like to keep them around. I used to suffer from migraines when I was a boy.'

'Had any migraines since you came back from Spain?'

'What do you mean?'

'I was just wondering whether your holiday had made you feel better or worse.'

Jet looked straight ahead. There was a Fiat ahead of them which weaved about the road a little, it looked as though the driver was looking for an address and was uncertain where it was. The driver seemed unconcerned about the impact this erratic behaviour was having on other traffic.

'It was just something I had to do, and now it's done.'

'So what's the plan now?'

'What do you mean?'

'You know what I mean.'

'I thought the plan was we went to the Energy Factory to see Jardine.'

Groom pressed the brake and the tyres screeched as the Audi avoided the urgent manoeuvring of the Fiat. 'Twat!' Groom pulled out and overtook the Fiat which was now pulling into the side of the busy road. As they passed the car they saw the elderly driver was engrossed in conversation with the woman in the passenger seat, who looked like his wife. They seemed to be in dispute over a map she had on her lap. Groom shook his fist at them as they passed, but Jet thought they had not noticed.

'You've got to admire people like that.' Jet watched the Fiat disappear past his nearside as he spoke.

'What, daft twats?'

'People totally unconcerned about anything else other than their own little world.'

'They're daft twats Jet. They should be looking out for others, not just thinking about themselves.'

'Maybe you're right.'

Groom pulled the Audi into a space in front of the Energy Factory behind a marked police car. Jet realised the car belonged to John Dawkin who was standing at the entrance to the club.

Jet and Groom walked over to where Dawkin stood guard.

'All right John?' Jet smiled as he approached.

'I'll be better when I can get away from here. Do you know what's happening yet?'

'We're just waiting for Sergeant Jardine to come down with the owner and we'll hand the place back to them. Now we know it's not part of a murder enquiry we're not interested in keeping it.'

'Good. It's not much of a job standing here just watching you lot come back and forth.'

'It'll be over soon.'

'Bad business with Steve Manson.'

'Tragic.'

'He was a good cop was Steve. He died a hero that's for sure.'

Dawkin had just finished his sentence when Jardine appeared with Hobson and Wilf Stone.

Groom smiled at them as they filed past and walked into the club. Stone was the last person to pass him. Groom waved a hand, 'After you Vera.' Stone made a slight growling noise as he passed Groom and walked into the club.

'John,' Groom raised his voice to Jardine.

'Oh yes.'

'Did you get the statement finished from Mr Hobson?'

'Oh yes, everything is done.'

'Good. Then we can release the premises and thank Mr Hobson for his co-operation. You never know, if Savage pleads guilty to assault we might not even need him to go to court and give evidence.'

Hobson had lost some of his finely groomed appearance as a result of his detention at the police station, but Jet thought he still held a superior air about him.

'I'm sure you gentlemen will understand if I don't invite you to stay for coffee, but there's a lot of work to be done to get the club open for business tonight.' Hobson's smile dropped from his face as he paused and looked at Groom. 'And you never know we might just be seeing each other again quite soon.'

Jet knew a threat when he heard one.

'I look forward to that.' Jet thought Groom was doing a good job of maintaining a brave face whilst watching Hobson escape prosecution.

'Well, all we have to do is give you the keys back and let you have a quick check to see if everything is the way you left it, we don't want any complaints after we're gone.'

Hobson cast his eyes around the club. 'I'm sure you've taken good care of it all for me.'

'We aim to please.' Jet thought he could still hear resignation in Groom's voice. 'John, if you could just check the safe with Mr Hobson, there was some cash in there.'

Jardine followed Hobson to the small strongroom and watched as Hobson opened the safe. He glanced inside and then fingered some of the cash bags that lay inside. 'Yes, it looks in order.'

'Oh yes, good.' Jardine produced a pink-coloured receipt. 'Could you just sign this for me to say it's all in order and we've handed the premises back to you?'

Jardine was pointing his pen towards Hobson who was just about to take it when Groom interrupted. 'We better just have a look in Mr Hobson's office first.'

Hobson looked annoyed at the formalities but followed Jardine into his office. Hobson moved towards the filing cabinets and opened one of the drawers. 'Are the files still here?'

'Oh yes. The files are back where they were before we came.'

'Good, then perhaps we can all get on.' Hobson moved to his desk picking up his own pen and taking a hold of the pink receipt.

'Just one last thing Mr Hobson.' Hobson rolled his eyes at Groom's voice.

'Yes.'

Groom turned to Jardine. 'We had better just check

the safe under the desk here.'

Groom lifted up the desk and slid it across the floor revealing the door to the compartment secreted in the floor. Jardine bent down and opened the door. He peered into the cavity and placed his hand inside and lifted out a piece of black card. Under it was a black ledger. Jardine lifted it out.

Groom looked surprised as he spoke. 'What's that John?'

Jardine flicked the pages of the heavy ledger. 'Oh yes. It looks like a business book.'

Groom looked through the book. 'We must have missed this one when we searched it the first time, John. It must have been concealed by that card.'

'That's ridiculous.' Hobson's composure seemed to have slipped.

'John, well done. Looking at this I'd say it's like one of those we saw earlier, but this one isn't part of any deal.' Groom looked at Hobson and gave a broad smile. 'John, I think under the circumstances you should arrest Mr Hobson on suspicion of extortion and incitement to assault.'

Jardine gave an uncharacteristic smile. 'Oh yes.'

Day Four – Afternoon

'Are you sure about this Jet?' Groom sounded uncharacteristically anxious.

Jet scratched his forehead. 'I think so.'

'We're about to put our careers on the line, so a bit more reassurance than think so would be comforting.'

'You think we've still got careers?'

'I hope you're right.'

'Me too.' Jet tried to grin but it didn't stay on his face for long. 'It all fits.'

Jet and Groom sat in the Detective Inspector's office, using the hard chairs Ormond had kept for visitors. Jet thought Ormond's empty desk had a sad look about it. The photograph of Ormond's one and only course at Bramshill National Police Training Centre had been removed from the wall and placed on top of the filing cabinet. The fresh faces of Inspectors on the course now stared their frozen false smiles at the ceiling.

The door opened and Ian Davison walked in and looked surprised. 'I didn't know you were using my office. I've got a meeting now.'

'We're not using it; we just need to have a word.' Groom got to his feet as he spoke, leaving Jet sitting with his clipboard on his lap.

'I haven't got the time, Jake Swinton's just in the

351

gents, we need to talk about the Community Centre. His offices were completely destroyed.'

Groom continued. 'I know, the incident room told us he was coming in to see you, we just wanted to have a few minutes.'

The office door pushed open again and Swinton peered in and stopped when he saw the three of them. 'Sorry, I'll come back.'

'No need, Jake.' Groom smiled. 'We just needed to speak to you for a second and thought we'd do it before your meeting with Ian here.'

'Sure.' Jake sat down. 'What can I do for you?'

'I was tidying up a few things and I wondered if you could clear something up for me.' Jet spoke this time and was looking at documents on the clipboard he held in front of him.

'No problem.'

'I'm doing some background work for the incident room. How long have you worked for NEGRA?'

'About five years.'

'Must be challenging work.' Jet looked up at Swinton and smiled.

'Yes it can be, but worthwhile.'

'Before NEGRA what did you do?'

'I worked at a chemical factory.'

'And before that?'

'I was at university. Why?'

'Just background. What did you study for your degree?'

'Chemistry.'

'That's quite a change of direction, from chemistry to co-ordinator for NEGRA.' Jet broadened his smile as he spoke.

'It's a good cause.'

'Do you know Terry Luton?'

'I knew of him; he did some work at the Community Centre and had a storeroom. Of course we didn't realise what he was doing in it.'

'That worried me a bit.'

'What worried you?'

'When you look at the amount of stuff he must have carried in and the work he must have done, it's strange no one got suspicious.'

'I don't think anyone really paid any attention. After all it's not something you'd expect is it?'

'I don't suppose so. Where were you when the bomb went off?'

'I was at the railway station. I had guests to pick up. Some people arrived late and I went to collect them.'

'It was a mistake. You know that?' Jet's tone changed and he now looked deadly serious.

Swinton looked taken aback by the suddenness of Jet's question. 'What are you talking about?'

'People arrived all day to go to the conference and yet

when I checked the only train you met was the one timed to arrive when the bomb went off.'

'What are you talking about?'

'It wasn't the only mistake you made.'

'What?'

'At the briefing when the Mondeo was first mentioned and was circulated, Luton made a call to me and pretended he'd seen the car near my house. It was designed to throw us off his trail.'

'So what?'

'The details of the Mondeo went out to the press and it was on the radio. But I checked with the radio station and he made the call before it was circulated.' Swinton looked pale. 'We now know the car was never near my house. So the only way he could have known about the Mondeo was if someone from the briefing had told him.' Jet looked directly at Swinton. 'You were at the briefing.'

'Yes with many other people.'

'Yes that's true. But when I saw this itemised phone record of the calls made to and from Luton's phone I had a look at the numbers and he actually received a call from your mobile phone just after the briefing.' Swinton remained silent as Jet paused and stared at him. Jet continued. 'Another mistake that. I suppose it never crossed your mind that anyone would even think about Luton's mobile phone. If he'd killed himself, as planned, then maybe nobody would have looked. We'd have a body and a Journal containing his detailed confession. Why would we want to look further for an accomplice? Why would we even think there was an accomplice? It was very clever.'

'He worked at the Community Centre, I had reason to ring him many times. His number is programmed in my phone like many people I work with.'

'Yes, I noticed you ring him a lot.'

'I could just have rang him by accident, it happens sometime when my phone is in my pocket. Haven't you ever had a call from someone you know and all you can hear is background noise and you know they've hit the button by accident?'

'Hell of a coincidence that you'd do it then.'

Swinton remained quiet.

'That brings me to your next mistake.' Jet paused and the room was silent as if everyone was holding their breath. 'As I've said, it was a very clever plan. Too clever. If Luton was dead we might not have thought too much about it, but the fact is, he's just not that bright. His father stopped him from going to school and he's been a gardener all of his working life, not really the type of person to come up with this scheme. He does seem like someone who could be manipulated easily by the right person though, perhaps by someone he felt close to. He hadn't had too many people to feel close to in the past. But he's not a person I would have thought would come up with this level of cunning on his own. To do this you need to be resourceful, it needed someone with education, planning and opportunity,' Jet paused for a second and slightly shuffled in his chair, then he settled and made direct eye contact with Swinton, 'someone like you.'

'Rubbish, that doesn't prove anything.'

'That brings me to you next mistake.'

Swinton stared hard at Jet.

'In his Journal Luton was very eloquent, he even referred to Oscar Wilde and *De Profundis*. He clearly had help to write it. You know, there wasn't a copy of *De Profundis* in Luton's house. I bet when we search your house we'll find a copy. Won't we?'

'There must have been millions of copies of that sold, it was written over a hundred years ago.'

'True, but it's all good evidence, isn't it? I bet when you met Luton, a damaged individual, someone who had been oppressed by their father, socially inept, you realised the potential. Luton must have been easy enough for you to manipulate. But he failed, didn't he? He didn't have your discipline. He's still alive.'

'This is madness.'

'He'll talk you know. Eventually, after he's been treated and counselled. He'll get the best of care from all sorts of doctors who will want to treat him. He'll be a celebrity and he'll talk to them. Even during the time he

attacked me he couldn't keep you a secret, kept saying
"we've" planned this. He'll talk eventually.'

'He won't say anything about me.'

'I'm not so sure about that. Tell me again how you
first met Luton?'

'He was contracted to do work in the grounds of the
Community Centre. I just knew him from the odd
occasion, when I said hello to him, when we were at
work.'

'Did you know Luton before you went to university?'

'No, why should I?'

'I saw you had two cautions for indecency offences, in
public places. They were committed when you were a
young man.'

'So what? Cautions so many years ago for things that
people would not blink an eye at these days.'

'You're three years older than Luton.'

'So what?'

'When Luton was arrested by me all those years ago,
an older man ran away. I checked the records, it was a
man not much older who had befriended him and
convinced him they could have sex in the safety of the
Gardens.'

Swinton looked plaintive and remained silent.

'Was that you?'

'Course not.'

'I think it probably was, and then all those years later

you saw him at the Community Centre and you became friends again. Only by that time he'd suffered at the hands of his father and he was very weak. Just right for you to take advantage of him. Where were we going to find Luton's body I wonder? Was he going to die at his home with his journal or in the explosion maybe? He'll tell us one day.'

'That's rubbish.' Swinton ran his hand along the back of his shirt collar, running his fingers between his neck and the inside of his shirt.

Jet watched and his eyes narrowed as he spoke again. 'I'll bet that you dictated some of that journal to him. For dramatic effect. After all, once this was all over you were going to be the centre of attention. Wasn't that the plan? Such an atrocity against the gay community and you as the organiser of the conference, one of the biggest victims. You could have made a lot of money out of this.' Jet watched as a bead of sweat formed on Swinton's forehead. 'I kept asking myself the question, why did he keep that journal, what was the real reason? It wasn't some grand plan to become a martyr after his death, you might have made him believe that, but it wasn't its real purpose. Its real purpose was to provide you with an alibi.'

'If he did have help then anyone could have done it.' Jet could see another small bead of sweat form on Swinton's forehead as he spoke.

'Your fingerprints are on the journal.' Jet could see a trickle of sweat make its way down Swinton's temple. 'I had prints you left on a glass in the briefing room compared with marks on the journal. You were careless Jake. I suppose you never really thought about an investigation after the bomb had killed all those people, but it didn't work out the way you thought it was going to.'

Swinton was shaking.

'All those mistakes. Someone as clever as you, someone with a degree in chemistry, who would be able to help Luton make the detonator for his bomb, know how to put the chemicals together; you made all those mistakes and they tighten the noose around your neck. You'd be the centre of attention, one of the few survivors of the atrocity against the gay community. You could embark on all sorts of tours, be a celebrity. You used Luton and planned to kill all of those people for personal fame and fortune.'

'It wasn't about money!' Swinton's outburst was loud and angry. 'It wasn't for me. It was the only way we were ever going to make real progress. I could arrange conference after conference, talking to ourselves until we were blue in the face, but who ever came and listened? No one of any importance, do you think we were ever going to make any progress at all, talking to each other? It was a waste of time, nothing has really moved on since they were throwing Oscar Wilde in prison. We're just queers. I did this so people would wake up and listen to us, to see how things are for us. It would raise emotions; shut people up like that stupid Priest. I did all of this to force people to think about it. Everyone will understand now. That's why we needed to make the sacrifice. Not for me.'

Swinton was shaking and the tears ran down his face.

Groom stood up as Swinton put his hands over his face. 'Jake Swinton, I am arresting you for the murder of PC Steve Manson.'

Groom took a hold of Swinton and stood him up. Groom looked at Davison and spoke. 'Inspector I think we should get this prisoner to the custody office.'

Davison did not speak and Jet thought he looked as startled as Swinton.

Groom nodded for Jet to take over holding Swinton. 'Jet, could you take him along the corridor to the custody suite. I'll just be a few seconds.'

Jet moved Swinton out of the room. Groom closed the door as they left the room then turned to face Davison. 'Jet's a clever bastard. He worked all that out from an itemised telephone bill.'

'Yes, it's a good collar.'

'Embarrassing for you though.'

'How do you reckon that?'

'Well you were Swinton's liaison officer through the

whole enquiry. He was planning mass murder and you were keeping him up to date with the investigation and you never suspected a thing. Very embarrassing. It wouldn't surprise me to find out that some of the information he used to execute his perverse plan was supplied by you.'

'We're all human, all make mistakes.'

'Like Ormond. He was human. Look what happened to him.'

'I'm not Ormond.'

Groom moved slowly forward towards Davison, stopping so close that he knew Davison could feel breath on his face as Groom lowered his voice to speak again. 'No you're not. Ormond wouldn't have been grassing other cops from the enquiry up to the Chief Constable's Staff Officer.'

Davison's face deepened a shade.

Groom's face remained close and his expression solemn as he continued. 'While Jet was looking at phone records he had a look at yours as well, to see when Swinton was speaking to you. And there on your records are calls you made to your pal Henry Hardwick, the Chief's Staff Officer. Every time Ormond did something he thought was right, to move the investigation on, you were there making sure he was being undermined every step of the way.'

'Nothing wrong with me ringing a friend.'

'I always knew you were a devious two-faced bastard, now everyone is going to know.'

'Are you threatening me?'

'No. A deal. You ask for a transfer out of Newcastle. You go and I'll not tell anyone about any of this.'

'What can you do?'

'Think about it. York alone will make your life a misery when he finds out you were grassing him up to the Chief. How could any of the cops here ever have confidence in you again, knowing they can't trust you?' Groom paused to allow a second for Davison to digest the thought. 'You go, and no one will have cause to keep thinking about the link between you and Swinton in the investigation. You can resume your career somewhere else. You stay and your career is dead in the water. I'll see to that.'

Davison did not say anything as Groom pulled away from him, turned and got a hold of the door handle. 'I'm going to help process our new prisoner. You do what you need to do to save your future.'

Groom closed the door behind him and Davison sat down at his desk.

At 5.00pm Jet stood outside the huge doors of St Stephen's Church.

'Odd.' Jet looked up at the door. 'First time they've

been closed.'

Groom turned the handle and the door opened with a firm shove.

Jet walked into the familiar tall building and felt a shiver as the cool air surrounded him. 'He said he'd be in the vestry.'

Groom followed as Jet walked down the aisle to the door he had seen the Priest walk out of during previous visits. The solid door was closed. Pinned to the centre of it was a white envelope with 'DC Whittle' written in neat black-ink handwriting. Jet pulled the envelope from the door. It felt heavy.

'Everyone's leaving you notes these days.' Groom said and looked on as Jet pulled out a key and a piece of paper. He unfolded the white paper and read it aloud to Groom.

Dear Constable Whittle,

Derek came to see me months ago. He had borrowed money from Gary Hobson. He got drunk one night and he lost it all gambling. Derek was a nice caring man but not very careful with his money. He bought the best of everything, expensive apartment, car, computers, cameras. He was alone for a long time living in Newcastle and spent a lot to console himself. It was not like him to gamble but he was lonely and suffered heavy losses. I think he was taken advantage of, such a kind trusting soul. Hobson threatened him for the money and extortionate interest. He was terrified. Hobson had sent Savage to see him and inflicted

*dreadful injuries. They kept coming back for more money.
Interest Hobson said. Derek trusted me, he turned to me as
his priest. I couldn't tell anyone, I made a promise. Hobson
always wanted more. I went to see Hobson myself and even
found out where Adam Savage lived and pleaded with them
to leave Derek alone. But they just wanted money.
Eventually Derek paid him off in full, but he had to take
money from his work to cover it. He was going to pay it back.
It was terrible. But something good did come of it; we
became friends. So it was not all bad. We grew too close.
Derek said he loved me. I told him on the last night I saw
him that it could never be. We had been at one of the
meetings we used to have at a pub around the corner. After
it we talked and Derek got upset. I told him it was against
all I believed. Now I know he was right and I was wrong.
He knew that I did love him, he could feel it. If only I had
shown the love I had for him. It could have been so different.
He would still be alive. He must have gone home and then
in the early hours of the morning went out again in search
of the affection I could not show him. Perhaps he was trying
to make me jealous. I'll never know. You cannot imagine the
conflict I have gone through these last days. I was so stupid.
I did my duty and spoke out as the church expected. But I
denied Derek. Like Judas. A coward. When you first came to
see me I should have told you then what I knew, but I was
worried about the reputation of the church and I was
frightened for myself. I did what I thought was right and*

after the first lie it became more and more difficult to tell the truth. Only now do I see how brave Derek was. Living and trying to love. Not denying who God made him. Being true to himself. Now all I can do is break my last solemn vow. God help me. Perhaps he will let me be with Derek after all. I would like to tell him that in my heart it is the only thing I really want.

The key is for the vestry door, I am inside. I have committed my last mortal sin. I trust my God will have the courage to show more forgiveness to me than I was able to.

P O'Brian.

Jet turned the key in the lock and walked through the oak door.

Jet looked at the body stretched from the roof beam. It was perfectly still. The cord around the neck looked as if it belonged to some religious garb. It reminded Jet of what Friar Tuck would have had around his waist in old television episodes of Robin Hood. Why did the name Richard Greene flash into his mind at this moment? The cord had been looped around a low beam and then secured to a large hook on the wall. A small stool lay on its side a metre away from the Priest's feet.

The Priest's head was hanging to the left. His tongue protruded and his eyeballs gazed up to the ceiling. Looking towards his God for guidance Jet thought, but did not share the notion.

'It's always the ones you think never in a million years.' Groom stared at the body as he spoke.

'He had more courage than I thought.'

'No Jet, less!' Groom's voice fumed. 'It would have taken courage to stay and make a difference here.' Groom turned from the body and stared in Jet's face. 'Courage is getting up every morning and making a difference. Making things better. This isn't courage Jet. This is letting people down. Giving up on yourself and those who mean something to you. Nothing courageous about that.'

Day Four - Evening

The phone rang on York's desk. He instinctively scooped it up and told the receiver his name.

'Chief Constable here.' York wished he had left the phone on its plastic cradle.

'Nice to hear from you Sir.' York smiled and felt the lies flow like fine wine.

'Brilliant work getting Hobson back on a charge sheet. I knew putting Davison on the case instead of that idiot Ormond would soon reap rewards.'

'Yes Sir, it was an inspired decision.'

'He'll go far that lad. He has the brain and desire that sadly some of your other staff seem to lack.'

'Quite.'

'Bad news though.'

'What's that?'

'There's a job come up here in the staff office and I'm told by Chief Inspector Hardwick that Davison's expressed an interest in it. So I'm going to transfer him up here so he can work for me. I know you'd want to keep him, but in the long run, this will serve the force much better. He'll serve in high rank in the future you know and we need to prepare him.'

'That is a shame.' York's smile broadened.

'Don't worry York, I'll look after him, his future is safe

367

with me.'

'Good to know.'

'I've also had the personnel department on to me, they tell me that Ormond has given notice to retire.'

'I thought he might go, he's got well over thirty years service in.'

'So you will be needing a new inspector.'

'Yes.'

'Personnel tell me the only qualified candidate is Mark Groom. Isn't he the halfwit who cocked up the press briefing a few days ago with that Priest?'

'Yes.'

'Sorry to take Davison off you and lumber you with Groom but do you think you could cope if we promote him?'

'We'll do our best to whip him into shape and make something out of him.'

'Good man.'

'Can I ask you if you've heard anything from your officers in Portugal yet?'

'It's gone cold. We can't find any trace of Harris anywhere. The Portuguese authorities don't seem to care because all they have is a missing person from England who's a criminal. So they're not interested in doing anything. They say he's probably just gone somewhere else to resume his life of crime.'

'I suppose it's possible.'

'Might be.'

'What about the address book that went missing from his mother-in-law?'

'No chance her making an identification. It was taken by a man in a suit wearing thick glasses. She doesn't even remember the colour of the suit. Nothing we can do. It's a missing address book. We only have her word that someone came to the house at the time it went missing. She's in her seventies. Until Harris turns up somewhere I don't think there is anything else we can do.'

'Well at least we'll be spared any embarrassing enquiries involving bent coppers.'

'Yes. Unless Harris turns up somewhere.'

'I suppose we have enough to worry about, other than missing persons from Portugal.'

'Quite.'

'Oh Sir, one last thing. If Davison goes and we promote Groom we'll have two vacancies for sergeants.'

York could hear the Chief rustle some papers on the other end of the phone. 'Yes, personnel did give me some details. Yes here we are. There's a man who I need to move from Gateshead for career development, Jardine. Gateshead say he's a good man but he would benefit from the change, I think he's been with you on this murder enquiry. His detective inspector has said the change has done him the world of good and it would suit everyone to make the move permanent.'

'Really, that's good of them to let experienced staff go like that.' The Chief did not pick up the irony in York's voice. Nor could he have known that York had just stopped smiling.

'Yes, they're forward thinking people at Gateshead that's for sure. You should send some of your officers across there, to have a look at their working practices.'

'Yes, I'll have a look at that. Perhaps with Jardine here now, we could learn from him.' The Chief did not pick up on that piece of irony either.

'The second will have to be a promotion. Who have you got on your list?'

It was York's turn to rustle papers as he opened the top drawer on his desk and opened the book he kept marked 'personnel'.

'For a detective sergeant the only qualified person I have is Whittle.'

'How do you feel about that?'

'OK. He's had a bad year with his wife's death but he's always been a sound operator. I'll keep a close eye on him. But what about the Portugal enquiry?'

'What does it matter? We can't prove anything. Can't stop things because we suspect he might have done something. Tell the personnel department I told you it was all right and to get the memos done. Might as well make it effective from next week.'

'Yes….' York said, and then heard the tone on the line

which meant the Chief had hung up. '....Sir.'

Jet was uncomfortably sat in the passenger seat of Groom's Audi as they headed towards Jet's home in Wallsend.

'When will the Fiesta be back on the road?'

Jet's mobile phone sang its tune and he reached in his pocket. As he was fumbling around he replied to Groom. 'They said tomorrow but I won't hold my breath.'

'I'll pick you up in the morning.'

'Whittle.' Jet shouted in his mobile. 'Yes, he's with me. Yes, I'll tell him. Yes we will.' Jet put the phone back in his pocket.

'What's up?'

'We've both been told to go to York's office first thing in the morning.'

'What for?'

'It was the control room passing a message from York, they don't know. What do you think?'

'I think we're probably in the shit again.'

Jet smiled. 'No change there then?'

'Not at all.'

'It could be a complaint from Hobson's solicitor.'

'Why would he complain?'

'Probably mystified about how we found an incriminating ledger in Hobson's secret cubbyhole after we had already searched it.'

'We're just human, we make mistakes.'

'Strange that the record made at the time we first seized the ledgers said just a number of books, not four or five. I thought there were five, so it's a good job you wrote it down and not me because it turns out there were only four, and so only four were covered by the deal with the CPS.'

'That'll teach him to make sure everything is covered next time he does a deal to save his own skin.'

'I searched that cubbyhole again you know. When I went back to the club. I had another look in, and it wasn't there.'

'As I said, we all make mistakes. In any case if you think about it, Hobson isn't going to make a complaint about it. His solicitor knows if he does, they'll have to disclose the fact there were another four ledgers. It's not much of a defence. No I think Hobson will realise the only thing to do is to keep his head down and be grateful he'll get a reduced sentence.'

Jet grinned at the thought. 'Suppose.'

'How did you know that Swinton's fingerprints were on the journal we found in Luton's place? I didn't know you'd taken prints off a glass in the briefing room.'

'I didn't. Educated guess.'

'You lied.' Groom shook his head. 'Tut tut.'

Jet's face straightened as he pondered the thought and

they were silent while the engine of the Audi raced as Groom weaved through the traffic on the Coast Road.

After a few minutes Groom glanced at Jet and spoke. 'Don't sweat it Jet, what you did was get one evil bastard off the streets.'

Jet remained quiet as he looked out the car window.

'Do you think Swinton did it in some misguided belief that he was going to make things better for the gay community?' Groom glanced at Jet again as he spoke.

Jet slowly shook his head. 'My money would be on the old faithful motive of self gain. It would certainly have made him the centre of attention, with books and television he'd have become rich and famous. Suppose we'll never really know.'

'He'll still be famous.'

'Not quite the attention I think he was looking for. Do you?'

'No Jet, I think he'd have preferred it differently. You did well today.'

As they travelled along the Coast Road they were getting close to Wallsend and Jet looked out to his left and saw the old Wills Factory. A remnant of the past, a huge building made to make cigarettes that employed the working class, now converted into apartments the working classes couldn't afford.

'You know, I came into this job to uphold the law, to work for justice.'

'That's what we do Jet.'

'Breaking or bending the rules, doesn't that make us the same as the criminals?'

'No, we don't do it for gain. We do it for justice, and with all the rules it's created for itself, sometimes it needs a helping hand. I told you Jet, it takes courage to stay here and do what's right.'

'A helping hand for justice.' The Wills Factory was now out of sight but Jet still looked out of the passenger window away from Groom as he spoke and pondered the thought. The smile returned to Jet's face and he looked at Groom, who was concentrating on the heavy traffic on the dual carriageway. 'Maybe there is a time for justice. You know, I think I can live with that.'

'Jet, that's really good to hear.'

ACKNOWLEDGEMENTS

I am eternally grateful for the work and guidance of Sheila Wakefield. Her support has been invaluable.

I am blessed with two very talented children, Andrew and Adelle. They always give freely of their time and gifts to help me out and I would be completely lost without them.

I would not have been able to write this novel without the help and support of my wife June.